I0661729

Out in Austin

LOVING LENNOX

KD ELLIS

Loving Lennox
ISBN # 978-1-80250-537-5
©Copyright KD Ellis 2023
Cover Art by Erin Dameron-Hill ©Copyright June 2023
Interior text design by Claire Siemaszkiewicz
Pride Publishing

LOVING
LENNOX

Dedication

To anyone who has struggled with addiction and pain—you are not alone. Together, we are strong.

Chapter One

The dumpster reeked of mold and urine. Ryland cringed at the thought of touching the lid, let alone diving inside for the day-old bread that he'd watched the man in the white apron chuck into it a few minutes ago. He used to think caviar and snails were the worst thing he'd ever have to eat.

The sharp hunger pains wreaking havoc on his belly quickly overcame his disgust. If it meant the cramps and aching would go away, he'd have eaten the bread out of the toilet at this point.

It was harder than he'd thought it would be to open the lid. Even when he stretched up on tiptoes, he couldn't quite get the heavy black plastic cover to stay open, and it fell more than once, nearly catching his fingers. He couldn't afford a hospital bill, and each time he had to yank his hands back, he grew even more nervous. Finally, though, he got it to stay.

But then it was a struggle to clamber up onto the narrow edge.

It smelled worse up here, with the added bonus of him being able to see the ruptured garbage bags hip deep in the bottom, spilling out rotted food and sticky, oozing trash. Ryland didn't want to even *begin* to guess what it was.

The loaves of bread, thankfully, were resting at the top. Riley could only hope the plastic wrappings had kept them safe for consumption. It wouldn't be the first time he'd gotten food poisoning since running away, but surely there was a limit to how many times he'd get lucky enough to survive it. He wished his fancy private school had taught him important things like that, rather than who the third President of the United States had been.

His real question was how he could get the bread out without actually getting *into* the dumpster — since once he was in, he was pretty sure he was going to be stuck there. Trash pickup had been two days before, leaving the dumpster just empty enough he'd never be able to climb out. Maybe if he was taller...or stronger.

Then again, if he'd been either of those things, he wouldn't have had to run away.

Finally, Riley decided to just lean forward and hope for the best. It was, unfortunately, nowhere near close enough to reach anything. Before he could come up with a better plan, though, an angry man yelled from far too close. "Hey, you! The fuck do you think you're doing in there? Get your ass down!"

Well, Ryland got down all right — very quickly and not entirely in the way he'd intended. But at least he had the rotund angry man to break his fall. The man grunted, but before he could grab Ryland with his flailing hands, Ryland was off, running toward the street at a dead sprint.

His heart thudding, he didn't stop moving until he reached the Walmart parking lot and the sound of footsteps had been lost somewhere behind him. His breath was ragged, and his chest was on fire, but he was—well, not safe. He was never safe on the streets, but at least he wasn't about to be beaten by a baseball bat or anything.

Ryland stared wistfully at the grocery doors but turned away. For the past three days, he'd been camping—if it could be called camping without a sleeping bag, tent or campfire—in the back of the lot, tucked between two piles of discarded pallets.

The blacktop was hot and hard, the semis spewed exhaust, thick and foul, whenever they drove in and out, and yesterday, he'd almost been impaled by a forklift. But at least here, nobody had stolen the last bit of change from his pocket, and he was yet to have woken up with a stranger's hand down his pants. The other homeless people he saw stayed on the opposite end of the parking lot, probably because it was farther from the building.

Riley crawled under his usual propped-up pallet, knowing it was too early to sleep but too tired to do anything else. Maybe things would turn around after a short nap.

* * * *

"Dude, you gotta wake up."

Rough hands forced Ryland awake, and immediately, he looked around for the fire or whatever emergency was causing the stranger to shake him like a nearly empty bottle of nail polish.

"Go away," Ryland said around a yawn when he didn't see anything worth worrying about in the darkened lot. It had to be nearing midnight.

"The cops are clearing us all out. Unless you want to spend the night in a holding cell, it's time to go." The stranger sounded serious enough that Ryland finally pushed himself to his feet and followed, his mind foggy. It didn't seem to matter how long he slept lately, he still always woke exhausted.

The stranger who'd woken him was younger than Ryland thought, he realized as he followed him across the parking lot and onto the sidewalk, skirting the flashing lights near the doors. Fifteen or so, Ryland guessed. Only a year or two older than Ryland, and almost as scrawny. The kid had floppy ginger-blond hair and crooked glasses, a hole-ridden backpack over his shoulders.

He also had a scowl on his face when he turned the corner, grabbing Ryland's arm and pulling him to a stop in the shadows of a boarded-up restaurant. "Are you new?"

"New to what?" Ryland asked, rubbing the sleep from his eyes as he yawned again.

"The streets," the strange boy answered, a pitying look on his face that made Riley scowl. "'Cause sorry-not-sorry, no throwaway I know would be able to sleep through those sirens."

"How'd you even know I was there?" Riley asked instead of answering, unwilling to admit that he wasn't cut out for life on the streets. He was going to make it, he had to. He refused to go home.

He was genuinely curious how the kid had known he was there, since he'd thought he was doing such a good job staying out of sight. The forklift operator hadn't even spotted him, and he'd nearly run Ryland over.

"I keep an eye on things. Saw you been going back there for the last few days and got curious. Where's your kit?"

"Kit?" Riley asked, confused.

"Blanket? Backpack? Change of underwear? Where's your shit, kid? Did it get stolen?"

Ryland felt his face turn scarlet, heat burning his cheeks. "Uh...yeah," he lied. "It got stolen." He would prefer not to admit that he'd left his backpack behind on the bus by accident. He'd been too worried about getting as far away from his dad as possible, as *quickly* as possible, to remember to grab it from the overhead compartment.

"And I suppose you need to eat, too," the stranger said, phrasing it more like a statement of fact than a question. Ryland's stomach growled immediately at the thought of food, too loud to deny.

The older boy sighed, shifting his backpack on his shoulders. "Fine. You can tag along with me, but you better pull your weight. You gotta pretty face, but it won't get you far if you don't learn how to use it." The stranger started walking, seeming to trust that Ryland would follow — or not really caring if he didn't.

Ryland jogged after the older boy. "What's your name? I'm Ryland."

The stranger stopped and sighed even louder, spinning on his heel to glare at him. "No, it's not. Not on the streets. You can be Billy or Johnny or Riley...but not Ryland. You leave your real name back at whatever home you left, unless you don't got no one looking for you — or I suppose unless you want to be found real quick."

"Riley... My name's Riley," Ryland—now Riley—corrected. He felt lighter as he said it, like the new name made him someone fresh, someone new.

"Nice to meet you, Riley. You can call me Sage." He held out his hand to shake, squeezing Riley's tight when he did. "First rule of the streets is don't trust no one."

Which...was a bit odd, coming from someone Riley was following blindly to an unknown location.

"So how do I know I can trust *you*?" Riley asked.

Sage grinned, wide and vicious, his blue eyes glinting under the streetlamps. "Exactly."

* * * *

The streets were scary, but not so much anymore, not since Riley started staying with Sage. The older boy had taken him under his wing—pseudo adopted him after that first night. He didn't realize how grateful he should be until he learned that Sage didn't usually pick up strays.

Riley didn't know why Sage was letting him tag along, but he slept easier now that he wasn't crashing alone. The basement of the flop house wasn't exactly safe, but no one messed with Sage, and by default, that meant no one messed with him.

Which was probably why the thought of Sage leaving him for the afternoon had him in a panic. As soon as Sage said he was heading out to make some money, Riley had freaked, clinging to Sage like a barnacle.

"Where are you going?" Riley asked, hating the sour notes of fear too easy to hear beneath his words.

Sage adjusted his tiny black shorts, tugging the waistband lower to widen the strip of pale skin between them and his hot pink crop top, but he didn't shove Riley off. "I'm going to get us something to eat. I want you to stay here."

Riley protested, but eventually Sage got fed up. As soon as he raised his voice, Riley backed down, letting him go and dropping down on Sage's sleeping bed in silence, his heart pounding. He shouldn't make Sage mad, not when so much of what he had right now — a too-hot place to sleep that kept him out of the sun, a soft sleeping bag to lie on, food — came from him.

Sage sighed and crouched down in front of him, his expression gentling. "I'm sorry I yelled, kid."

Riley liked it when Sage called him that. It was like he was acknowledging that Riley didn't have to have everything figured out. He could make mistakes, and Sage would help him.

Sage continued talking, "But where I'm going isn't particularly nice, and I can't watch my back and yours at the same time."

Riley nodded, but his stomach dropped at the thought of Sage going somewhere dangerous. So, he waited until Sage was out of the room to stand up and creep along after him.

Sage never had to know Riley was following, but if he got in trouble, Riley wanted to be able to help.

It was late — that time of night when the restaurants were closing down, but the bars were just getting busy and the sidewalks were just crowded enough to give Riley cover. He stayed just close enough to keep the neon pink shirt in his view.

When they got where they were going — the corner of Twelfth and Chicon — he didn't understand, not at first. It didn't seem dangerous. The white bricks behind Sage looked freshly painted, a brilliant contrast to Sage's bright clothing.

Riley didn't dare get any closer, knowing that if he did, he'd risk getting spotted. Instead, he stayed by the bus station, trusting in the shadows to keep him out of sight. Then, he watched.

He didn't understand why Sage kept walking up to cars that slowed down, rolling his hips and trailing his fingers over his skin. He'd lean into passenger windows, exchange a few words, then the car would drive away.

He didn't understand, until he did, but by then it was too late. Sage climbed into the car, and it drove away, turning into an alley a few streets down. By the time Riley, out of breath from running, sprinted around the corner, Sage was climbing out of the backseat, his hair mussed as he pulled his shorts up.

Sage's gaze met his and narrowed.

Riley swallowed around the lump in his throat, cringing when Sage mouthed, "*Go home.*"

He looked angry, but more than that, Riley thought there was a hint of shame hiding under the expression, which made him feel so much worse. It was the only reason he ducked back around the corner, his heart pounding, and headed back to the squat.

Chapter Two

Sage was still angry.

Maybe he wouldn't be, if Riley would just suck it up and apologize, but instead he'd dug in his heels. After all, Riley had pointed out, it was dangerous to get into cars with strangers, and the least Sage should do was let Riley come with him. If anything happened, he could go for help.

"Who's going to help a whore?" Sage had just said bitterly, walking away to force an end to the discussion.

So Riley kept following Sage, and Sage kept catching him—and it left a rather sour note to their friendship.

Most nights, Riley just watched, his heart pounding in fear, wondering if *that* night was the one when it would all go wrong. So far, the worst he'd seen was a man backhand Sage, then drive off before Riley could even holler.

Tonight, though, his skin crawled like he'd been infested by ants as he watched Sage walk up to the window of an expensive black Cadillac. Maybe it was the dent in the bumper that had him uneasy, or maybe it was the way the well-dressed man inside seemed determined to keep his face out of view.

Whatever it was, he'd never felt like this when Sage worked before. Riley hesitated, knowing Sage would be pissed if Riley cost him a well-paying client over something so obscure as a bad feeling, and by the time he stepped forward, Sage was in the car.

Riley watched the taillights drive, speeding past Sage's usual alley. He wasn't fast enough to keep them in sight, losing the car as it turned a corner.

All he could see was Sage's panicked face and him pounding his hands on the back window then, the car was gone.

Riley waited until morning, but Sage never came back.

Chapter Three

Two years — and some months — later

It was mid-July and nearly noon, and the Austin streets felt like a brick oven. Riley's threadbare shirt — the best he could find at his favorite Goodwill, the one just off Norwood Park Boulevard — was too thin to prevent the metal lamppost from almost branding his skin. It would be better across the street, where the fancy boutiques with their etched-glass windows cast long shadows and the bricks stayed cool.

Unfortunately, the managers — though, really, at this point he might say 'manager', since they were basically all the same well-dressed white man with a sour expression — had chased him away with a broom earlier this morning.

It was too late for the early-to-workers, and too early for the pay-to-players, the men who would bend him over a dumpster for the price of his dinner. And it was definitely too hot today to even attempt to squeeze in a nap, so he'd set out the metal can he'd salvaged from his pork-and-beans dinner a few months back and decided to kill time begging. He hoped he would be lucky enough to get at least an hour before too many businesses complained and the cops showed up to shoo him away.

Can't have street trash lowering the curb appeal.

Riley'd learned two years ago how little the cops cared about people like him.

So far, Riley had managed to stay under their radar for half an hour, but he had only a fistful of change to show for it. He was tired and sore but mostly bored. It just sucked that he wasn't getting much traction here, because the boutiques were high-end and the shoppers well-off.

He could move streets, but if *these* shoppers, with their Jimmy Choos and Balenciagas padded with spending money wouldn't spare more than quarters, he doubted the thriftier shoppers elsewhere would turn him a better profit.

It left a hollow ache in his stomach, deeper than the gnawing hunger that went hand in hand with eating only one meal a day. If he couldn't get money from begging, he'd be forced to turn back to his *other* tricks.

He really wasn't feeling up to it today. Riley was pretty sure he'd overworked himself. He was still sore from a particularly forceful client last week, and even though the fissures in his butt—which, *gross*—had finally started to heal, now he was…*itchy*. It was nearly impossible not to squirm. The stomachache Riley had woken up with this morning made him even less inclined to tricking.

Maybe he should do what some of the other boys did and make a sign outta cardboard. He could prop it up beside him. They claimed it made them more money, but all he'd seen it do was get them boosted by the cops even faster.

Riley rolled his head to the side as a yawn threatened, smothering it against his shoulder, then glared at the 'Help Wanted' notice on the laundromat by the corner.

He passed by dozens of signs a day, each one mocking him. Nobody wanted to hire him without at least two forms of identification, but he didn't have any. Besides, even if he did, most of the stores had a minimum age of employment. Riley wouldn't turn sixteen for another few months, not until smack dab in the heart of winter.

By then, the weather would drop to the forties, and he'd be freezing—if he hadn't already starved to death.

He sighed and tore his gaze from the laundromat, turning back to the sidewalk just in time to watch a pair of hot pink shoes kick over his can. Coins spilled in one direction while the metal container went the other.

"Come on, man. What the heck?" Riley cursed and flopped on his side to grab the can, but he wasn't quick enough. It jumped the curb and rolled out into the street, where it was promptly run over by a cab. Riley stared after it numbly before the sound of a coin hitting metal triggered him back into action.

He started to scramble after the change instead, gathering up what he could and shoving it into the pocket of his jeans. He hoped the holes in them were small enough not to let any escape, as too many had already rolled into the grates.

"Shit, sorry," the pink-haired man said, crouching down to help. "I wasn't paying attention." Riley watched his hands carefully to make sure he didn't pocket them, but there wasn't much left anyway. He took the few coins the man held out, then glared at the sewer drains.

Great, he thought. *Even the rats have more money than me now.*

Out loud, he said, "Clearly." He gave up and dropped back against the hot metal post. "Whatever. Probably just pennies anyway." He shoved his thumb through his only remaining belt loop, trying to act like he didn't care.

Like those last few pennies might not have been the difference between selling his mouth or his ass.

"Can I buy you lunch? Or, um...a coffee?" the man said abruptly, his gaze trailing over Riley's body like a hot brand. Reluctantly, Riley appraised him. If he was going to have to do it anyway, now or later wouldn't really matter. The man was attractive—younger and better dressed than Riley's typical clients. Actually, not much older than Riley, if he had to guess. Young twenties at the absolute oldest.

Riley was used to the overweight men with saggy stomachs and pit stains, the ones who liked to make him hide his face while they called him "Good girl." Like if they said "girl" loud enough, he'd grow a vagina, and they wouldn't be gay.

Or, worse, the well-dressed men who liked to pinch his sides and leave bruises—the ones with too-white teeth and eyes like razor blades, capable of cutting him with just a glance.

"Sure." Riley pushed himself to his feet and hiked up his pants. They left miles of ankle exposed at the bottom but gaped around his waist. They were the last remaining things he had from *before.* "I know a place."

The man was well-dressed, and *his* jeans looked like the kind that cost more than a bottle of high-end Scotch. Riley's ass might be sore but maybe if he was good enough, he could ask the man for a few dollars extra — enough for dinner *and* a tube of hemorrhoid cream from the drug store.

If he had a computer and a few extra bucks, he'd buy stock in it, since they certainly made enough money off him.

The man followed Riley into a nearby alley. The dumpsters on this side of town were washed semi-regularly and only smelled kinda foul. They'd have to be quicker, though, because the businesses this way actually gave a shit if people fucked by 'em.

"So how do you want to do this? You want a blow job, or…" Riley grabbed the waistband of his jeans and went to shove them down. Even during a blowie, most of his customers wanted to see his ass.

But the man stumbled back, his hands raised like Riley had pulled a gun. "No! Shit, sorry! I actually meant lunch, not…" He trailed off, seeming barely able to say the words.

"People never mean lunch when they say lunch…" Riley wondered if the man was getting cold feet. It happened. Not often, but sometimes, especially with first-timers. And this one didn't look like the kind of guy to frequent corners on the regular. He was, if Riley was honest with himself, kinda hot. Probably, he got laid often enough on his own merits.

"Look, kid — "

"Not a kid," Riley cut him off.

He wasn't a *kid.*

Kids got to keep going to school and sleep on bunk beds and have sleepovers. *Kids* got to have their first kiss playing spin the bottle, not for the price of a favor passed from one man to another, neither of whom gave a shit what he wanted.

"I'm sixteen," Riley lied, dragging his mind away from the past. He was close enough anyway. "And I've been taking care of myself for years, so fuck off." If the man wasn't going to buy his ass, then Riley needed to get back to work somewhere else, so he shoved past him toward the street.

The man didn't let him get far. His hand formed an iron manacle on Riley's arm, jerking him to a stop. Riley froze for a split second before he yanked free.

He stumbled until he slammed into the brick behind him, his heart pounding. Memories flashed through Riley's head of other tricks and other hands — and of hands against windows as a car drove away.

"Sorry, sorry." Again, the man lifted his hands. Like somehow, that would convince Riley he wasn't a threat, despite his grabby hands. "Let me take you to lunch. Real lunch, with actual food."

Riley was missing something. Maybe the man wanted to bribe him with lunch then talk himself up as a pimp? It wouldn't be the first time someone tried, and Riley wasn't *that* stupid. He'd seen it too many times. Boys and girls who sold their ass just to give all their profit away in hopes of avoiding a beating. Riley was a free agent.

"Why? If you don't want my ass" — which Riley still thought unlikely — "what's in it for you?"

"Well, kid," the man started to say. Riley tensed, mouth opening to interrupt, but the man waved a hand to cut off the tirade Riley was preparing to give. "Okay, sorry, not a kid. But it's not like I know your name, dude, so what else am I supposed to call you?"

The pink-haired man cocked his hip and rested his hand rather flamboyantly on top of it. Something about the move made Riley relax, but only slightly.

Riley answered immediately, "Riley. You can call me Riley."

"Great. Well, *Riley*, I get to apologize for kicking over what was probably your lunch fund, and I get company for what would otherwise have been a boring meal at a taco stand or Tex-Mex or something. Nobody is sticking their dick in anyone, I promise."

After several moments of silence, Riley finally spoke, though his shoulders remained tense and his feet stayed pointing toward the alley, one step away from fleeing. "I guess you can buy me lunch. But I'm not fucking you. You promised."

Chapter Four

Lennox looked around his new apartment. The ad clipped haphazardly to the corkboard outside the Registrar's Office had read 'off-campus student housing' and he'd mistakenly assumed that meant a well-maintained dorm. Instead, he got...this.

Apparently, 'fully furnished' meant a living room with a springy couch and an off-keel coffee table, a kitchen that consisted of a microwave and a whiny fridge, and a tiny table with two rickety chairs squeezed into what was claiming to be a dining nook — if by nook, Lennox decided, it meant what used to be a closet but had at some point lost its doors. The rusty hinges were still visible, glaring at him over the back of the squished-in chairs.

It was a far cry from the house his parents had rented for him last year that he'd clearly underappreciated.

Lennox hadn't realized that he would only be allowed to keep living in it if he majored in pre-med. He *should* have known the Registrar was sending his parents copies of his transcripts every semester. For some odd reason, he'd thought that his grades were between him and the school...

Not him, the school and his parents. But of course, they paid his tuition and that, apparently, entitled them to his transcripts.

When his mom had asked Lennox — over the phone, thank God, so at least he didn't have to look her in the eyes during the lecture — why his new schedule was 'littered' with history classes about the Renaissance and the Enlightenment, he'd had to stutter his way through an explanation that he'd changed his major...at the beginning of last semester. And to subjects he didn't even *like* that much, but at least were better than the boring biology classes he'd been taking before.

Lennox figured — incorrectly — they'd be happy that he was at least getting a law degree. And that *he'd* be happy he wasn't falling asleep in his classes anymore — or having to pick up extra study sessions that went on until all hours of the morning with stuffy kids in sweater vests just to keep his C average.

And, *maybe*, he'd actually be able to *use* it someday. What on earth was he going to do with a medical license? Sure, he spent a lot of his free time in emergency rooms...but mostly because walking across a flat floor was a treacherous endeavor. Just last week he'd tripped in the art room and plunged a pair of embroidery scissors into his thigh.

He hadn't even been sewing. He'd just been putting them away for his friend Avea, whose wheelchair made navigating the narrow, and yet somehow still considered 'accessible', aisles difficult.

"Dude," a loud, gruff voice said from behind him, and Lennox jumped. "Are you going to stand in the doorway the whole time or let me get by?"

Flushing, Lennox sidestepped quickly out of the way, banging his elbow into the doorframe. He glanced at his new roommate, hoping he hadn't noticed, but the man was smirking. The landlord who took his application had told him his roommate's name was Mike and that he was a senior.

The only *other* thing Lennox knew about him was that he played...some sport, which he only knew because Mike was wearing a Texas Longhorns' jersey.

"Sorry." Lennox plastered on a bright smile of his own to hide his embarrassment. The luggage Mike was carrying looked like it weighed more than Lennox's whole body. He'd have no trouble making mincemeat of his face.

His new roommate just waved the apology off. "No biggie, man, just these bags are H. A. S."

"H. A. S.?" The acronym was one Lennox had never heard of, but unless it was medical terminology — hell, even then — he wasn't surprised. His parents might speak English fluently, but only in public. At home, he was expected to converse in Japanese. He had to 'respect their heritage'.

"Heavy as shit," Mike answered after a boisterous laugh. "You got a preference which room you want?"

Lennox shrugged. It was probably best if he kept whatever *preferences* he had to himself. "Not really." From the brief tour he'd taken when he'd signed the lease agreement, they were both the same — tiny as a prison cell with the stench of pot clinging to the drywall — just on opposite sides of the narrow hall. They'd have to share a bathroom.

"Then I'm taking this one," Mike decided, heading straight for the room on the right. "I heard there's a sorority next door, maybe one of the chicks will forget to close her curtains and I can cancel my *O.F.* subscription for the real thing."

"Of?" Lennox was going to need a subscription to Urban Dictionary — if that was even still a thing — to keep up with the conversation.

"*OnlyFans*? Come on, you can't tell me you've never heard of it. OnlyFans! The camming site?" Mike stared at him from the doorway, no longer seeming to notice the heavy weight in his hands. "You know... You pay to watch girls take their clothes off, maybe diddle the devil's doorbell? Sometimes live stream?"

Lennox stared blankly, and Mike shook his head. "Oh, you poor summer child. Don't worry. I'll hold off on canceling until you get a taste. We'll pop your cherry yet!" Mike chuckled and finally headed into his room.

Lennox grimaced now that the man couldn't see him. He had no desire to see boobs — not accidentally through a window, not on a laptop, and definitely never in person. He hoped his new roommate didn't have an issue with gays, because he was queer as a riverbend.

At least he was smart enough to keep *that* a secret from his uber-traditional parents.

Lennox scooped his duffel bags up off the floor and headed into the remaining bedroom. He dropped them by the dresser to unpack later, then collapsed onto his bed with a groan. At least Mama had insisted that his father let him keep his furniture, because he wasn't sure he'd be able to handle lying in someone else's mattress funk.

It's not like he'd even wanted to go to college in the first place, he mused, staring at the water-stained ceiling. That had been entirely his parents' decision, like most of the other things in his life.

At five, they'd assigned the neighbor boy, Ryan, to be his new best friend — even though Ryan was two years older than him and still wet the bed like a baby. At twelve, they paid for his braces to fix his overbite, but refused to let the orthodontist correct his snaggletooth. At sixteen, they'd bought him his first car, a giant gas-guzzling SUV, not willing to be shown up by their colleagues. He'd quietly traded it in for a second-hand Prius last year.

So he shouldn't be surprised that his career choice wasn't really a choice — not according to them, anyway. He was *going* to get his medical degree, whether he wanted it or not. He'd had to literally get on his knees and beg just to be allowed to go to school in Texas, instead of attending New York University as they expected. In the end, they only agreed because 'living away from home was a learning experience.' Really, he wanted to be closer to his sister.

Mama cried when she had to return the 'Proud Parents of an NYU Honor Student' bumper sticker. Heaven forbid, Lennox attend a college of *his* choice, not the one she'd picked out for him in kindergarten. He was certain that if Mama could get away with it, she would pick out his future spouse, too.

She expected him to marry a woman from a nice family.

Like his sister Ally had.

Lennox snorted at the sudden thought, the irony not lost on him at all. When they told his older sister how important it was she *"maintain the family image"* and marry well, he knew what that meant. They both did. *Marry rich.*

And Ally had.

She married one of the best pediatric surgeons in the country. Their parents were ecstatic—until they realized two things.

Dr. Bryer lived in Texas, not New York City. A fact they could live with.

And Dr. Bryer was a woman—a fact they could not.

His parents hadn't spoken to—or allowed him to speak *of*—Ally since.

He wished he knew how she was doing.

"Dude!" Mike banged on his door, the flimsy wood rattling in its frame. "You gotta come see the rack on this chick!"

Lennox sighed. "Nah, man, I'm really tired. Think I'm going to crash," he hollered back, adopting the closest thing to a dude-bro voice he could manage.

"Suit yourself then, I guess," Mike replied. Maybe Lennox should just...tell him? He'd never outed himself before, but he could treat it like a band-aid... Just blurt it out and get it over with.

"Mike, I'm a homosexual." *Too formal.*

"Mike, I'm gayer than a two-dollar bill." *Too antiquated, he might not understand.*

"Mike, I am a proud member of the alphab—"

"I get it, you're gay," Mike hollered from the hallway, the booming voice making him flinch. "Just don't leave any pocket rockets in the shower."

"What?" Lennox hollered back. "Why would I leave a toy rocket in the bathroom? Why would I *have* a toy rocket in the bathroom? I mean, maybe a toy boat..."

"A back door plunger? A selfie stick? Wand of plentiful pleasure? Dude, your fucking dildo, got it?"

Mike laughed, then Lennox heard him smack the door for emphasis.

"Oh!" Lennox blurted, grateful no one could see how red he turned. "I um...I don't have one? So, no worries. I won't leave...*that*...in the shower."

"Wait, seriously?" Before Lennox could protest, Mike pushed open the door and peered into Lennox's room. He looked honestly shocked. "What self-respecting gay man doesn't have a dildo? I mean, no offense, but I'm like, *totally* straight, and I have a really nice one. Not too long, not too thick, hits the spot just..." Mike did a chef's kiss with his fingers. "Perfect."

Lennox must have looked shocked, because Mike grinned and stepped fully inside the room, leaning against the frame with far too much casualness for the conversation. Personally, Lennox wanted to find a hole in the floor and shove his face in it like a teeny-tiny ostrich.

Mike's grin stretched. "What, you think only you gays like ass play? I mean, just because I like pussy doesn't mean I don't have a prostate. I'm just saying, between you and me? Ain't much better than a girl sucking you off and slipping a finger —"

"Okay," Lennox interrupted, cringing slightly at the thought. He didn't need to picture his roommate with *anyone's* fingers slipping *anywhere*. "Yep, I get it. I imagine that would be...nice?"

"Well, I mean *you'd* want a *boy* sucking you off and sticking *his* fingers —"

"O-kay, yep, I get it." Lennox's voice was high-pitched. He'd spent the previous twenty years of his life carefully avoiding *any* talk about sex, and boys, and most *especially*, sex *with* boys.

"Great! Then you understand why you absolutely *have* to have a dildo. Don't worry, you're in luck. A buddy of mine works part-time at the Pleasure Emporium." Mike gyrated his hips obscenely before clapping his hands. He started for the living room without waiting for Lennox to agree, and when Lennox followed him out, Mike was already sitting on the couch, putting his tennis shoes on.

"I really don't think —"

"Trust me. Once you try one, you'll never go back to the boring old rub'n'tug again. Come on." Mike held the door open. "I'll even drive."

"Oh, sure. That sounds...nice," Lennox said, his voice faint. Reluctantly, he followed the larger man out of the apartment. Maybe he should have kept pretending to be straight...

He doubled down on that thought when Mike parked his suburban outside the Pleasure Emporium.

He gulped at the thought of going in *there*. The sign was large and flashing, with a triple X glowing neon pink in the window. Of course, Mike hopped out with no problem, strolling toward the door like there was nothing to be ashamed of.

Which, Lennox acknowledged, there really wasn't. He was a grown man. He was living on his own, in an apartment he actually had to pay for. Well, kind of. He was using the trust fund he'd inherited from his grandparents to keep up with rent until he found a job, but still. His parents weren't paying it, so it counted.

And best of all, he was half a country away from them, so there was no way they'd ever need to know that he was at an...*adult* store.

Buying a dildo.

With his straight roommate.

God, when had his life turned into the start of a comedy romance? Lennox snickered as he got out of the car, trying to imagine how the film would go but unable to imagine Mike as the leading man. It helped take his mind off what he was about to do, at least.

Well, until he ended up red in the face, standing next to Mike in front of a wall stacked with dildos — big ones and small ones, dildos that vibrated and ones shaped like tentacles, dildos in boxes and dildos on hooks and one particularly large one suction cupped to the wall.

"You should start with something small," Mike decided, nudging Lennox away from the box labeled 'Monster Fucker' toward a more natural-looking one — or at least, one that *claimed* to feel like 'the real thing'. Lennox still thought it looked far too large and far too demanding to fit in his ass.

"What about this one?" Lennox asked, grabbing a smaller one from the shelf above. It was hot pink and slightly curved.

"Oh, one of my girlfriends had that model, and she *loved* it. Said it's got two speeds — '*I'm coming*', and '*good God, make it fucking stop!*'" Mike barked out a laugh.

Lennox couldn't help it. He had to laugh as well. He almost put the box back, uncertain if he wanted to play with the dildo now that he'd be thinking of Mike and his girlfriend every time he tried to use it. But in the end, it came with such a good recommendation... He stuck it under his arm.

"Good choice, man," Mike said agreeably, grabbing a *much* larger dildo, this one unpackaged except for the cardboard backing. He gave it an experimental tug, twisting his wrist on the upstroke.

Lennox looked away from the vulgar scene, a confused sort of erection starting in his pants. Since he wasn't watching, he jumped when Mike tossed a different case at him, fumbling it and barely keeping it from hitting the ground. "You should get those, too."

"What are they?" Lennox asked, finally clutching the box and turning it over to see the front. He felt his face heat as he saw the label. In giant print across the front, it read, 'Lovehoney Bumper Booty Bundle Anal Sex Toy kit—for Beginners'.

He almost dropped it again when he saw the white sticker in the corner. "It's sixty dollars!"

"Yeah, but it's a six-piece set. By the time you've worked your way through it, you should be able to upgrade to one of these babies," Mike bonked him on the head with the large dildo he'd been obscenely fondling. Then, he tapped the plastic over one of the black silicone plugs in the box. "*This* one vibrates."

Lennox decided not to ask how he knew that.

He also decided *not* to ask why Mike had a loyalty card to hand over when they checked out.

Some things you just *didn't* need to know about your roommate.

Though now that Lennox knew how Mike masturbated, maybe they'd already crossed that line.

Chapter Five

Riley left dinner stuffed full and forty dollars richer. He didn't even have to put out for it. And to top it all off, he had the address to an LGBTQ youth shelter in his pocket. He doubted they'd have room for him. He'd tried a few when he first hit the streets with no luck. The ones that *did* have beds were generally saving them for someone younger — or didn't want to risk housing a kid who refused to give his last name.

Best-case scenario, they had a bed.

Worst-case, he'd trick in a new part of town for a few days.

Which might be a good thing, because he'd started getting a few too many searching glances from cops.

With just his ratty backpack — the only thing he'd managed to keep of Sage's — holding everything he owned thrown over his shoulder, Riley scoured the map outside the bus stop, squinting at the small street names to find the one he was looking for. The nearest stop to the shelter would drop him off three blocks away.

He wasn't nervous until he stood outside the Victorian with its large, wraparound porch. Two teens were horsing around in the driveway, throwing a basketball at each other instead of the hoop attached above the garage door.

Unlike him, the boys were clean — both their bodies *and* their clothes — which looked like they fit, unlike Riley's, which hung off his near-skeletal frame like a garbage bag.

He didn't belong here.

His hole-strewn shoes whispered that he should just turn and leave, and he was about to listen when one of the boys dropped the ball and spotted him. "Hey!" the taller of the two teens called, waving him over.

Riley approached slowly, his hands wedged into his pockets. "Hey."

"You here for the Drop-in Center or the Rainbow House?" The boy had hair the color of a banana. Not blond, but...neon yellow. There was *no* way it was natural. Riley had a hard time looking away from it to meet the boy's brown eyes.

"Um..." Riley dragged his gaze down again. "Some guy said the Rainbow House? Is this it?" To him, the sprawling blue Victorian with perfect little white shutters didn't look like any youth shelter he'd ever seen. He'd expected a *factory* feel, or...or a church. This looked...nice.

"Yeah, you're in the right place. Want me to walk you in?"

"I guess," Riley agreed, stomach churning with nerves. "Yeah."

The shorter kid stayed in the driveway, dribbling the basketball, while the other guy grabbed Riley's arm. Riley flinched but didn't pull away.

The blond boy was a talker. He rambled the entire way up the porch into the house, bouncing from topic to topic without waiting for a reply. Riley learned the boy called himself Tweety, though his real name was Lorenzo, that he was seventeen and counting, and that he hated lollipops but they were the only thing that kept him from smoking.

Riley discovered *that* when the boy pulled a pair of suckers from the pocket of his blue basketball shorts and held one out for him.

He'd also learned that, despite his nickname, Tweety was petrified of birds…and dogs. And some fish, but only the ones with the eyes that looked like they were staring at you — which Riley thought was *all* fish, but Tweety disagreed.

Tweety was still trying to explain the difference when they approached a desk in the entryway. Riley found it too endearing to interrupt, but the pink-haired anime girl on the other side must have been used to it. She waited for Tweety to take a breath before quickly stepping into the conversation, her words making Riley realize she wasn't one of the residents but some kind of staff. "Lorenzo, it's your turn to help with laundry. Why don't you go find Ms. Beca and start gathering towels while I help your friend here?"

"But, Ms. Ally, what if he has questions? You know I'm *great* at answering questions! I can show him to his bed, tell him about the chore chart, help him meet the other kids and tell him the rules, then he can sit next to me during dinner and maybe he can help me sort the laundry — and what if he needs a nightlight? Or tucked in? Or—"

"Lorenzo," Ms. Ally interrupted with an exasperated sigh. "Ms. Beca will be done with the laundry by the time you go help her if you don't hurry up."

"Yeah, I know, but—" Tweety pouted.

"Laundry now, talk later." Ms. Ally shooed Tweety away with a smile creeping over her lips.

"Ugh, no fair! I never get to do *anything* fun! What if he makes a new best friend without me and I'm all stuck in the laundry room smelling like soap and sadness, crying into dryer sheets because I have no friends! All because *you* made me do laundry instead of—"

"You'll have Ms. Beca. I'm sure she'll be your friend," Ms. Ally suggested.

"I don't want a girlfriend. I want a boyfriend," Lorenzo wailed. "I mean...not a boyfriend. A friend, who is a boy, who can be my boy slash friend and do things that boys who are friends do—like...paint each other's nails, do each other's hair and talk about *boys*! Not girls!"

Riley couldn't hold in his snicker. He slapped his hand over his mouth when both Lorenzo, who had honest-to-God tears forming on his lashes, and Ms. Ally turned to look at him. "Sorry..."

"See? He already *gets* me, Ms. Ally! How could you tear us apart like this? Our friendship is destined by the sparkly rainbow glitter gods!" Tweety stamped his foot. It was kinda hilarious to see what Riley would have assumed was a muscle head, what with the tank top and basketball shorts and, you know...muscles, rhapsodizing on about glitter and rainbows.

Fuck stereotypes.

"I promise that your friend —" Ms. Ally started.

"*Best* friend," Tweety interrupted, crossing his arms with a mulish expression.

"Best friend," Ms. Ally corrected, "will still be here, filling out paperwork, by the time you get done helping Ms. Beca. Unless you don't go get started, then he really *might* have to start meeting people without you."

Tweety hesitated, literally rocking on his heels before he huffed. He stabbed his finger at Riley. "Don't go anywhere without me. I have so much to tell you."

"Uh...sure?" Riley agreed, already fearing that maybe he might regret it. Tweety seemed like someone who had a *lot* of energy to spare...and Riley wasn't sure he'd be able to keep up. Also, he still didn't know if they'd even have a bed for him, so he might be gone long before the boy returned.

Ms. Ally watched Lorenzo leave, shaking her head. "That boy," she said, before turning back to Riley. Her expression gentled. "You, my friend, are going to have your hands full. Lucky for you, we have a bed open in the room across the hall from him, so you won't have to share. Well, not with Lorenzo anyway. I think we can put you with Gray. Unless —" Ms. Ally stopped, biting her lip as she looked him over. "I'm so sorry, dear, I didn't ask your name or anything. You *do* identify as a boy, right? We have one more bed open in the wing for people who are transitioning?"

"I'm not trans," Riley answered. "So you *do* have beds open? I can stay?"

"Of course, honey. We try really hard not to turn anyone away, so even if we didn't have a bed, we'd make sure to find you something." Ms. Ally, with her bright smile, hair and wide eyes, looked like the angel on the sign across from the cathedral he liked to sleep behind — not in coloring, but in presence. He might hate churches, but sometimes the nuns gave away free food. As long as he avoided the priests with their starched collars, he could stomach it sometimes.

"We do have some paperwork to fill out, but don't worry. I'll help you through every step."

"I don't have ID," Riley admitted, his heart dropping as he realized paperwork likely meant legal forms, which meant birth certificates, social security numbers and *last names.*

"Don't worry, we have forms for that, too. You'd be surprised how common this problem is," she said.

"I'm not going back home." Riley folded his arms around his chest like a shield. "You can't make me, and if you try to, I'll just run away. I've done it before."

"Nobody will make you go anywhere you don't want to. Well, except to the doctor for a physical, but the center covers the cost for that. And I suppose if you *really* don't want to go, we could try to convince the doctor to make a house call. He does for emergencies. We just try to avoid it."

"I think...um, yeah, a doctor would be good?" It was embarrassing, but a doctor would have seen *everything* before, right? And it wasn't like he hadn't shown his asshole to too many men to count already.

"Great! I'll call and get an appointment set up as soon as we get all the paperwork filled out and you settled in your room. Why don't you come with me to my office?"

Chapter Six

As grateful as Riley was that the shelter was springing for a doctor, he was terrified to hear what they had to say. It's what had him clutching the thin paper gown they'd forced him into—with words only, no physical contact—like it would somehow make the doctor come in with only good n—

"Well, I have good news and bad news," the doctor said as he reentered the exam room, flipping through the chart on his clipboard. He was younger than Riley expected, which had made the whole anal swab and bend-and-cough situation just that much more awkward.

"Am I sick?" Riley asked, biting his lip hard to stop the next question. *Am I dying?*

"Yes, that's the bad news, unfortunately. But the good news is that it's curable, so I don't want you to worry." Dr. Townsley pulled over his stool so he could sit at Riley's side. His expression was gentle, sympathetic—and did nothing to stem Riley's nerves.

What kind of doctor told someone they were sick by saying they have good news and bad news? Like…it wasn't an 'oopsie, I broke your favorite mug, but we have Gorilla Glue in the cabinet' kind of conversation?

"What is it?" Riley asked, digging his fingernails into his forearms. "It's not…"

"You have several anal fissures that are healing nicely on their own, but I'll send you home with a cream to apply, just to speed that along. You are also dehydrated and malnourished, but I'm confident that the Rainbow House will do well in addressing those issues. What I'm most concerned with is the results of your STI panel."

The doctor had barely finished speaking but Riley didn't want to hear it. Just the *word* STI had him cringing, burying his face in his hands as he started to shake.

"Take a deep breath, hold it… There you go, that's it." Dr. Townsley talked him through his anxiety attack. It took a few minutes, but finally Riley's breathing slowed down. "Better now?"

Riley shrugged but gave a small nod. It was, of course, a lie. No one was *better* after hearing they had bad news on an STI panel.

"Good, that's good. Now, most of your tests came back normal, but you do have gonorrhea. Wait! Take a breath," Dr. Townsley hurried to say as Riley's breath caught in his lungs again. "It's a common diagnosis and completely treatable with a round of antibiotics. Just make sure you take every dose and abstain from sexual activity until at least a week after you finish treatment. We'll have you come back for a check-up in two weeks, just to be certain, but I am fully confident that you should experience no long-term effects."

"I thought only girls could get that?" Riley asked.

"It's a common misconception. I can send you home with a pamphlet, if you'd like. I'd also suggest you stop by the reception desk after you check out for some condom samples, if you're going to continue to be sexually active," Dr. Townsley said.

Riley tensed, but the doctor didn't say it like an accusation or like it was something that Riley should be ashamed of, so after a few seconds he nodded and relaxed.

He didn't plan on fucking anyone again anytime soon, but maybe he'd grab a handful or two, just in case things at the Rainbow House fell through.

He left the doctor's office with his script and the condoms, joining Ms. Beca in the lobby a bit sheepishly, embarrassed to admit that he needed the antibiotic. Unlike with Ms. Ally, he felt nervous around her. She was nice enough, but something about her made him think of his old nanny, a cold woman who'd spent more time on her phone than watching him. Unfortunately, Ms. Ally was busy, and he'd not had a choice.

Despite his worry, Ms. Beca took the prescription with a smile that didn't judge. She picked up his scrip for him and even treated him to a fast-food ice cream cone before driving him back to the Rainbow House.

Tweety met him at the door, bouncing on the balls of his feet. "You're back! Finally, you were gone *forever*. Do you want to play Mario Kart with me? Or we could get out the old Nintendo 64 and play Donkey Kong? I'll even be Diddy Kong so you can go first?"

"Um…" Riley turned to look at Ms. Beca. "Is it okay, or do I have to do chores first?"

"We'll assign you chores next week, once you've settled in. I don't see a problem with you going to the game room. Just make sure you go to the nurse before dinner for your new med," Ms. Beca said, waving him away with a smile that softened the lines around her eyes.

Riley waited for the moment when Tweety asked *why* he was on a med and he'd have to admit the truth, but Tweety just grabbed his hand and dragged him along behind him, already rambling about his favorite levels.

* * * *

Later that night, Riley scrambled up the ladder to the top bunk and flopped down on his comforter. It was a few minutes shy of curfew, and he held his breath as he waited. Finally, the alarm for lights out sounded, and he released a sigh.

He really liked spending the day with Tweety, but the kid was *exhausting*. If Riley didn't know that it was impossible to smuggle in drugs or alcohol — and if they weren't randomly drug tested at least once a month — he'd have assumed the other boy was on speed. That, or snorting Ritalin, because no one should have this much energy *naturally*.

Riley got tired just watching him.

Ten minutes after he collapsed boneless on his mattress, a quiet knock sounded on the door. "Riley?" Tweety whispered through the wood. "Are you still up?"

Riley groaned and almost rolled off the bed as he sought out the ladder with his feet. He climbed down carefully and tiptoed to the door. "It's late. You should be in bed."

"I can't sleep. Can I come in?"

"Won't we get in trouble?" Riley hesitated, shifting his weight as his heartbeat quickened. He didn't want to risk getting kicked back out onto the street, no matter *how* lonely Tweety was.

"Not if we're quiet," Tweety promised.

Riley glanced at the bottom bunk. His roommate was lying curled up on his side, facing the wall with his comforter pulled over his head. Reluctantly, Riley cracked open the door.

"Gray's asleep," he warned Tweety, holding it open just far enough to let the boy slip in.

"He won't care that I'm in here." Tweety waved off the concern as he shuffled over to Riley's bed. He made climbing the ladder look easy as he scrambled up onto the mattress, crawling under the comforter and scooching close to the wall. "I've always wanted to have a sleepover."

"Don't you have a roommate, too?" Riley pointed out as he climbed back into bed, rolling to face Tweety.

"Yeah, but he's *boring*. He wants me to stay in my own bed and only touch my own stuff — and it's not the same," he pouted.

"I mean, I'm going to be pretty boring, too, you know. I have to help with breakfast in the morning, so I really do need to get to sleep." Riley couldn't hold back his yawn.

"You can go to sleep now. I can be quiet. And your bed is really comfortable, so it won't even be that hard. Like, I think you got a special mattress or something, because mine is all lumpy and squeaks if I bounce on it." Tweety abruptly shifted, wiggling up and down so the mattress felt like it was vibrating. Riley clenched the edge of the frame, immediately fearing being tossed off.

Or, worse, the whole thing breaking and crushing the older kid below him. "Yours doesn't make a sound."

"I wish *you* wouldn't make a sound," Riley's roommate finally snapped, his voice echoing through the quiet room. "Go to *sleep*! Or go back to your own room!"

"I'll go to sleep, I promise. I'm just so excited," Tweety replied. "It's like one of those TV shows that—"

An angry Gray poked his face over the side of the bed and tossed a lumpy pillow right at Tweety's face. Riley bit his lip on a laugh. *Is this a threat to smother us if we don't be quiet?*

"Shutting up now," Tweety said, grabbing the pillow and shoving it under his head with a laugh.

Chapter Seven

Two weeks after the trip-that-shall-not-be-spoken-of, Lennox sat rather uncomfortably on one end of the couch. He'd decided just a few minutes earlier that he'd graduated butt plugs too soon, withdrawing the medium-sized plug with a yelp that he hoped to God Mike hadn't heard. From the smirk on his roommate's face, he didn't think that he'd gotten that lucky.

Now, Mike sprawled on the other end of the sofa, his hairy thighs peeking out from the hem of his basketball shorts—not that Lennox was looking.

"My girlfriend is coming over tonight," Mike said conversationally right before taking a giant bite of the pepperoni-pickle-and-pineapple pizza, his eyes still fixated on the sports-ball game on TV, where someone had just scored a touchdown in the goal-ball-basket thing.

Lennox could have sworn that his roommate had broken up with someone a few days earlier, since all he could hear was crying, moaning and things falling down in the kitchen.

"You have a girlfriend?" Lennox asked around his own bite, almost choking when his haste to swallow made it slide down the wrong pipe. He took a drink of the vile beer to wash it down, a momentary pang of homesickness making him wish for *nihonshu* instead.

"Yeah, kind of. It's an open relationship. You know how it goes." Mike shrugged.

"Uh...sure?" Lennox hesitantly agreed. He didn't *really* know how that went. He'd never actually dated anyone, always too busy studying—or pretending to study—so his parents didn't question why he never wanted to ask out "*that pretty Asian girl down the street.*"

"She'll be here after the game," Mike continued, still staring at the screen. There were three minutes left of the third inning.

"Okay," Lennox said, confused. Mike seemed to be hinting at something Lennox didn't understand.

Finally, Mike sighed and looked toward him, an apology in his eyes. "Dude, do you think you could uh...find somewhere else to go? For a few hours? Wendy gets really frisky, and while *I* don't care if you hear us, she won't do nothing if she thinks you can hear her, if you know what I mean..."

"Oh. Oh! Yeah, sure, no problem, I'll just...um." Lennox flushed and dropped the crust of his pizza on his plate, standing up to carry it to the kitchen. "I'll go visit my sister." He'd always been planning on heading out to the Center where she worked eventually...but he'd been putting it off for the past few years, always afraid his parents would find out somehow and cut him off.

Which they'd done anyway, so he guessed now he had no more excuses.

"Hey, Lenny?" Mike hesitated. Lennox winced at the silly nickname but turned back anyway. "You think you could clean up your dishes in the kitchen before you go? And maybe pick up some of..." Mike waved a hand at the scattered detritus that seemed to follow Lennox everywhere.

The precarious stack of textbooks teetering on the edge of the coffee table, the paints uncapped on the bookshelf, the random sock near the base of the entertainment stand...

"Oh, yeah, I can do that. Sorry... I guess I got distracted." Lennox felt a tendril of shame coiling in his belly. Of course Mike was too nice to tell him he was cluttering the place up, but Lennox wasn't used to sharing space. No one cared if he didn't pick up after himself in the house his parents had been letting him use, since he'd lived alone, and back in New York, his mom had a cleaning lady who came in twice a week.

Mama was always so proud of his mess, happy that her 'precious baby boy' was too busy studying to worry about something so minuscule as cleaning.

Lennox tidied up quickly, forcing himself to stay on task as he carted his belongings back to his bedroom to drop on his mattress. It took a few trips, but by the time the buzzer for the front door sounded, the apartment looked...*less* cluttered.

He'd forgotten the dishes, but Mike waved him away before he could wash them. He slipped on his shoes and opened the door, skirting past the busty redhead on the stoop with an awkward wave. He wasn't even down the stairs before Mike was greeting her with a loud, wet kiss and dragging her inside.

Her laughter echoed in the entryway before the door cut it off.

Lennox pulled out his phone to open his sister's profile page on SpaceyFace. He took a moment, scrolling through her previous posts until he found the name of the youth shelter he'd heard she'd opened shortly after moving to the city.

He couldn't help noticing the several pictures of her and her wife—always happy, always smiling...even when they both looked tired.

He forced himself to scroll back down to the shelter name, and a quick search online got him the address. He plugged it into a rideshare app. He hadn't gathered the courage to ride the bus yet, though it was on his list of 'Someday Things'. Then, he finished walking down to the sidewalk to wait.

When the car finally pulled up, he almost wished it hadn't.

The old man was so short he could barely see over the wheel, with Coke-bottle glasses and a habit of scrunching up his nose when he was trying to see. None of this was the problem.

It was the scent memory still lodged in his nasal cavities from the *last* trip he'd taken with this driver that filled him with regret.

Unfortunately, the man's car still smelled just as strongly of menthol and skunkweed.

He held his breath as long as he could, but when the car finally dropped him off outside a blue Victorian house, he was fairly sure he'd gotten a contact buzz. He practically tumbled out onto the sidewalk. Though, honestly, it *could* be his natural clumsiness.

Regardless, he was blaming the marijuana.

He waved halfheartedly as the chatty man pulled away from the curb, driving so slow he may as well have been reversing, then turned back to the house. It looked too small to house the number of homeless youths a city like Austin must have, but maybe that was because the Rainbow Center only catered to LGBTQ youth.

Or, the less naïve part of him spoke up, *there simply isn't enough funding to support a bigger place.*

As he walked up the uneven sidewalk, it became even more obvious that the real answer was money.

Oh, the house was lovely, he supposed, certainly not completely falling apart. At least, it wasn't in any worse shape than the others in the neighborhood — but he saw the peeling paint on the white shutters and the way the porch railing bowed near the center, one heavy hand away from coming loose.

Near the stairs, an older teen boy in baggy jeans and a sweater despite the heat hovered behind a pink-haired woman in overalls. While he held the railing, she struck the base — more likely, he realized, a nail — with a small hammer, clearly trying to DIY-it back to health.

The woman looked up when he approached, a friendly smile on her lips. Her dark brown eyes were wide and lined with glitter that shimmered in the sun, distracting him long enough that it took him several long seconds to see past the happiness and recognize…

"Ally?"

Chapter Eight

Ally's smile faltered, and she straightened quickly to her feet. "Lennox? What are you doing here? Does Mama know you're here? Because I already told Papa I'm not going to come back for his charity dinners and put on a happy smile and pretend to be straight for the donors at his firm. I—"

"No, they don't know I'm here," Lennox interrupted, eyeing the hammer still clutched, white-knuckled, in her hand.

She followed his gaze, then cursed under her breath, quickly tucking it away into a toolbox and turning to the boy beside her. "Gray, why don't you go inside and wash up? I think we're about done for the day, anyway."

The kid shoved his hands farther into the pocket of his oversized sweater. "I can finish without you, if you want?"

"No, but thank you, I appreciate the offer. I think I'm going to have to go to the lumber yard anyway, as I doubt this is salvageable." Ally's smile was fond as the boy hesitated before finally walking away, staring suspiciously over his shoulder at Lennox — like he thought Ally was in danger and he, despite his lanky build, was going to protect her.

It was sweet, even if she didn't need protection from him. Even if Lennox *wanted* to cause trouble — which he didn't — he was still just as svelte as the teen. He could barely swat a fly. The only difference between him now and when they'd last seen each other was the clip-on earrings he was trying out. She'd been able to pin him down since they had been adolescents.

Lennox plastered on an uncomfortable smile and shifted his weight. Ally didn't seem excited to see him, or happy. She sounded suspicious, if anything.

Maybe he shouldn't have come.

Maybe she didn't miss him the way he missed her. After all, she was ten years older than him, the planned baby in comparison to his 'oops'.

Of course, Mama and Papa had shunted her aside as soon as they had their 'precious boy', not that he'd realized the change as a child until he was almost in his teens and saw the difference in the way they were treated.

He wouldn't blame her if she wanted nothing to do with him.

"I heard you were going to school at the university here." Ally finally broke the tense silence just as Lennox had decided to leave. He could always go kill time at the library. "Are you enjoying it?"

Lennox shrugged and looked down at his feet, not really wanting to talk about himself when he felt like he had so much to apologize for. "It's okay. I like some of my history classes but..."

"It's not art." Ally sounded sympathetic, and when he glanced up, her smile was gentle. She didn't look angry anymore. "I'm sorry. I know our parents are shit."

Immediately, she cringed, glancing around like she was worried about being overheard, then relaxing. "Sorry, but you have no idea how sneaky teenagers are. They like to pop out of the woodwork like whack-a-moles at the *most* inconvenient times. Would you like to come in? You can't go into the dorm area, but we can go to the kitchen and grab a coffee?"

"Sure." Lennox hated coffee, but he would drink it to be polite.

"How do you take it?" she asked as she led him inside, down a hallway past a desk and past what looked like a game room. It was a struggle, but he managed not to stare in, despite his overwhelming curiosity. He hadn't seen an actual Pac-Man game in years.

"Um..." Lennox stuttered around an answer. He knew he didn't want the bitter motor cleaner that was black coffee but wasn't sure if adding milk would make it any better.

Ally laughed. "How about we start with a bunch of sugar, then we can doctor it up from there."

In the end, he settled on several heaping scoops of sugar and some flavored cream to make it palatable. By then, it was lukewarm. Nothing to write home about, but the expression on Ally's face as she sipped her own caramel-laced was so orgasmic it made him uncomfortable to see.

They sat in silence for a long stretch, him nursing his coffee, her savoring hers. Finally, though, he broke the quiet. "How's Jada?"

Ally shrugged, but her smile softened at the mention of her wife, the love still clear as day in her expression. "She's been busy. They're putting in a new pediatric wing, and she's been consulting with the architects a lot. And I mean, her hours were never all that reasonable to begin with, so we're a bit like ships in the night, you know?"

"You're still happy, though?" Lennox twirled his spoon in his coffee, pushing the sugar sludge around the bottom.

"I couldn't ask for a better wife. Don't worry, we're solid," Ally promised.

"I'm glad." Lennox shifted in his chair. "So, um…a youth center, huh?"

"What can I say? It was a cause that spoke to my heart and luckily, Jiji and Baba left us enough of an inheritance that I could follow through with it." Lennox felt a bit guilty at the mention of the trust their grandparents left them. She was spending hers on this place, and he was using his to…what? Spite their parents?

"Oh, Lennox," Ally gushed, hurrying over to the table to drop into the chair beside him. "You should see some of these kids. Listen to their stories…" She shook her head, her eyes burning into him. "They are so much stronger, so much *braver*, than I would have been at their age."

"I don't know… I think you're pretty damn brave, Ally-*Kuma*." His Ally bear. He missed sneaking into her room during thunderstorms, and the way she'd brush his hair at bedtime.

"You haven't called me that since you were knee-high," Ally mused, reaching out and, after what seemed both a moment and a lifetime's hesitation, ruffling his hair. "It's really good to see you, Noxy-*Hachi.*"

Her little bee. She'd jokingly said it was because he never stopped buzzing around her.

The old nickname sent warm fuzzies through his chest. "I...I really missed you, Ally."

"I missed you too, Bug."

The soft moment was broken when two boys in bathing trunks stumbled into the kitchen, one after the other. The one in front had neon yellow hair, and peals of laughter spilled loudly from his mouth. The blond boy behind him was beet red and dragging his feet like he was being pulled into a firing range.

"Tweety," the second boy spat.

"Ms. Ally, Riley and I are *starving*! I told him you wouldn't mind if we grab a snack. You don't, right? Because I know Ms. Beca made banana bread yesterday and I only got a really tiny little piece, so we can have another one, right? And maybe some lemonade? And it would be fine..."

"Slow down, Tweety. I think..." Ally tried to say.

"We could take it out into the backyard and set up the sprinklers and have a picnic..."

"Tweety, we're having dinner in a few hours. Maybe..." Ally's eye twitched, the same way it used to whenever Lennox did something silly, and she was trying not to laugh.

"Because Riley's never had a picnic before, or at least not here, and it's definitely going to be different here, right?" The kid named Tweety sucked in a breath.

Ally jumped into the silence. "You'll have to wait until dinner for the banana bread or else all the kids will want some. But yes, you may go turn on the sprinkler in the backyard."

The other boy, the red-faced one, kept staring at Lennox, but tore his gaze away when he realized he'd been caught. Lennox laughed as the two teenagers darted into the backyard.

Ally sighed and leaned back in her chair, shaking her head as she watched the door bang shut. "Careful. That used to be you, Bug, before Papa convinced you to act like his little mini-me."

Lennox flushed, shame rising in his chest as the smile slid from his face. He dropped his gaze as the memory flooded him.

Six-year-old Lennox, clumsy with his big feet and even bigger shoes. He clutched his art project in tiny hands, proud of the big, gold ribbon stuck carefully on the corner. He couldn't wait to show Papa. He'd spent dozens and dozens of minutes at his desk, even skipping a whole half *of recess, just to finish it.*

The big yellow house on the paper was too small, but he liked that. Papa looked like a giant, a great big superhero standing beside Mama. And he'd been so careful drawing Ally in her pretty pink dress, the new one that she got just last week with it's pretty sparkly tutu and great big bow.

He knew he wasn't supposed to bother Papa in his office, but this was different. *This was* special, *and he just knew Papa wouldn't mind.*

Papa was going to be so proud of him.

Lennox flinched, struggling not to dwell on the way Papa had ripped the painting from his hands and thrown it into the trash, but not before telling him he'd never amount to anything if he didn't get more serious about school instead of wasting his time on crap. Lennox had thrown away his crayons and picked out his very first blazer, just like the one Papa wore.

He hadn't given up art for good — but he'd given it up for years. Even now, he got antsy when he picked up a paintbrush, like his father was looming over his shoulder, casting a shadow on the canvas.

"Oh, Bug, I'm sorry. I was just teasing. I know he was hard on you. I always counted myself lucky I was born a girl, or he'd have had those same expectations for me," Ally said, reaching out to squeeze his hand.

Lennox plastered on a smile. "It's okay. I'm over it. Papa was probably right, anyway. They aren't called 'starving artists' for nothing, right?"

Chapter Nine

Riley barely held back his questions until they were outside. The guy in the kitchen looked a bit nerdy with his button-down shirt and black trousers, but there was something about him that kept drawing Riley's eyes.

"Who was *that*?" Riley finally blurted as the kitchen door slammed shut behind them and he and Tweety tumbled into the grass. The backyard was overgrown, but not in an unkempt way. It was wild and free, like a slice of the wilderness.

"Hm? I don't know. I've never seen him before. Too old to be a resident, though. Could be a donor, I guess, because he looked like he's got money. Did you see his shoes? Fancy stuff, that. Anyway, donors stop in occasionally to make sure their money's being well spent. Like this one guy, a lawyer? He likes to make sure that there's always dance equipment, and sometimes he comes for the kids to put on little recitals."

Riley tried really hard not to think of how weird it was, some old man coming to watch kids dance. Before he could get the image out of his head, Tweety was going on, "And this really old woman is always super worried about the number of books available. Thinks a kid who's stuck in a book is less likely to be robbing gas stations, which I *guess* makes sense," Tweety continued rambling about all the various people who gave money and stuff to the Center as he hooked up the sprinklers to the long, green hose.

"Careful, the water comes out hot," Tweety finally broke from his lecture to warn him.

And it did, spluttering out a sun-warmed spray into the grass. Riley didn't care. It wasn't hot enough to blister his skin, even if it was a tad uncomfortable. After spending so long struggling just to find clean enough water to drink, dancing in it felt freeing, like it was finally washing the stain of the streets off his skin. He closed his eyes and tilted his face beneath the mist, feeling the way it kissed his cheeks.

Tweety was talking and part of Riley was listening, nodding along and smiling when the conversation warranted, but the rest of him was calm...safe. He didn't even care when Gray slunk out of the house and scolded them for wasting water, guilting them into shutting the sprinkler off.

Instead, they sprawled out on the cement, towels rolled under their heads like pillows, and basked in the sun.

"Oh, boys..." Ms. Ally's voice woke him from his sleepy haze, and he startled, looking up to see her staring down at him with pity.

Riley blinked, glancing at Tweety. The other boy was passed out, his tan skin just a few shades darker.

He didn't see why Ms. Ally sounded so concerned...until he looked down and saw his chest.

He'd have gone pale if it were possible, but his skin was so flushed and red that no one would have been able to tell.

"Shit," he cursed, his voice whiny. He should have *known* to put on sunscreen, fair as he was, but he honestly hadn't thought of it. After all, he hadn't had the time or ability to lounge around outside in years. On the street, even in summer he was fully covered, ankle-to-wrist. He couldn't risk his cold weather clothes getting stolen if his bag got grabbed.

"Come inside, and we'll get you in a cool bath. I think I have some aloe in the fridge..." Ms. Ally trailed off with a wince. "And maybe we should get you some Motrin..."

Tweety woke with a snort, stretching his arms up. "Oh, Ms. Ally! Is it dinnertime? I was ju— Holy shit! Dude, Riley, I've never *seen* anyone so red! Does it hurt?"

"Not now, Tweety. Can you go inside and ask Ms. Beca to bring the Motrin to the upstairs bath? And maybe grab Riley some baggy clothes to wear?" Ms. Ally asked. Tweety bounced up and sprinted inside, ignoring Ms. Ally's call to use walking feet. She just sighed and urged Riley inside. She had him pause in the kitchen so she could grab a bottle of green gel out of the fridge. The shaggy-haired man from earlier was still sitting at the breakfast table, an empty mug in front of him. Riley was staring, which was how he noticed those pretty brown eyes widen at the sight of him.

"Oh boy, I hope you're a back-sleeper, or it's going to be a long week," the man said without appearing to think about it.

"Lennox, that's not helpful," Ms. Ally said, and to Riley's surprise, the man blushed nearly as red as Riley.

"Sorry, Sis."

It explained their relationship and, now that Riley had the clue, he felt a bit silly. He could see the resemblance far too easily. They had the same eyes. "I am," Riley blurted. "A back-sleeper, I mean."

Lennox, Riley decided, had a nice smile.

Unfortunately, that was the moment Ms. Ally ushered him upstairs. She rapped on the door to the bathroom, only opening it when no one answered. Riley could see a stack of clothes on the counter next to a pair of white oblong tablets. "I know it might be tempting but be careful not to make it too cold, just keep it nice and cool. Put this on when you're done, it'll help...a little." She pressed the aloe gel into his hands.

Riley barely remembered to lock the bathroom door before he got undressed. As much as the idea of an ice-cold bath lured him in like a siren call, he knew better than to ignore Ms. Ally's warning.

He grimaced as he swallowed the tablets dry, the chalky taste sticking to his tongue, then started filling the tub. His skin felt hot and dry, stretched tight over his wiry muscles, like it belonged to someone else — or, maybe, like it was his old skin, returned to him from childhood, two sizes too small, shrunk in the wash and abandoned at the bottom of a dresser drawer.

He hissed as he sank into the water. At least the sunburn wasn't too sore yet, though he could tell from the heat radiating off his skin that he would be miserable later.

Riley almost smiled. There was something freeing about knowing that the only reason this week would suck was because of a measly *sunburn*—not because of a rough client, a sore ass or running from the cops.

Riley settled deeper in the tub. For the first time since coming to the Rainbow Center—hell, for the first time since he'd fled his parents' house—he was able to relax. It took him several long seconds to identify the warm feeling in his chest. It was safety.

Security. Something he hadn't had in...well, ever.

Eventually, the water felt too cold, even with the heat pouring from him, and he dragged himself out of the tub, his muscles like soup. And though the clothing was, as promised, too large, the drag of it against his skin still sucked big old donkey balls. He was just this side of tender, and he felt like he was walking bowlegged as he made his way back down the suddenly too-steep stairs to the kitchen.

Ms. Ally was sitting at the table with her brother again.

"Can I eat in here with you?" Riley blurted, having no desire to eat in the larger dining area where other residents threw elbows to get to the best roll or the last scoop of beans. "Just tonight? And...maybe tomorrow?" Riley practiced his best puppy-dog eyes, the ones that sometimes convinced old ladies on the street to give him an extra dollar.

Ms. Ally smirked but nodded. "I already saved you a plate. It's in the microwave."

"Thanks!" Riley barely kept himself from bouncing as he spun on his heel to grab it. He didn't even care that it was sloppy joes, a meal that reminded him too much of last summer when he had scrounged a dozen cans from a garbage can and ate nothing else for weeks.

Today, it tasted like his old summer camp cookout— one of the few fond memories he held of his childhood.

* * * *

Lennox stared at the younger boy as the kid washed his plate at the sink. He couldn't remember a time when he'd ever felt that…comfortable in his own skin. The boy was humming something under his breath, a smile on his chapped, sun-cracked lips. Even burnt to a near crisp, he looked happy.

Lennox didn't remember what 'happy' felt like.

He wasn't even old enough to drink but he knew obligation and debt, rules and regulations — how to put on a fake face to appease his parents.

He didn't know 'happy'.

"He's too young for you," Ally murmured, a playful grin on her lips.

"I *know*," Lennox answered immediately, his cheeks burning. He wasn't staring because of *that*. "He's practically a *baby*, Ally!" Lennox whined, sounding like a baby himself.

Ally laughed. "Oh, I know. I'm just teasing. But don't think I didn't notice that you never said anything about *him* being a 'he'. You know I'm here if you ever want to talk, right?"

Lennox stayed quiet, not speaking until the boy waved and left the two of them alone. He sighed, slouching back in his chair. "It's ironic, isn't it? Mama and Papa hate faggots so much, and they ended up with two of us?"

Ally grimaced. "I hate that word."

"Yeah. Me, too." Lennox ran a hand through his hair. "But Papa says it all the time. You know what he said when I told him I didn't want to go to prom?"

"I can guess," Ally muttered, her voice dark.

"*'What are you, a faggot?'*" Lennox parroted, rolling his eyes. "I really, *really* wanted to tell him to shove my tux up his ass and buy me a dress instead."

"As satisfying as *I* would have found that, I'm glad you didn't. They'd have cut you off, just like they did me."

"Does that make me a horrible person? I feel like it does. I mean...I'm pretending to be their perfect, straight-A *straight* son, just so they pay my tuition and my rent. And now they aren't even *paying* my rent. I'm staying at this off-campus apartment with a football player, of all people. Though, I guess I can't complain. He seems really friendly, even if he did kick me out so he could hook up with his girlfriend." Lennox trailed off, unsure if that made it sound like he was only here because he didn't have a choice, which wasn't true.

"It doesn't make you a horrible person at all. You shouldn't have to be straight to go to college. But putting that aside, if the rules of the game aren't fair, then sometimes you have to break them. If staying in the closet makes sure you have a roof over your head, then you do what you gotta do. But, little brother..." Ally reached out and grabbed his hand, giving it a reassuring squeeze. "If you want out, I'll support you in a heartbeat. Jada and I have a futon—you can stay on it as long as you need, rent free. And I've still got enough in my trust to cover your tuition, if it comes to that."

Lennox teared up as he shook his head. "I can't do that, but it means a lot that you would offer. I want you to use that to keep helping these kids. I've been thinking, and Mama and Papa are back in New York. I think...I think I can start learning how to be *me*, whoever that is... Our parents...they don't love *me*.

They only love who they think I am, you know? I don't think I care if I have to keep pretending with them. They don't deserve to know the real me anyway."

"Damn right they don't."

Chapter Ten

Four years later

"But... But, Ally," Lennox whined at his sister, "Mike *just* moved out. Like...last year." Plopping down on his armchair, he had to hold back his wince when a paintbrush stabbed him in the ass—and not in the fun way.

Ally sighed, and the sound spread a phantom itch over Lennox's arms. His sister had a big heart, and Lennox hated disappointing her. He was going to cave, he knew it. He *always* caved when it came to Ally. Staying in Austin after he passed the Bar exam was the best decision he'd ever made, even if it meant accepting the 'just-forget-we-cut-you-off-that-one-semester' apology house his parents 'gifted' him with right before the graduation ceremony. He was lucky they passed over the deed beforehand, considering what they'd seen *after*.

"I know, Lennox. Trust me. I get that you like your space." Ally glanced around his messy living room, reaching out to nudge one of the dirty plates on the coffee table a bit farther away from her. "But the kid's having a rough time. I *worry* about him. He's aging out, and he doesn't have anywhere to go. I shouldn't even be talking to you about this, so that right there should prove how worried I am." She batted her eyes at him.

"Doesn't the Rainbow House have a system in place for this kind of situation?" Lennox asked with last-ditch desperation, running his fingers through his shaggy black hair. Unfortunately, he only remembered afterward that his fingers were still coated in the remnants of his last project. The brilliant blue paint caked the strands.

"We try, but there's only so much we can do. Next Step housing is all full. We don't have anything opening for six months, and the policies at the Rainbow House absolutely will not let anyone over the age of twenty stay, as it's not safe for the other kids. He's only got a few months left. You wouldn't *really* make him live on the streets again, would you, Lennox?" Ally pouted, going far enough to conjure crocodile tears. He knew they weren't real—and she knew that he knew, since she could never cry without her face turning blotchy and red—but she also knew he couldn't resist them.

"Tell me about him?" Lennox finally asked, grimacing when Ally's face broke into a wide smile, as if there had been any chance he wouldn't cave.

"His name is Riley. He turns twenty next week. He's a great kid. Actually, I think you met him? That first time you came to visit? Kid with the sunburn? I promise he's quiet, stays out of trouble, does his chores without complaining." Ally paused, fixing him with a stern glare. "Which does not mean you can use him as your personal maid, Lenny."

Lennox shuddered. "You know I hate that name. Only old people are called Lenny. And *boring* ones."

Ally grinned, not looking at all apologetic. "Sorry, Lennox. Old habits."

Lennox let it go. "Does the kid at least have a job?"

"Yeah, he works part-time at an animal shelter," Ally explained.

Lennox did the math. Unless the shelter was one of those fancy private ones that catered to the rich and famous — doubtful — it wouldn't pay much, especially if he was only part-time. He didn't think that the kid could afford what Ally was suggesting he ask for rent. Maybe he should cut it in half.

"It'll take me a few days to clean up the spare room," Lennox finally broke. He'd been meaning to do it for months, ever since Mike had moved in full-time with his girlfriend from college, but he could never seem to get around to it.

Ally eyed him nervously, then glanced toward the door down the hall. "Please tell me you didn't get another cat..."

"That was not my fault! I was twelve!" Lennox winced as his voice pitched higher at the end, creeping into the territory of a lisp he'd spent a decade trying to hide. His parents wanted a straight son — a straight, *manly* son with a law degree. They got...a son with a law degree...which he was pretty sure he'd stored somewhere in the house — or the shed.

"Yeah, and we almost had to move, your room smelled so bad." Ally snickered.

"I hate you." Lennox moaned. "You never let me live anything down." It really wasn't his fault. How was he supposed to know the skinny creature wasn't a cat? Skunks were supposed to have *stripes*, not *spots.*

Ally's phone buzzed, and she tugged it out of her pocket, her smile wilting. "I have to go. I have a meeting at four. Can you have the room ready by Friday?"

It was Tuesday. Lennox could have the room done by Friday...as long as he didn't get distracted. "Yeah. Totally. No problem." He nodded.

"I mean it, Lennox. If I send him over, it better be ready." Ally lost the joking tone. "Riley's been through a lot already. I don't want to regret sending him to you."

"You won't. The room will be done by Friday. Promise."

"You know today's Wednesday, right?" Ally pressed.

"Of course," Lennox lied, mentally rearranging his plans for the week.

* * * *

Lennox glared at the clock on his phone and spewed another handful of curses. It had to be lying to him, right? One minute, it was Wednesday, and he had plenty of time to de-clutter and set up the spare room, then, *bang!*

Friday showed up out of nowhere.

And of course, everyone seemed to have had the same plans for the day as he did, because he was stuck in the checkout lane. The mom in front of him had three kids—one was picking his nose, one was having a screaming contest with himself and the oldest had kicked Lennox twice already. And behind him was a steel-haired man in a business suit. Mr. Briefcase took one look at Lennox's glitter eyeliner and visibly stepped back.

It reminded Lennox of his father, down to the stuck-up designer tie expertly twisted around his neck, which was the only thing that made Lennox do it. He'd swear to it later if anyone asked, on the Bible and everything — not that anyone would ask, because being gay — or *super* gay — wasn't a crime, not yet anyway, not unless some of those stuck-up religious twats like his parents got *their* way.

It was just a little harmless flirting, a bit of prancing. An artfully limp wrist and some batted eyes, until the man turned red and fled, abandoning his cart and everything.

"Don't worry, honey," Lennox hollered after the man. "It's not a cold. You can't catch it!"

It was like the man couldn't hear him, because he just walked faster. The cashier, however, snorted.

Lennox now had less than two hours to get himself back to his house, throw the sheets currently buried somewhere in his cart — along with shampoo, bath soap, toothbrush and anything else he could think a boy might need, since he knew it was unlikely the kid would have much — onto the bed and hopefully clean up the living room.

Two hours and a handful of minutes later, Lennox abandoned his car in the driveway rather than pulling it into the garage. He should have known better than to take Lareina Drive. He could never pass the Cathedral of Junk without slowing down, and slowing down always led him to parking, for 'just one picture'. Which…generally ended up with him taking a tour.

He scooped the bags out of the backseat and hurried up the sidewalk. He hated making more than one trip, and he *really* wanted to get everything put away before Riley got here.

Unfortunately, he noticed the kid standing awkwardly on his porch at the same time he felt one of the bag's plastic handles start to stretch. Gravity yanked at it, the sheer white plastic going thin like cellophane, until it tore free, sending shampoo, deodorant and body wash tumbling into the grass.

And in his fumbling attempt to catch as much as possible, he managed to drop the rest of the bags, skin his knee on the edge of the sidewalk and look like a complete idiot.

Good going, Lennox, he scolded himself. Chagrined, he started scooping everything back into the nearest bag. A pair of hands joined his, nails painted in miniature Pride flags.

Lennox meant to apologize…he really did. He even opened his mouth with the words readied on his lips. What emerged instead made him die just a little bit inside.

"Oh-my-God-I-love-your-nails-where-did-you-get-them-done?"

Lennox looked up, his eyes meeting the kid's. Except…the guy wasn't *really* a kid. A dark swath of hair tumbled down, shadowing his wide blue eyes. Like Lennox's, they were lined with makeup, though Riley's didn't glitter. He found himself staring, until he realized Riley was talking.

"What?" Lennox asked, his face warming as he realized what he was doing.

It was a bad habit he'd developed in childhood, tuning out sounds to concentrate on the images instead.

It was like his brain could only focus on one thing at a time.

He'd always preferred to see the beauty.

Riley's lips — *is he wearing lip gloss?* Lennox forced his mind away from wondering what it tasted like — curved up in a smirk. "That's what I said."

"Oh." Lennox felt his face heat farther. Riley was going to think he was an idiot. But maybe that was for the best... Lennox had already thought at least three inappropriate things about his house guest. "Your nails are cool. Who did them?" Lennox repeated.

This time, it was Riley who blushed. "I did. It's not that hard, just Sharpie. I could do yours for you — I mean, if you want? I'm sure you don't want the rainbow. You probably want—"

"No, the rainbow's fine," Lennox interrupted.

"I wasn't trying to ask if you're— I mean, if you are, it's okay. So am I. But you know that, of course. Ms. Ally would have said—" Riley grew more flustered as he spoke. It was adorable. Lennox was going to stop him, but he got stuck staring instead. Riley had perfect teeth.

"Can I paint you?" Lennox asked, then immediately realized how that sounded. "*Oh my God,* I'm sorry, that probably sounded *so* creepy. I'm a painter, I swear. I paint portraits and fruit. I didn't mean paint you like...like a French girl kind of painting. Not that I think there's anything wrong with that, but that's not what I meant." Lennox would have covered his face if his hands weren't full. He *did* paint those kind of paintings sometimes, though.

"Don't worry. I didn't think you were a creeper. Though you are kneeling in your front yard holding a box of condoms, so..." Riley laughed.

Lennox looked down at the box he was clenching like a lifeline and choked. God, could this be any more mortifying? He shoved the box into the bag he was gripping in his other hand. "Those aren't mine! I mean, I bought them, but they were for you. Not that I want you to use them with me, that's not what I meant." That sounded bad, like he didn't think Riley was appealing.

He corrected himself again. "I mean, I *would* use them with you. I don't mean that you're not attractive. You're very attractive. I just meant that you didn't *have* to — I'm just going to shut up now."

Was it getting hot outside? He felt like he was standing in an oven, in the desert, *on* the sun.

Riley's perfect teeth were digging into his lip, holding back what was probably a very loud laugh. "Can I help you carry any of those?" Riley changed the subject, reaching for the handles of some of the bags. Lennox stood up rather than passing them over.

"I've got them. I wanted to have them all put away and everything for you before you got here, but I'm late. I'm *so* late. I was painting and I lost track of time then I had to go to the store and apparently so did *everybody* else — and the traffic gods hate me, so I hit every red light, then I wanted to look at a bunch of trash, but it's like...*art* trash, not trash-trash. I really meant to be on time." Lennox couldn't stop rambling.

"It's fine. I just got here myself." Riley replied, following him across the yard and up onto the porch.

Lennox grimaced. "Still, I promised Ally I would pretend to be a mature and responsible adult for the day." Lennox shifted the bags again to grab his keys out of his pocket and unlock the door. He dropped the bags on the floor inside before turning back to Riley.

Lennox grinned. "Can we start over?"

Chapter Eleven

"Can we start over?" Lennox had asked.

Then, before Riley could even agree, Lennox slammed the door in his face.

It left him with a rather odd feeling in his belly. Part of him was stunned by the abruptness, but another part of him was amused, while a still smaller part felt nervous, uncertain if this was the moment that he'd find himself walking the streets again.

Riley didn't know what he expected, but this certainly wasn't it. When Ms. Ally had suggested Riley rent her younger brother's spare room, he'd expected Lennox to be...well, more like the cardigan-wearing man with crazy hair he'd met all those years ago in the kitchen. He had a foggy memory of finding the man mildly attractive but never really gave him much thought after that. He'd seen the man again, of course, but normally only for a few seconds in the distance.

The only other thing Ms. Ally said was that Lennox was an artist and that sometimes, he got lost in his own little world. Riley had assumed that meant when he was working, he didn't like distractions.

He hadn't thought that it meant Lennox would show up a half hour late, wearing glittery eyeliner that did distracting things to his amber-specked eyes, with a strip of blue paint in his dark hair.

Riley stared at the smooth wood, his teeth digging into his lip. He must have missed something. Was it something he said? Had Lennox actually hated his Pride nails and just not wanted to say anything?

Unlikely, considering the man's sister ran an LGBTQ youth shelter.

A few awkward seconds later, just as Riley was about to pull his phone out and call Ms. Ally for help, Lennox cracked the door open a few inches and peered through the gap. "You're supposed to knock." Then, the door was slammed shut a second time.

Riley knocked.

Immediately, Lennox threw the door open wide. "Hello, you must be Riley! You're late, you should have been here" — Lennox peered at his bare wrist — "several minutes ago."

Riley couldn't help smiling. "Sorry."

"Oh, no worries. I was just um…" Lennox peered down at the bag of groceries. "Hmm. I suppose I should have put those away first. Ah well. You'll just have to pretend you don't see them, and that you don't see me finishing getting the room all set. You can do that, right?" The look Lennox shot him was so hopeful that Riley couldn't do anything but nod. "Great!" Lennox stood in the doorway for a long moment before frowning. "Why are you still on the porch?"

"You haven't invited me in," Riley answered.

"Oh, shit! Sorry, I mean…" Lennox frowned. "Shoot. Yeah, come on in."

Riley scooped up the trash bag that held everything he owned in the world and stepped around Lennox. "You can swear. I'm not a kid."

"No, I know. I just..." Lennox ran a hand through his hair, looking guilty. "I told my sister I'd be good. She seems to think I'm not responsible. I *think* she thinks I'll corrupt you or something."

Riley blinked. Before he could reply, Lennox scooped the bags back up from the floor and moved on.

"I'll show you to your room. I meant to have it all set up, but like I said...I screwed the pooch with that one." Lennox stopped, then spun around. "Not literally, I don't even have a dog. But I promise, and if I did, I would treat him respectfully. Or her, I suppose, though...definitely the wrong equipment. But a boy dog would still have the wrong equipment, so I guess I don't need to specify. I'll...stop talking now." He lifted his hand, two fingers up. "Scout's honor."

Then he spun around and kept moving down the hall. Riley stood still for a moment, still processing the accidental segue into animal buggery, before he shook his head, chalked it up to a bit of endearing social ineptitude and followed. Lennox was still speaking. "I'll throw the sheets on the bed and leave the rest of the stuff for you. There's an attached bathroom and everything, so you'll have your own space."

"You don't have to do that. I can take care of it myself," Riley interrupted. He didn't need anyone to make his bed for him, even if it would provide a bit of material to his mental spank bank, watching the cutie stretch across his mattress.

Lennox shot a grateful look over his shoulder as they continued down the long hallway. "Thank God. I've never quite got the whole bed-making thing down. I normally just kind of...throw the sheets on the mattress and hope they land straight. Hospital corners aren't my thing."

They passed a living room off the hall to the right and a galley kitchen to the left before reaching a flight of stairs. Riley followed Lennox up.

On the second floor, Lennox nodded at each of the doors as they passed. "That's my home studio, I work in there when I don't feel like leaving the house — which is more often than it probably should be, if I'm honest, unless I feel like going out dancing. Then, it's *much* less often than advisable. And that's my room," Lennox darted forward to grab the handle of the open door, grocery bags swaying dangerously on his wrist.

He yanked it closed, but not before Riley caught a glimpse of the disaster inside. "I have to clean it." Lennox giggled a bit nervously. "Let's just move on. This" — Lennox juggled the bags over to his other arm to push open the door at the end of the hall — "is yours."

Riley stepped in and immediately wondered if there'd been a mistake. Surely this was like…the master bedroom, not a guest room. The bed was big enough he could lie spread-eagled and still not be able to reach either end.

And he didn't even have to share it.

Lennox dropped the bags on the bare mattress. "This is all yours. I wasn't sure what you'd need, so I got a bit of everything."

Riley flushed, embarrassment battling with pleasure. "You really didn't have to do that."

"Nah, I know." Lennox shrugged. "But I wanted to. I *love* shopping. I just always choose the worst times."

It was hard to argue with the bright smile the man was giving him. "Oh, well…um, thanks."

"You get settled in." Lennox stepped out into the hallway. "I'll be in my studio for a bit. Help yourself to whatever you need. There's food in the fridge—or at least I think there is. I probably should have grabbed some while I was out, but...hm. That really would have been a good idea, wouldn't it? I guess we'll order takeout for dinner. Until then, feel free to use the TV...or whatever. What's mine is yours. *Mi casa es tu casserole*, as the saying goes." Lennox didn't wait for a response—specifically, that it was definitely *not* how the saying went—he just waved and headed down the hall. Riley stared after him.

Yeah, Lennox was *definitely* not what he'd expected.

Riley's phone dinged and he dragged it out of his pocket, already knowing who it would be. There was only one person who messaged him, except for work. He flopped down on his belly on the bed and stared at the message from Tweety.

How's the new digs? Pics or it didn't happen!

Riley laughed out loud, rolling his eyes as he texted back.

Dude, it's a new apartment, not a one-night stand.

Still, Riley snapped a picture of the bedroom, trying to fit as much in the frame as he could, and sent it.

Damn, nice!

Immediately after, a long string of texts followed, dinging his phone one after another. Even in text form, Tweety was loquacious.

In the brief space between two messages, Riley hurried to type out a message.

How's Dallas? The team treating you okay?

Tweety had moved to Dallas to play basketball with the Wranglers, a junior team with a good track record of sending players to the Mavericks. As much as Riley hated that his friend now lived almost three hours away, he was happy for him. The Mavs had a great reputation for being gay-friendly, thanks to their work with Athlete Ally, and it was Tweety's ultimate goal to join them as a rookie player.

Riley would never begrudge him that, not even if it meant their midnight talks where they'd planned out their move to a tiny apartment together after they aged out of the Rainbow House had never come to fruition.

Amazing! OMG, I saw a real live cowboy! He was still in his jersey and all sweaty and damn! You should have seen his ass in his football girdle. If I'd had a quarter...XD

Typical Tweety.

* * * *

Riley woke up the next morning and Lennox was already gone. Unlike Riley, who worked afternoons and nights, Lennox was clearly an early riser. Riley would have to remind himself to be quiet when he came home in the evening. He didn't want to be a disturbance. Besides, this way he could almost pretend he was living alone.

He tried to tell himself that it was a good thing...not disappointing at *all*. He *definitely* didn't want to spend more time around the hot little artist. It wasn't a good idea to get a crush on his landlord. The illusion of living alone was *definitely* a good thing...for sure.

He almost had himself convinced, then he stepped into the kitchen. He was pretty sure it was supposed to be a kitchen, anyway. He'd only seen it from the archway yesterday, since they'd eaten out of takeout containers on the couch the night before.

It looked more like a do-it-yourself project gone wrong. The sink was cluttered with plates and bowls and coffee-stained mugs. Clean dishes were piled precariously in random stacks on the counters, like Lennox had been rearranging the cabinets and forgotten to finish. Several boxes of open cereal were left on the little counter space that remained, along with a jug of what had to be rancid milk.

Riley didn't know whether to laugh or grimace.

Instead, he eyed the clock and decided he had enough time to tidy up a little before getting ready for work. He worked a double today — his shift at the animal shelter immediately following the job he hated — and he couldn't afford to be late, especially not now, with rent to add to his skimpy budget. Ever since the shelter had lost half its funding, thanks to city-wide budget cuts, he'd been getting fewer and fewer hours. He didn't want to, but he'd picked up a job washing dishes at an Italian restaurant downtown as soon as he'd learned he wouldn't be able to get into Next Step housing.

Gotta pay those bills, even if it meant getting screamed at by the chefs, leered at by the manager and completely ignored by the wait staff, who just chucked dishes at him and scurried away like rats fleeing a sinking ship.

At least it meant he had enough practice to scour the dishes here quickly, though he didn't have time to let them drip dry. After several minutes yanking out random drawers to find weird things instead of towels, he finally found one tucked underneath a stack of takeout menus.

In the end, it was easier to take *all* the dishes out of the cabinets and start over fresh. Riley was mostly finished returning all of them to spots that made more sense when he found the note tucked underneath one of the half-empty cereal boxes. The elegant handwriting looked out of place on the crumpled napkin.

Riley,
Don't *do the dishes. It's my mess, I'll take care of it later. Have a good day doing…whatever you do. :)*
L

Riley was already almost finished with them anyway, and besides, if he didn't take care of them now, the thought of them just sitting there would bother him all evening.

He scrawled his own note at the bottom of the napkin, his own handwriting significantly messier.

Too late. *Dishes washed and put away.*
− R
P.S. I think I reorganized your cupboards?

He stuck the note under a letter magnet on the front of the fridge then left the kitchen, intent on exploring the rest of the house while he had the chance. It wasn't snooping. He wasn't going to go through Lennox's drawers or anything. He was just curious. After spending four years at the Rainbow House and the three before that on the streets, he couldn't help wondering how people could fill up an entire house with things. He'd shared a dresser with his roommate, and living on the top bunk meant he couldn't store anything beneath it.

Since, you know, Gray might have gotten angry at having to give up his bed for Riley's shit and all.

An hour later, Riley had figured out only that Lennox had good, if a bit eclectic, taste. Everything matched in a weird, unexpected sort of way. If he hadn't known Lennox was an artist, the house would have given it away. Finally, though, he had to stop exploring to get changed into his uniform. Black dress pants and a white button-down shirt he'd cover in an apron when he got there.

The walk to Antonio's was manageable. He swiped a hand through his hair, straightening it the best he could, then tucked his shirt in for the third time. Once inside, he stopped at his locker to tug on his apron before moving into the bustling kitchen.

"You're late, boy," Santoni, the head chef, hollered from his place by the stove. The man was perpetually frowning, though the pinched expression was often shadowed by his well-trimmed beard.

Riley paused, his apron half-tied. He glanced at the clock over the swinging doors that led to the dining room. "My shift doesn't start for another ten minutes."

"Well, go work on the dishes, then," Santoni snapped.

"Yes, sir." Riley started toward the industrial three-compartment sink in the back. He could already see the warzone waiting for him, as if no one had touched them since he'd left yesterday.

As he walked past, David, the only Kitchen Porter who deigned to acknowledge him, muttered, "Johnny never showed for his shift."

Riley's slumped his shoulders. That explained both Santoni's mood and the pile of dishes cascading over the entire surface of the sink. Johnny was the front manager's nephew and as such, allowed to come and go as he pleased, provided the owner wasn't there.

Riley finally got the caked-on dishes finished just as the lunch rush ended — in time for the bussers to cart in a whole new pile.

By the time his shift finally ended — ten unpaid minutes after it was supposed to, thanks to his allegedly unapproved potty break before dinner — Riley's feet were throbbing, and his hands were chafed near to bleeding. But he had a hundred untaxed dollars in his pocket. It would be going straight to rent, like most of his paychecks for the rest of the month, but that didn't stop his growing sense of achievement.

This time, he was going to do better. He wasn't a scared little boy anymore.

He waved goodbye to the few of his coworkers who actually spoke to him as he hung his apron up on the hook, then slipped into the alley behind the restaurant. Mr. Corbin — the owner, who Riley had seen at a distance but rarely spoke to — preferred the kitchen staff to leave out of the back. Riley knew that the wait staff was hired more for their looks than skill, and anyone not up to Mr. Corbin's standards was kept out of customers' view.

Riley knew he was attractive enough to work the front. The front manager, *call-me-Antonio-but-my-name-is-really-Conner*, had told him enough times that he'd be willing to let him interview — provided Riley lost the glitter, stripped the paint off his nails and spent a few minutes on his knees in the stockroom whenever the man needed his penis inspected.

The pay might be better out front, but if Riley was going back to that life, he'd make more money on the corner.

Riley refused to go back.

So instead, he washed dishes.

The alley dumped him out onto a clean, brightly lit sidewalk. Riley followed it toward the bus stop. He glanced longingly at the waiting bench but then continued past. As much as he hated traveling Austin on foot, especially after a long shift, he needed to save his money. The animal shelter wasn't too far to walk.

Riley quickened his pace as he left behind the safer, more tourist friendly neighborhoods. Not that he would call any of these areas bad, really. They were nothing compared to his old haunts, where the shadows between streetlights were deep. There, dealers peddled their wares and street walkers peddled themselves.

Riley's gaze drifted north. It had been years since he'd been one of them. He wondered if any of them would recognize him now, his guilt stirring. He'd gotten out, thanks to a stranger and the address he'd scrawled on a napkin. He'd seen the man again, right here at the shelter, but couldn't get his words of gratitude free of his lips.

Riley saw the man's face, a bit older but smiling beneath a shock of pink hair, for the rest of the day. He could almost taste the pizza they'd shared as he locked the shelter door and cleaned the animal cages, as he walked the dogs and scooped poop out of litter boxes.

He wondered if the pink-haired stranger knew he'd saved Riley's life that day—if he'd somehow seen how close Riley had been to ending it all. Riley had a name for him now, thanks to the news segment he'd seen months and months ago, the one that drove Riley back to drinking.

Shiloh Beckett.

A man with a trust fund larger than the GDP of a small nation.

As soon as he realized that the stranger had a face the *rest* of the country would recognize on sight, his kindling desire to send the man a "thank you" card died to ashes. That forty dollars and scrawled address may have saved Riley's life, but it probably meant nothing to Shiloh Beckett.

* * * *

Riley quietly unlocked the front door and slipped inside, fully expecting to find the house silent. Surely, this late in the evening, Lennox was already sleeping, especially considering his early start this morning.

He heard Lennox holler before he'd even stepped into the hallway and headed toward the living room. He froze in the archway, his keys dangling off his fingers, forgotten.

Lennox was definitely awake, though what on earth he was doing was an entirely different question.

Chapter Twelve

Lennox twisted as he heard the front door shut, his muscles sagging in relief. Holding himself in this position wasn't as simple as it should be. Maybe he needed to take up yoga?

"Riley! Great, you're home. Um...help?" At least, he hoped it was Riley, otherwise this was going to be rather embarrassing. Or...more embarrassing. He didn't want Riley to see him like this, but it was better than a burglar...probably.

"How did you manage *that*?" Riley's voice grew louder as he came through the archway, his confusion easy to hear.

"It was super easy," Lennox admitted, feeling heat stain his cheeks. "Way easier than it should have been. I was just trying to glue *this*" — he lifted the artificial daisy that was glued to his left hand — "to my new sculpture. But the whole bottle spilled, and it went everywhere. And I was trying to clean it up then I slipped..." Lennox shrugged, gesturing at his jeans, which were *maybe* just a *little* glued to the floor. "I'm stuck."

"Um..." A laugh slipped out of Riley's mouth, though he covered it quickly. "How strong is this glue?"

Lennox wiggled, trying to peel up enough of the fabric to get free, but he was well and truly stuck. He'd started using the insta-bond kind for...reasons. Also, it saved him time...usually, when it didn't make him emulate a mouse in a glue trap — which, don't even get him started on how inhumane those things were.

"I'm going to die here," he moaned with what he considered the perfect level of drama for the situation.

"I'll bring you food and water you like a plant," Riley promised solemnly, though Lennox swore he could see a smirk hiding. His lips *definitely* twitched.

"Killed by my art!" Lennox moaned louder, ignoring the kind offer.

"Have you tried taking your pants off?" Riley suggested, crouching beside him and eyeing his predicament a bit critically. Like, surely *anyone* could have gotten themselves into this situation, right?

"No, why would I take my pants off?" Lennox wiggled again. *Still stuck.*

"Because then your pants would still be glued to the floor, but you wouldn't be. Maybe they'd make a good rug?" Riley's smile spread wider. Lennox found himself staring. Riley had a nice smile.

"You just want me to see me in my underwear," Lennox pouted, snapping out of the daze. The moue became a grin when Riley's cheeks turned champagne pink. "I guess I'll do it...but just for you — not at all because I've had to pee for like...two hours." Lennox unsnapped the button of his jeans and wiggled his hips, trying to slip free.

"You've been stuck here for two hours?" Riley sounded incredulous.

This time, it was Lennox who flushed. It was probably closer to four, if he were being honest, but he'd only had to pee for the last two. "Yeah, yeah, I know. And I didn't think to just take my pants off. How silly am I?" Lennox feigned a carefree laugh, like it didn't hurt to admit to his stupidity at all. "This is exactly why I didn't want to go to college." Finally, he pulled his ankles free from the tangled material. "At least my panties are cute. Look at this little bow."

Riley appeared to choke on whatever words he was about to say but didn't deny it—which was good, because then Lennox would have had to call him a liar since he *knew* they were adorable. He'd examined his ass from all angles in them just this morning. He was wearing one of his favorites, a green scrap of lace that cupped him delicately. Spoiler... His ass looked great.

"Do you...?" Riley cleared his throat, his face scarlet. Well, not really scarlet... It was more currant-colored, but that wasn't important. Unless he tried to paint the way Riley looked at this moment—which he might, later—*then,* it was allowed to be important. Riley kept speaking, distracting Lennox from his tangent. "Is there something that will get this off your skin?" Riley gently tugged at the flower still clinging to Lennox's hand.

"You don't think I should keep it like that? It could be a trend. I could be a hit on Insta." Lennox tugged at the faux flower. He was pretty sure... *Nope. Definitely stuck.* He sighed and admitted, "I have nail polish remover in the bathroom."

"I'll go get it," Riley said and stood.

"But then it'll mess up my nails!" Lennox whined and flopped back onto the ground again. "Oh!" He jerked back up. "But then you could do them for me, right? In the flags? Like yours?"

Riley just laughed and disappeared down the hall.

Lennox hollered after him, "Hey! You didn't answer!"

* * * *

Twenty-two minutes later, Riley finally headed up to bed, leaving Lennox with his failed art project in the living room. He couldn't stop staring at the pretty rainbow flags newly decorating his fingernails.

Riley, despite not answering, had indeed fixed them for him. He'd even liberally doused Lennox's pants with nail polish remover so that they could unstick them from the floor. Lennox had two-finger pinched the foul-smelling things to get them to the washer, but at least they didn't have to turn his pants into a rug.

Though now something in the back of his head was insisting it would be a brilliant idea to design a rug made from clothing...like a bear rug, but human. He mentally filed it away in the 'maybe' section of his brain and turned back to his current project. This time, he carefully moved it upstairs to his studio, instead of the living room. He'd also been a lot more cautious when trying to open the bottle of glue. Sticking himself to the floor once was an accident. Twice was a pattern.

And since this might possibly have been the third time he'd managed it... Well, nobody needed to know he'd stopped wearing his old Chucks because he'd stepped in slightly less-quick-drying glue, and they'd ended up permanently adhered to the shoe rack. He'd hoped using the insta-stuff would fix the issue.

Live and learn, right?

He carefully screwed the lid back onto the glue and set it on the shelf by the paint. Holding his hands in front of it, like that would somehow stop it from exploding, he took a slow step back. When the glue stayed safely where he'd left it, he pumped his fists into the air and whooped.

Except his arm banged into the wall, turning his whoop into a cry of pain and sending him hopping around the room, his hand clasped over his elbow. He tipped over a cup of paintbrushes and a little tray of beads, knocked his shin into the leg of his easel and stubbed his toe.

He rubbed his new aches, before turning a cautious eye back to the shelf. He grinned. The glue remained in place.

Of course, now the floor was covered in hundreds of tiny plastic beads, but they should be easy enough to clean up.

And they were, until he stretched his arm under his paint shelf to chase the last few and bumped it, sending dozens of bottles of paint tumbling down.

At least only three opened.

Chapter Thirteen

Having a roommate again wasn't as bad as Lennox anticipated. He tried—really, he did—to not use Riley like a servant. He kept telling the younger man to stop cleaning up after him, that he would get to it when he remembered, but Riley would just nod, smile—and do it anyway.

He had to admit that it was rather nice not coming home to a messy house, even if it did take him a bit of time to get used to having dishes in the cupboard where they went and clean towels in the hall linen closet.

Linen...maybe *that* was what his newest painting was missing. It was pretty enough but the darks seemed *too* dark, and the lights a bit too white. Maybe if he added some linen-colored paint, it would improve the contrast?

Lennox dropped his half-eaten sandwich on the table and strolled back to his study to start mixing.

"Lenny!"

Lennox jerked at the unexpected shout far too close to him, bumping into his easel with an outflung elbow that had his canvas wobbling. Lennox held his breath, then released it when it finally stabilized, unharmed. He spun on his heel to glare at his best friend and former roommate—emphasis on *former*—as in, he probably shouldn't be tromping around the house like a sneaky elephant startling people. Unfortunately, Mike was already glaring at *him,* and with his muscles and height, it was far more intimidating. "Dude, you have *got* to start locking your door!"

"It *was* locked," Lennox protested, though, honestly…it probably wasn't. He knew Riley had spun the little knob before he headed out to work but then Lennox had gone out to grab the mail and he'd gotten distracted by the neighbor lady screaming at her boyfriend of the week and chucking garbage bags of clothes out onto the lawn and…well, who could blame him for forgetting after that?

"Sure, and I'm Leonard Nimoy." Mike rolled his eyes, then shoved at Lennox's shoulder. "You don't exactly live in Kansas, you know."

"What are you doing here? Did you forget your address? Are you *drunk*? Cause Wendy's going to be real mad that you spent all that money on a new dining room table if you never come home to use it." Lennox tried to keep his face sympathetic, but he'd never had a good poker face and felt the smirk slide out.

"Don't be an asshole." Mike grinned. "It's not like I never visit."

"So you *say,* but I haven't seen your ugly mug here since you threw up in the sink." Lennox dropped his paintbrush in the cleaning solution and started for the kitchen. "This one, right here"—he pointed at it as he passed, like Mike would have forgotten— "I don't have any more of your beer since you've abandoned me for the domestic life, but I've got..." He yanked open the fridge and stared at the unfamiliar contents.

Riley must have gone shopping.

"Tea? Or orange juice."

"Bleh, I'll take a water. But hey! Your fridge actually looks like it belongs to a real, grown adult now. What'd you do, mug someone passing by with their groceries?" Mike opened the cupboard below the sink, then stared at the cleaning supplies now stored where Lennox used to keep the drinkware. "Well, I suppose that is a better place for them..." Mike said, voice nonplussed. "Dude! Where're the cups?"

"Up there." Lennox pointed to the cabinet right next to the fridge. "Riley reorganized everything."

"So let me get this straight," Mike started to say.

"No, I'm still gay," Lennox said with as *straight* of a face as he could.

"Ha. Ha. You're a fucking comedian."

"No, I'm an artist."

"A real Steven Wright," Mike pushed on, shaking his head. "God save us from fools and religion."

Lennox laughed. "Let me guess, another visit from the Jehovah's Witness?"

"No, them I can handle. Real polite people. And we had the Latter-Day's in for coffee, a few of them even left with Wendy's pamphlets on Wicca. No, it's the goddamn Girl Scouts."

Lennox's laughter exploded out of him, and he gave up on grabbing a drink, shutting the fridge to lean against it. "The *Girl* Scouts?"

"Yeah, those little fuckers are *scary*. Have you seen them in their little...military outfits, with the badges and the sashes?" Mike shuddered. "I had to buy three boxes of Thin Mints, and you know I don't even like them."

"What did you think was going to happen?" Lennox asked, hopping up on the counter and swinging his feet. "They going to shank you if you don't hand over the cash?"

"If they don't, you know Wendy would. All I hear every time one of those little bastards knocks on the door is *'when I was a Girl Scout...'* and *'oh, our daughter would look so cute in those skirts!'"* Mike grimaced and took a long swig of his water.

"Oh, is Wendy pregnant?"

"No! And she keeps saying she doesn't want kids. I've asked her, because you know I've always wanted a little rugrat to play ball with, but she keeps saying we're not ready for that yet. And I guess I get it, because babies are small and I'm pretty sure you're not supposed to drop them, and just last week I fumbled a vase and I'm *still* sweeping up glass from the strangest places." Despite his protests, Mike looked sad.

Lennox sobered up, walking over to his friend and placing a comforting hand on his shoulder. "Sorry, Mike. It's little comfort but I think you'll be a great dad."

Mike shrugged. "Maybe not, but better than mine was at least. You think she'll change her mind?"

"I hope so."

"I think I'm going to propose."

"Shit, really? Mike, that's awesome. Not just 'cause of the kid thing, though, right?" Lennox hesitated, excited for his friend but also nervous. Marriage was a big deal, not something to get into unless you *really* wanted it.

"No, of course not, Dude! Lenny, I love her—like, really love her. I can't see myself with anyone else. I mean, I *can*, 'cause you know we still fool around sometimes, but...not like forever." Mike looked so serious that Lennox didn't even have the heart to tease him. He'd known the pair practiced consensual non-monogamy practically since they met, and it worked for them, which was all that mattered.

"That's good. I'm really happy for you both."

"You think she'll say yes?" Mike's voice shook, the words plaintive and begging for reassurance.

Lennox, however, didn't have the heart to lie. "I hope she does, but...I don't know. Wendy's never really talked about wanting to get married, has she? But I think even if she says no, it won't be because she doesn't love you."

"Yeah...yeah, I guess you're right." For a second, Mike looked sad, but then he cheered up quickly. "We don't need some piece of paper from 'the man' to tell us what we are anyway."

"'The *man*'?" Lennox laughed. "What are you, *Harold and Kumar?*"

"No, I know exactly where I left my car."

"That's '*Dude, Where's My Car?*'" Lennox said.

"No, I just said I know where my car is," Mike answered, but he winked big enough that Lennox knew it was a joke.

"Seriously, though," Lennox said, "I hope it works out for you."

"Me too." Mike sighed. "Well...Mario Kart?"

"Mario Kart."

Chapter Fourteen

"But where will they go?" Riley stared at the kennels, each one housing a dog with no other options. And the cat room was even fuller, cages doubled or tripled in occupancy when the cat would allow it. Two weeks wasn't enough time to adopt them all out, not nearly — not when some of these animals had been here for months and months.

Angie looked uncomfortable, refusing to meet his eyes. She was getting on in age and she'd been talking about retirement since Riley had hired on, but he thought they'd have longer. "Funding's gone, hon. There's nothing I can do. I called around, and there's a few shelters willing to take some in. I'm going to waive the adoption fees on the rest, so hopefully..." Angie trailed off, worry lining her face.

She knew as well as he did that some of these animals would never get adopted, even if they were literally giving them away. They were too old or too ugly, barked too much or were too aloof. He knew better than anyone what it was like to be mistreated and unloved, and how hard it was to trust humans afterward. Families wanted puppies and kittens, not animals with fully formed personalities and trauma.

"How many are they taking?" Riley asked.

Not enough, was the answer, though she tried to sugar coat it in numbers and hopeful dreams that were just that...dreams. Like him, she had to know that it wasn't enough.

Riley went back to work, careful to spend extra time passing out scritches to the dogs and treats to the cats, like that could in some way assuage his guilt. It didn't, especially when he knew that as much as he cared for these animals, it wasn't just *their* impending homelessness on his mind, but his.

Without the hours he got here, his finances would be tighter than ever. He could swing it for a month, maybe two, but definitely not more than that. He barely acknowledged Angie's half-hearted goodbye.

Maybe he could pick up a few extra hours at the restaurant, if Johnny kept calling off. There were always dishes to wash, after all.

Riley ignored the little voice in the back of his head telling him he knew exactly where to go for some extra cash, and he picked up the broom, sweeping the litter off the cement floor.

He wasn't going back to that life.

Riley lingered as long as he could, but eventually, the alarm would set itself automatically and he didn't want to explain to Angie why he had to disarm it. Instead, he packed up and headed home.

Riley wasn't even fully inside when he heard a loud *crash* come from Lennox's studio. He kicked the front door closed with his heel before hurrying toward the sound. He could tell they'd had company at some point because there were two controllers on the coffee table and the detritus of what looked like a pizza party strewn around the living room.

But the only car in the driveway was Lennox's, so…

He hesitated only a second before he twisted the knob. Lennox hadn't told him not to, but Riley had avoided entering this room specifically because something about it felt…private. Like going inside was invading Lennox's privacy.

When another crash sounded, though, he pushed the door open and stepped inside. He'd expected a level of chaos like the rest of the house, and to some extent, he wasn't surprised. It was definitely a work room — paint dribbled then dried on the floor, paintbrushes scattered on every surface, but it was more orderly than he expected.

It took him only a second to spot Lennox, alone, wrangling with a large, off-balance tripod. It was a light, he realized as he hurried over to assist.

"Thanks," Lennox said as they finally got it stable and turned on, stepping back to eye it critically. "I don't remember it being so heavy last time, but maybe I'm crazy."

Riley went to make a joke but swallowed it when he realized now that he wasn't hurrying to keep Lennox from getting crushed, what Lennox was wearing.

Or more accurately, what he *wasn't*.

"Oh, um…I should…" Riley waved vaguely toward the door, unable to tear his eyes free from Lennox's bare chest. He didn't have an eight-pack, wasn't sculpted like a gym god. He was lithe like a swimmer and nearly hairless, his nipples standing erect — begging to be bitten. His lacy pink hipsters did nothing to hide his dick, which looked even larger against his tight little body.

If Riley were to press his body against the man's, they'd be the same size. And if Lennox were kneeling... Riley groaned and finally jerked his gaze away, looking up to meet the man's eyes. Lennox seemed oblivious to his perusal. He smiled at Riley as if he wasn't nearly nude. "Actually, can you stay? I thought I could figure this out on my own, but someone to hold the camera would be amazing!"

"Camera?" Riley nearly groaned at the thought. "Um, sure."

"You're a lifesaver," Lennox gushed before crossing the studio in his bare feet to grab a fancy camera off the shelf, carrying it back over. "All you have to do is look through here then press the button. Don't worry if the shots aren't perfect, I'm mostly using them for reference. It's just much easier than trying to set up a bunch of mirrors to see myself in then trying to pose and paint at the same time. I've done that before, and it was super *not* efficient."

"I bet." Riley could barely find his voice. Lennox wanted him to take photographs while he was wearing...that? He cleared his throat and tried to sound normal. "You're working on self-portraits, then?"

"Only by default. I'm working on a series of paintings about BDSM for a show and I...kind of forgot to advertise for a model?" Lennox shrugged but his skin turned pink like he was embarrassed.

It was so typically Lennox, forgetful and absentminded, and Riley loved — *liked* him all the more for it.

"I can take the pictures for you, no problem." Riley lifted the camera, already imagining what Lennox would look like on his knees for him, all dolled up and pliant. But...he found nearly as much allure in the thought of kneeling for the pretty man while he put paint to canvas, a feeling that felt foreign in his chest.

He had to remind himself that this was Lennox's job, and the man wouldn't be looking at him like *that*.

"Next time, though...maybe I could model for you?" Riley suggested.

Lennox's pupils widened. Riley watched his Adam's apple bob as he swallowed. "Um, yeah. If you want, I'd...I'd like that. I'd pay you, of course...for modeling," Lennox said quickly, like maybe his mind had gone somewhere else. That, of course, made Riley's mind follow the same thought. Accepting money for work done on his knees...

"No," Riley said, more abruptly than he'd intended. To soften the harsh word, he smiled and added, "Consider it a favor among friends."

"I...yeah, okay. Friends?" Lennox's voice lifted near the end. He ran his hands down his bare sides like he was nervous.

"Yeah. I mean, if you want? I'd like to be, anyway." Riley didn't have many friends...just Tweety. He'd never quite been able to see the other kids at the shelter as anything but competition—competition for attention from Ms. Ally and the other counselors, for food, for a bed. Like him, most of them were survivors. They'd have stabbed him in the back for an extra blanket if it wouldn't have gotten them kicked out. He could see it in their eyes—and knew they could see it in his.

It made it difficult to form a lasting friendship.

Or any kind of friendship.

He would forever be grateful for Tweety's persistence. Without him barreling through all of Riley's carefully erected walls, he'd still be alone. He missed his best friend more than he'd expected.

"I'd like that, too," Lennox said, then cleared his throat. "I guess...let's get started then? Um...how do you want me?"

"Well," — Riley grinned — "it's your photo, but if I had to pick? I'd say on your knees."

Lennox turned ruby red and stammered, "Yeah, it is my photo, isn't it? But...yeah. On my knees. I can do that, you're probably right. I mean, that would be..."

"Lennox," Riley interrupted, heat flooding him at the sight of the man so flustered. It made him feel big and strong. Two things he definitely was not, but maybe...for Lennox...he could be? It was a thought he knew he shouldn't have but once it struck, he couldn't shake it. "Take a breath. There you go. Good. Now why don't you kneel for me, pretty boy, so we can take your picture?"

The words slipped out without his permission, drawn from his core — a part of him long dormant, wakened by Lennox's clear submissiveness. It grew stronger when Lennox dropped to his knees immediately, his body stilling in the perfect picture of obedient grace.

For the first time since Riley had met him, Lennox was unmoving, his fingers not twitching toward paint brushes or pencils, his eyes downcast to the floor, breathing smooth — like being put on his knees calmed his racing thoughts.

Riley never thought he'd get to explore this part of himself that he'd always known was there, not after his years on the street when johns wanted boys who'd beg and plead and break — not give orders, never that. Even if now, it wasn't real, just…just a show for the camera. But it *felt* real.

Riley appreciated the beautiful sight for a moment longer than appropriate between friends, then lifted the camera. He took several shots, from multiple angles, doing his best to capture the right lighting and shadows for Lennox to use later.

He reluctantly lowered the camera when he'd gotten a dozen good ones, holding it in front of the bulge that had formed in his jeans like a screen. "I think we got it."

Lennox was slow to look up, blinking at him like he was coming out of a daze, his skin blossoming pink like a flower. "Oh. Yeah, you're probably right. Thanks?" It came out sounding like a question, then he licked his lips.

Riley barely bit back his groan, practically shoving the camera at Lennox as he made his excuse to leave. "I have to…go shower, yeah. Um, long day." Then he spun on his heel and hurried out of the studio.

He'd barely closed himself in the bathroom when he shoved his hand into the waistband of his jeans, squeezing his aching dick at the base as he drew in several deep breaths.

They didn't help, and the pressure only delayed the inevitable. He shoved his pants down his thighs and gripped his cock, stroking himself quickly with a pressure that almost hurt, biting the side of his fist to dampen the loud moans and animalistic grunts spilling from his throat.

He hadn't felt like this — this frenzied, crashing pleasure — since he was a young teen, before the streets opened his eyes to the reality of sex and power.

Namely...that sex was messy and painful, and power belonged to everyone else but him. Now, though...

With his pants tight as tourniquets around his thighs and memories of Lennox on his knees trapped behind his eyelids, he found himself pulled inexorably and unstoppably toward climax. He couldn't have held it off or drawn it out longer if he tried.

His body shook with his orgasm and his head flew back, striking the wood of the door in a burst of pain that did little to dim the blind pleasure he was swimming in. Cum painted his hand and splattered to the tiles in front of him like a Pollock painting. Boneless, he stumbled to the sink to rinse his hands.

"Riley?" Lennox called from the hallway, then the door burst open.

Chapter Fifteen

Lennox had never fallen so fast. He'd been told — by his one and only Dom, anyway — that he was a terrible sub.

Which, to be fair to the man...

Lennox *was*.

Kneeling on cold laminate made his knees hurt and, too often than not, he forgot to be silent and still, all the hallmarks of a 'good' sub. And it wasn't like he had much opportunity to Dom, since people saw a young, effeminate Asian twink and made assumptions.

Maybe he fell so easily today because it was the first time he'd knelt in his studio, and the carpet was thick, intentionally so. He spent most of his day in here standing, and he didn't plan on a joint replacement at the ripe old age of thirty. It was stained with paint, and clumped together by glue in places, but his knees didn't notice.

Or, maybe, it was because Riley wasn't a taller, stronger man who could break his arm with a snap of his fingers if he chose to. Most Doms, he'd found during his forays into BDSM clubs, seemed to spend most of their time in the gym or at a fast-food restaurant, and while there was nothing *wrong* with either of those things, large men made him squeamish.

Lennox knew he'd been lucky, blessed even, that he'd never been a victim of physical violence. Austin was a pretty safe city. He'd never been mugged or assaulted, and the few homophobes he'd run into seemed content to sneer and throw insults. And his parents might be cold and distant, but they'd never lifted a hand in anger.

He had no excuse for his irrational skittishness around large men—no personal history to blame it on, no traumatic backstory—just the knowledge, gained from books and crime shows on TV, of what could happen.

Riley didn't trigger his primal fear. He'd felt safe, kneeling here for Riley. He'd sank toward subspace like a poorly thrown skipping stone in a quiet lake, until he was yanked free by Riley's abrupt departure.

He blinked his way back to the surface, feeling the chill of the air-conditioned room for the first time, surprised to realize he was hard. Pre-cum left his panties sticky and damp against his skin.

The abandonment left him off center as he shakily stood, his head muggy. This wasn't a scene, just a favor between friends, and he had no right to expect Riley to stay and give aftercare. Riley might not have even realized the dominance he'd asserted, if he wasn't in the lifestyle.

Which, Riley realized, pressing a hand to his face with a groan, he likely wasn't, not at his age. At nineteen, Lennox had barely been able to find his way around his own dick, let alone the world of kink.

Lennox was the...well, not adult, since Riley was also an adult...a more adultier-adult than Lennox, if he were honest with himself. But Lennox was the one with the experience, limited though it may be, and if he was feeling the effects of a scene cut off midway, he had to assume Riley was feeling *something*.

It was his responsibility to make sure Riley was okay with what had just happened, even if it was relatively tame to anyone *else's* standard. He grabbed his pink silk kimono and tied it on, not bothering to pull on his slippers before he stepped into the hallway, just in time to hear a loud thump, followed by a pained groan, from the bathroom.

Maybe, he overreacted.

Maybe, he panicked just a little, thinking Riley slipped in the shower or tripped on the slidey bathmat Lennox kept meaning to replace.

He barged into the bathroom to find Riley, not bleeding on the floor in the shower, but standing, his pants pulled down and dick dangling half hard against his bare thighs. Riley's hand was moving toward the running sink, glistening with a pearly fluid Lennox knew was semen.

Clearly, their little mock-scene in the studio had a similar effect on Riley as it had on him. Was *that* the reason he'd run from the room so quickly? Lennox sucked in a breath, jerking his gaze up to Riley's when he realized Riley's dick was swelling again. "I... Sorry... I heard... I thought you fell."

Riley was silent, eyes piercing into his as he rinsed his hands and spun off the water. Lennox could practically feel the heat as his gaze trailed over his body, down to the erection tenting the front of his robe. Riley looked hesitant for a second before something resolved, and when he met Lennox's gaze again, they were smoldering. "Want help with that?"

He did. *God,* he did.

A whimper slid from his lips, and his nod was jerky. His knees threatened to give beneath him. Lennox swayed but then Riley was there. His pants were pulled back up but unfastened, and Riley gripped his hips to keep him steady. His hands were strong and hot, and one slid up, parting Lennox's silk robe to flick over his nipple.

It sent a shock through his body, like being tasered, if such a thing could be pleasurable, and Lennox cried out, arching into the touch. Riley chuckled, releasing his nipple after giving it another pinch. Lennox got a moment of relief but then Riley had his hand curled around Lennox's throat instead.

With a firm pressure, not hard enough to cut off his breath, Riley guided him back until he hit the door. And the look on his face...? His eyes looked nearly black with want.

Then Riley slid his other hand lower, dipping under the tie of the kimono to cup his dick through the lace panties. There was no shyness in the move at all. It was like Riley knew exactly what he wanted — and what he seemingly wanted was to take Lennox apart piece by piece. He stroked Lennox's dick with a teasing patience, just slow enough to leave him wanting more.

Lennox panted, thrusting his hips into Riley's palm. "Please, I need...more, please. Take me out?"

"Is that what you want? Wanna fuck my hand?" Riley's voice deepened to a throaty growl that made Lennox shake. And there was something in his eyes, something unexplainable.

He nodded, biting his lip on another groan. "That, yes...I want it. Please, Riley, let me fuck your hand. I'll be good." He *shouldn't* want this, not with his roommate... If Riley regretted it after, it could screw everything up. But Lennox lived in the present, not the future, and now, at this moment, he wanted this — wanted Riley and the smooth heat of his hand. Then, he wanted to repay the favor, let Riley put him on his knees again.

Riley grinned and it lit up his face, so pretty Lennox *almost* didn't notice when Riley let him go to untie the robe and shove his panties down his thighs. His dick bobbed free until Riley grasped it with his right hand and returned his left back to Lennox's throat.

He felt the pressure of Riley's palm when he swallowed, and it made him sway, pleasure coursing through his veins like a current. Riley started jerking him in sync with each thrust of his hips, a tease that had Lennox whining and pre-cum leaking from his dick like a faucet. He'd thrust his hips forward just as Riley dragged his hand back, almost pulling away, then sinking back down when Lennox retreated.

Murmured pleas fell from his lips without thought or care, words without meaning. He didn't understand how the simple touch of Riley's hand could be working him up like this. He'd had full-blown intercourse that left him less hot. A hand job should barely be foreplay at this point in his life.

Lennox was proud to call himself a bit of a slut.

Riley's hand made him feel like a virgin again.

Especially when Riley smirked and added a twist of his wrist to the downward stroke, and a flick of his thumb over Lennox's crown on the way back up. "You like that, baby?"

Lennox nodded, his chin bumping Riley's forearm, and the reminder of the hand around his throat was all it took. He shuddered, crying out as he shot his seed into Riley's still-moving hand.

"Oh, naughty boy," Riley chuckled, stroking Lennox well past the point of sensitivity, not releasing him even when Lennox whimpered. "I wanted to taste you."

Lennox shuddered. "I...I'm sorry?" His brain felt like it was offline, all white noise and painful pleasure.

"You'll just have to come for me again, pretty boy. I know you can do it," Riley's smile was sharp and dominant, his words a demand Lennox wanted nothing more than to follow.

"It hurts," he whimpered—and it did, but he didn't want Riley to stop. His body shook with each stroke of the skin on his sensitive cock. When he looked down, he sucked in a breath. Riley's hand was small, like his. The rainbows on his nails looked even brighter against the smooth skin of Lennox's cock.

"Tell me to stop, and I will," Riley said.

Lennox shook his head, "No, don't, please. I... It hurts, but I want it."

"I thought you did, pretty boy. You want to be good for me, don't you? Want me to wrap my lips around your dick and suck you dry. But you gotta get hard again for me, baby. I know you can."

God, Riley was so mean, gripping his dick just a bit too tight and stroking him just a little too slow—and Lennox loved it. How did Riley know that would turn him on? Was it tattooed on his body, how much he loved to be used and owned? How a little bit of discomfort made it feel that much more real?

Riley scratched his nail lightly underneath his crown and the flare of pain had him hardening so quickly that he felt dizzy, held up only by the door and Riley's hand.

"There you are, good boy," Riley purred. Then he dropped to his knees and swallowed Lennox down in one go, taking him in to the root. Lennox could feel the tip of Riley's nose brush against pelvis, and Lennox's balls pressed tight to Riley's chin.

"Oh God," Lennox cried out, fisting his hands in Riley's hair instinctively, and Riley froze. Lennox froze as well, wondering if he'd gone too far. Before he could drop his hands, Riley chuckled. His throat spasmed around Lennox's dick like a vibrating Fleshlight but better — tight and warm and wet.

He was already close, his dick throbbing, and they'd just started. Riley's twinkling eyes staring up at him didn't make it any easier to hold off, then the man cupped his balls, rolling them in his palms. The sound that came out of Lennox's mouth was one he'd never made before — high-pitched and keening, an anguished not-quite scream that crossed the line between pleasure and pain.

It was just a blow job, so it shouldn't feel like...like *this*. Like he was at some pinnacle moment in his life, some tipping point and everything after this was going to change.

It wasn't rational, so he shoved the feeling down, concentrating instead on the way Riley flicked his tongue just under his crown, the softness of the young man's lips on his skin. The way his hair felt like silk under his fingers.

"I'm... God, I'm *close*," Lennox moaned, throwing his head back against the door and gritting his teeth. The thought of coming scared him unreasonably, the fear of meeting what came after.

Riley pulled back, blowing a stream of cool air over his oversensitive skin, and Lennox had to see. He looked down, meeting Riley's dark eyes as Riley said, "Come for me, pretty boy. Let me taste you." He curled his fist around the base of Lennox's dick and gave him a firm stroke, then another. "Come on my face."

Riley opened his mouth and stuck out his tongue, their eyes locked in a heated gaze. Two firm strokes and Lennox cried out, unable to hold back. His climax ripped through him like a hurricane, cum erupting like a geyser. The first shot landed on Riley's cheek, milky white as it dripped down his skin, then Riley shifted on his knees to catch the last few spurts on his tongue, holding it out for Lennox's viewing pleasure for several seconds before he pulled it back into his mouth and swallowed.

"Delicious," Riley purred. He stayed on his knees, slipping his hand into his unfastened jeans to draw out his dick. It was swollen, the head purple and shiny with pre-cum as he started to jack himself.

Something in Lennox flipped and his spine straightened. He was a switch, submissive and dominant equally, and maybe it was that Riley was still on his knees. Maybe it was that now, with every drop of cum sucked from his body, his mind was clear enough to want to return the favor.

He didn't much care the reason. Lennox stepped forward, looming over Riley as much as someone his height could, and nudged Riley's hand off his dick with his toe. "Who said you could play with that?"

Riley laughed. "Who said *you* had a choice?"

"There's always a choice, sweetheart. If you'd rather jack yourself off, I can go back to my studio. But, if *you* can be a good boy now and leave that pretty dick alone, I'll give you a reward," Lennox offered.

Riley looked up at him through his dark lashes, and it was easy to see him thinking, debating…weighing the decision like he had a scale behind his eyes. "What kind of reward?" He stilled his hand but didn't remove it, leaving his fingers curled around the thick shaft.

"Take your hand off, and I'll show you."

The moment stretched, and just when Lennox thought he wasn't going to, Riley removed his hand, curling it into a fist on his thigh instead. His dick bobbed in the open vee of his jeans. "I can be good."

"I can be good, *Sir*," Lennox corrected, testing the water for a mental riptide, hoping he wasn't stepping into the undertow of a painful past.

Riley's cheeks turned pink, but he didn't look angry. "I can be good, *Sir*."

"Good boy," Lennox praised as he lowered himself down onto his knees, straddling Riley's spread thighs so he was kneeling half in the other man's lap, his soft cock dangling beside Riley's hard one. Lennox hummed as he curled his fingers around it.

"Look how thick you are," Lennox said, struggling to keep his voice bland and uninterested, when inwardly, he felt his mouth water at the thought of it stretching out his hole. Riley wasn't particularly long, maybe an inch or so shorter than Lennox's seven inches, but the girth? He couldn't wait to feel the burn.

Lennox pushed Riley onto his back, careful to make sure he landed on the fluffy bathmat instead of the cold tiles, then leaned over to tug open the bottom drawer — ironically where he kept all his bottoming supplies — of the cabinet. He had to stretch for it, but he was able to dig out a travel-size bottle of lube and his emergency strip of condoms.

He held up the latter for Riley's inspection. "I'm on PrEP…"

"Me, too," Riley panted, his fists still clenched by his sides, like he had to force himself to not reach for his dick…or for Lennox's. "But…"

"Say no more." Lennox grinned, ripping open one of the foil packets and making quick work of suiting Riley up. Then, he flipped open the lube. He dribbled it over his fingers, then rubbed his hands together to warm it. He could see Riley's throat bob as he swallowed, nerves flaring in his eyes.

"You're going to feel so good stretching my hole, sweetheart," Lennox said, and his words seemed to calm whatever momentary fear Riley had. He filed it away to analyze later.

He coated Riley's dick with lube, jacking him slowly to keep him on edge, and he shifted forward on his knees a bit so he could reach his right hand around himself, working his hole open as quickly as he could without risking damage. It was still a bit of a process, but the groan that escaped from Riley's mouth at the sound of Lennox's hiss made it worth it.

When he thought he was open enough, he smirked down at Riley. "I want your hands on my hips, Riley. I'm going to ride your cock like it's my personal toy."

"You're not hard," Riley panted through gritted teeth as Lennox shifted over him, angling the man's cock until the tip pressed against his hole. Still, Riley obediently grabbed Lennox's hips in a grip tight enough to leave bruises.

"Don't worry. I'll get there," Lennox promised. He could already feel the blood struggling to fill his dick again. "Love your pretty dick, and it's going to feel so good inside me." Slowly, Lennox sank down, just enough that the head of the thick dick finally popped inside with a pleasant burn. "Feel how tight I am? Is my hole strangling you?"

"God, *yes*," Riley moaned, his fingers flexing against Lennox's hips like he was fighting the urge to drag him down, to plunge into his ass in a single solid thrust. "So tight, Sir. Feels good."

Lennox took another inch, biting back a groan. Finally, his dick was plumping up again. "See how good you're making me feel, Riley baby? Making me hard all over again, never come this much." He should have stretched himself more, given himself more than three fingers, but he wanted this too badly. The burn was just shy of too much as he lowered himself agonizingly slowly, until finally, he was fully seated. He could feel Riley's balls flush with his ass.

He allowed himself time to adjust, dropping his hands onto Riley's chest and flicking his nipples. "You turn pink so easily, sweetheart," Lennox mused as he scratched his fingertips down Riley's abs, leaving behind little pink scratches. Oh, he didn't break the skin, he would *never* do that without negotiations before the scene, but he liked seeing the marks, regardless.

"It's the pale skin," Riley panted, his head thrown back. Every tendon in his neck stood out prominently, drawn tight. Lennox couldn't resist. He traced them with his fingers, strumming them like a guitar string until Riley moaned, arching his back off the floor and his whole body shaking. For a second, Lennox thought he came, before he realized the man was still hard and throbbing in his ass.

"Oh, good boy, waiting for permission," Lennox praised, rewarding him with a twist of his hips. He clenched his ass tight around the shaft impaling him. "You can come, baby. Go ahead and breed me. Mark me up from the inside." It was just a fantasy, but the dirty words spilling from his mouth worked. That, or his ass milking Riley's dick was just too good. Either way, one of them worked.

Riley cried out, his whole body going tense as he pumped his hot seed into the condom.

Lennox kept shifting his hips, bouncing up and down until the other man grew too soft and slid from his ass with a wet *plop*. Lennox jacked himself off until he coated Riley's abs with his cum.

Muscles weak and shaky, he collapsed down beside Riley, his breath coming in heavy pants. "Love your dick," Lennox praised.

"Love your ass." Riley snickered. Neither of them moved, until Riley moved his hand to take Lennox's. It felt…nice.

Chapter Sixteen

Of course, the best evening he'd had in a while would be followed by the worst morning.

Riley's alarm didn't go off, so he woke up to four missed calls from Antonio's and a voicemail where an irate Santoni told him not to bother showing up today. With as angry as he sounded, Riley would be lucky if they let him show back up at all, which was hardly fair considering the number of times *other* people were allowed to not be there.

And when he swallowed, his throat hurt.

He tried to ignore it as he swung his heavy legs — God, he felt like he was dragging bags of cement around on his ankles — out of bed, and as he brushed his teeth in the bathroom and made breakfast in the kitchen, but then he sneezed into his glass, and he couldn't anymore.

He was *definitely* sick.

He *hated* being sick.

Of course, if he'd been feeling better, or been less stressed out, he probably wouldn't have broken down sobbing into his milk, sending Lennox into a panic of his own.

"I'm just sick," Riley mumbled around the lump in his throat. Maybe it was nerves, or maybe it was a giant wad of mucus, who could tell? "Go paint. I'll just die in my room."

Instead, Lennox hustled him off to the couch and coddled him, wrapping him in a soft throw blanket Riley didn't have the heart to throw off, even if it was ungodly hot in the house and his forehead was literally dripping sweat. It stung his eyes until Lennox wiped it away.

Of course, an hour later Riley was shivering.

But then Lennox brought in a bowl of steaming hot chicken noodle soup and spoon fed him, and…suddenly, being sick didn't feel so bad.

He changed his mind when he started throwing up.

Nope, being sick still sucked.

But Lennox took care of him for three whole days.

Of course, then *Lennox* caught the bug, and it was Riley cleaning up puke, but…for some reason, he found he didn't mind.

Weird.

* * * *

"Hey, Riley? Can you help me for a sec? I need someone to hold my dick," Lennox yelled from his studio out to the kitchen. Seconds later, he heard glass shatter and realized what he'd said. "Duck! I meant duck!"

Riley peeked his head into the studio with a smirk. "Hold your duck?"

"Um…" Lennox felt his face turn hot as a barbecue grill as he lifted the rubber ducky. "I need to glue it to this chandelier here…but every time I let it go, it falls down…"

The chandelier was an old one he'd found at a flea market, one with the dangling crystals he'd always thought looked like water drops. He was between art projects now, since he'd finished editing the photos Riley had taken for him this morning and prepped the canvases, but he had to wait for the gesso to dry before he could start the next step.

He figured it was as good a time as any to work on this. It wasn't his typical style, and he doubted he'd be able to sell it, but once the idea had hit, he couldn't quite get rid of it. He'd decided to just…go with the flow. Worst case scenario, it joined the rest of his misfit pieces in the attic.

"I mean, I'd hold your dick again, too, if you ask me nicely," Riley teased, coming in to stand beside him. "Why are you gluing ducks to a chandelier?"

"It's a Bombay *Duck* chandelier," Lennox said as he squeezed a dollop of glue on the bottom of the ducky and held it out to Riley.

Riley took it, rather hesitantly Lennox noticed, then hovered it over one of the dangling crystals. "Here?" Lennox would tell him he didn't need to be so nervous, that this was just a side project, but Riley looked too cute concentrating on the little duckie.

"Yep. Just hold it on until it sets. Like this." Lennox squeezed glue on a second one and held it onto another crystal. Riley was staring at him, a small smile tugging on the corner of his lips. Lennox felt his skin flush and blurted the first thing that came into his head. "Have you ever seen ducks hunt?"

Riley blinked, his smile slipping. "No? Don't they just eat bread old ladies at the park feed them?"

"Actually, it's really not good for them to eat bread. If they eat too much, they can get bone deformities. They should actually eat insects and grass and stuff," Lennox said, and Riley quirked his lips back up. "Did you know— Oh wait, I was telling you how they hunt. They turn upside down in the water so all you can see is their little tuft of tail and feet. I personally think it looks like they're drowning, and it can't be all that fun sitting there with your head underwater and your butt sticking in the air."

Riley chuckled. "I don't know. I can think of a few things to do with your ass up in the air..."

Lennox stammered, heat flooding his chest. He hadn't been sure over the past week if he should bring up their little rendezvous in the bathroom, or if Riley would prefer to ignore it, and between the throwing up and the...other stuff...figuring it out hadn't been a priority. Now he had his answer. "I, um...yeah, I could...there's a few things I can think of, too..."

"Hey, Lennox?" Riley leaned forward, and Lennox couldn't help staring at his lips as they came closer, wanting to steal them in a kiss.

"Yeah?" His voice sounded breathy.

"Is your hand supposed to be glued to the duck?" Riley asked.

"What?" Lennox jerked, glancing down at his hand which was, indeed...glued to the rubber duck. Again. "Shit."

Riley laughed. "I thought we talked about being more careful around glue, baby. Hold on. I'll..." Riley stopped speaking and glanced down at his own hand. Lennox looked as well.

Then, he laughed. Riley's fingers were also stuck. In the same amused tone of voice, Lennox said, "Riley, I thought we talked about this."

"Oh, shut up!" Riley turned pink. "It must have oozed out or something."

"You said ooze." Lennox snickered, his mind dropping farther in the gutter as he imagined the feeling of Riley's cum oozing from his hole someday.

"You're such a child," Riley said, but he was smiling.

"Come on. You know you were thinking it, too."

"Not until you said it," Riley groaned. "Look what you've done." He angled his hips, showing off the erection tenting the front of his hot pink skinny jeans. His dick made a mouthwatering bulge.

Lennox gestured to his groin, where his own hardening erection was starting to dig into his zipper. "Seems we're both in the same...*sticky* situation."

"Not yet, we aren't," Riley said, voice husky. "But we could be, if you ask me nicely."

"Hey, Riley." Lennox's voice was breathy as he shifted closer. "Make me get all sticky?"

"Grab me that nail polish remover," Riley ordered, gesturing to the bottle sitting on the table beside him.

Lennox scrambled to obey, fumbling for the bottle and practically shoving it into the younger man's hand. Riley shoved it between his knees so he could unscrew it with his free hand, sloshing half of it over his fingers before setting it down. Lennox watched him rub the foul-smelling acetone over his skin until it softened the glue enough that he could pull free.

Lennox waited for Riley to dump the bottle over his hand next, but instead, Riley smirked, leaving him stuck. "Tell me to stop, and I will," Riley said, reaching for Lennox's free hand. "Okay?"

"Okay," Lennox agreed.

Riley guided Lennox's hand to the bulge in his jeans, letting him feel his girth.

"I'm going to take myself out, and you're going to jerk me off. Do a good job, and I'll blow you after." Riley winked, letting Lennox know that more than likely, he was getting blown anyway. Still, he shivered at the thought that he had to do good to get rewarded.

"Yes, Riley," he agreed. Riley grinned and tugged down his zipper, pulling out his dick and wrapping Lennox's hand around it. Lennox thought he was going to release him, but he didn't. Riley kept his fingers curled around Lennox's.

Lennox moaned when Riley made him move his hand, using it like a toy to pleasure himself. It didn't give Lennox the same sense of accomplishment he typically felt pleasuring someone, because...he wasn't doing it, Lennox was. Instead, he felt used and dirty and somehow...perfect.

Riley stroked himself off until he shot his cum all over Lennox's hand with a grunt. By now, Lennox was painfully hard, his zipper biting into his dick. It was, he supposed, a bad day to have gone commando.

Or a great day, because Riley dropped to his knees and yanked his jeans down, baring him in one smooth move. "Look at you, all hard and waiting. Did you like that, Lennox? Being a dirty boy, letting me *use* you to get myself off?"

"Yes, Riley," Lennox admitted. If his skin got any hotter, it was going to melt off.

"Maybe sometime, I should put you on your knees and you can just be my little cock warmer." There was something in Riley's face as he said it, like he was questioning himself, worried maybe he was going too far. The way his face tipped slightly, the hesitation in his voice.

"Please, Riley, let me do it, I want to. I'll keep your dick so warm that you'll never want to take it out," Lennox moaned, hoping his words would reassure the young man. He knew what he wanted, and he wasn't afraid to say otherwise.

The hesitation disappeared and Riley smirked. "What a good boy you are. Do you think you were good enough to earn a reward, or should I punish you instead?"

"How…how would you punish me?" Lennox asked.

"I could put you over my lap and spank you like a naughty boy," Riley suggested, his eyes twinkling.

"Can I still come?" Lennox pleaded, hips jerking forward at the thought of Riley's hand on his bare ass.

"Naughty boys don't get to come, Lennox. Naughty boys have to stay needy and wanting until they've been good again." A bead of pre-cum seeped from Lennox's dick, sliding down his shaft.

He moaned at the thought of being denied, forced to wait. What would Riley consider being a good boy? Giving him a foot massage before bed? He could imagine rubbing his thumbs over the balls of Riley's feet after a long day at work, smoothing lotion over his delicate ankles and long toes.

Or, maybe, making him a sandwich to take with him for lunch, so that when he opened his lunch bag, he had a meal made by *him,* with his own hands — mayonnaise spread evenly from crust to crust, turkey folded pristinely between the bread…made with care.

Would Riley make Lennox do chores? Clean his room, do his laundry…make his bed so they could come back in and mess it up? The thought of Riley putting him on his knees to scrub the bathroom floor shouldn't be that hot. He *hated* cleaning. It was boring and took too much mental energy to do right. But the thought of Riley telling him to do it, putting him on his knees…scolding him for laziness and praising him for his effort…

He couldn't help it. He didn't mean to. Without Riley even touching him, he was coming, seed splattering on the younger man's face without warning. "I'm sorry, sorry," he mumbled as he spasmed, his body shaking with pleasure.

Riley chuckled. "I see someone likes the thought of a punishment. Tell me, what was it that tipped you over, sweetheart?" As he asked, Riley swiped the pearly fluid from his skin, sucking it off his fingers like the sweetest candy.

Should he admit it? Would it be too much for Riley, the thing that made this all awkward? He bit his lip, then Riley was standing, invading his space as he backed him up against the table with stormy eyes. Riley grabbed the nail polish remover and carefully started removing the glue from Lennox's hand, but it was clear he was still giving Lennox every ounce of his attention.

His voice was gritty when he finally spoke, just after freeing Lennox's skin. "Tell me now, Lennox. Be a good boy."

"I…I was thinking of making you lunch, and…and giving you a foot massage after you get out of work, and…and you giving me chores to do." He turned his face away, feeling it heat again.

"Hm," Riley hummed, and when Lennox peeked back over at him, he didn't look disgusted. Instead, he had a small grin on his lips. "It sounds like you want to make me feel good, baby — and maybe for me to give you some rules."

"I...I like rules," Lennox admitted. "I get caught up in...well, *here,* sometimes," — Lennox waved his hand, gesturing at his studio — "and in my head. I can forget to eat if I don't set alarms." An embarrassed laugh slipped from his lips at the confession.

"Nothing to be ashamed of," Riley said softly, his fingers gentle on Lennox's cheek as he carefully turned his face back to his. "We all need help with things. Do you know how long it took me to remember to take the trash out when I first got off the streets? Ms. Ally had to remind me every week for months."

"It... But... I shouldn't find it erotic, though!" Lennox blurted. "That's weird, isn't it?"

"Lennox, baby. None of *this"* — Riley gestured between the two of them — "is exactly normal, is it?"

"I...guess not," Lennox conceded.

"I don't care what anyone else thinks about what we do here. If you want me to give you chores, or homework, or an eating schedule, then that's my choice. And if that makes this" — Riley reached out and gripped Lennox's dick, still soft, though struggling to harden already — "stiff as a steel bar, then I guess I'll have myself a toy to play with, won't I?"

Lennox shivered. "But would you like it?"

"If you haven't noticed, sweetheart, I'm a bit of a control freak sometimes. I don't mind cleaning up after you," Riley clarified, "but yeah, I like the idea of punishing you when you're naughty and leave your dishes in the sink or your towels in the hallway. Putting this pretty ass" — he reached around to squeeze the ass in question and Lennox moaned — "over my knee and turning it red when you forget to eat dinner? Trust me, baby. It won't be a hardship at all. And" – Riley's grin turned devious—"if sometimes you want to put *me* over *your* knees, I can't say I'd complain."

"Shit," Lennox cursed as he started to harden again. "You're going to murder me."

"Nobody's ever died from too many orgasms." Riley laughed.

"I feel like that's a lie." Lennox frowned, struggling to think with Riley's hand still on his dick.

"Lennox? Shut up." Riley dropped back down to his knees and swallowed him down, and Lennox couldn't even be insulted, as he was too busy crying out with pleasure.

Riley was going to kill him, but what a way to go.

Chapter Seventeen

Later that evening, Riley leaned against the open door of the studio, smiling as he watched Lennox paint. He was intent on his canvas, his tongue peeking out between his teeth. Riley couldn't see what he was working on, but from the scarlet paint streaked through Lennox's hair, he guessed it had a lot of red.

Riley almost regretted interrupting.

"Lennox," he purred, straightening up. He strutted into the room like he was on a catwalk, enjoying the way Lennox's eyes widened when he looked up and saw him. It was nice to realize that Lennox, even in the middle of painting, could look at him like that.

Like he was the last scoop of his favorite ice cream.

"Huh?" Lennox said, blinking slowly as he dipped his gaze down Riley's body.

"Like what you see?" Riley asked, cocking his hip. He was basically naked. The only thing separating him from nudity was the lacy teal panties gently cupping his slowly growing erection. They were made for women, and he'd bought—okay, *stolen,* but he'd been a lot younger then and it hadn't seemed like that big of a deal at the time—from the bargain bin of Victoria's Secret, but he still thought they looked hot.

From the expression on Lennox's face and the heat in his eyes, Lennox agreed. He straightened, and there was something in the set of his shoulders that made Riley's knees go weak.

It wasn't what he'd expected when he walked in. He'd been feeling toppy, had big plans to put Lennox on his knees for a pre-dinner snack, but now…

"Tell me to stop and I will," Lennox said, a promise in his smile.

"What are you going to do to me?" Riley asked, his voice thready.

"Kneel for me, and I'll show you."

Riley hit the floor, grateful for the carpeting that kept him from splitting his knees open. He arched his back, pulling his shoulders back for Lennox's perusal, even if he couldn't convince himself to lower his eyes or tip his head in deference. He needed to *see* him, to see the man he was choosing to trust enough to put him on his knees.

"Good boy. Remember…all you have to do is say 'stop'."

He didn't need the reminder, but he was grateful for it, nonetheless. It reassured him that Lennox, even without knowing his past and his trauma, cared. "Yes, Sir. I understand."

Lennox carded his fingers through his hair, and Riley leaned into the touch. It was gentle but still, somehow, dominant. "Such a good boy. I'm going to paint you."

A shiver spread over his skin. *Yes.* He wanted that.

Except Lennox didn't grab a canvas like he expected. Instead, he grabbed a palette and started filling it from tubes of watercolor paint. Then he walked, slow and deliberate, over to the shelf that homed all his paintbrushes. They were separated by size and color, placed with the care of a parent into their little holders.

Riley could hear him humming, though he couldn't place the song. Lennox ran his fingertips over the bristles of several brushes thoughtfully before shaking his head and returning them.

In the end, he picked up three to keep, carrying them back over to Riley. Lennox set the palette on the nearest shelf and circled Riley. Losing sight of him made Riley tense but immediately, Lennox started speaking.

"I love how smooth your skin is, so pretty and pale. It pinks up so quickly and is such a lovely contrast to your dark hair." Lennox ran his fingers through it again, tugging lightly on the strands until Riley let his head fall back, his neck exposed. A second later, he shivered as the rough bristles of a paintbrush traced along the column of his throat, leaving behind a cool wetness.

Paint, he realized, though he hadn't noticed Lennox dipping the brush into it.

"You're the perfect canvas. Skin like linen." The paintbrush dipped into the hollow of his throat below his Adam's apple, swirling in slow, teasing strokes. Riley swallowed, feeling the pressure of the bristles.

He let out an uncomfortable laugh, the tension too…real. "Should I be worried you're going to turn me into a lampshade, Mr. Bryer?"

"It's actually Nakayama. Bryer is Ally's married name," Lennox corrected, his voice teasing. Riley flushed with embarrassment at the mistake, something so simple he should have realized, but Lennox didn't mock him. He just laughed, trailing paint down the center of Riley's chest. "Feel free to keep calling me Mister, though. It's hot."

"Mr. Nakayama," Riley experimented, then let out a gasp when Lennox leaned over him, dragging the bristles roughly over his left nipple. He wanted to look, to see what color Lennox was covering him in, but if he moved his head, he knew he'd smear the paint on his throat.

Riley stayed where Lennox put him.

"And no need to worry, sweetheart. I'm going to turn you into my masterpiece — my Sistine Chapel, my David, my *Pietà*." Lennox finally circled around in front of him, the palette back in his hands. Riley tried to watch, his anticipation swelling. He was just barely able to see from this angle, and somehow, that made everything even more intense.

It was like being blindfolded without the fear and danger. All he'd need to do to return his field of vision was bring his head down. The only thing keeping him from doing it was his own choice...his own unwillingness to smear the paint.

Bondage of his own making.

Riley's dick throbbed in his panties.

"So beautiful in watercolor," Lennox murmured, almost like he was speaking to himself. Riley closed his eyes, relaxing into the feel of the paintbrush on his skin. It was an extension of Lennox's hand, as intimate as fingertips. He knew how well Lennox treated his materials, the care he took washing and conditioning his brushes. That Lennox felt his skin worthy to paint on...

"Mr. Nakayama, I *need*..." Riley trailed off, not even sure *what* he needed. Touch, or...something. Something *more*. "*God.*" He shuddered as Lennox leaned forward, dragging his nose along Riley's chin and inhaling.

"Tell me what you need, Riley." Lennox teased him with the paintbrush, dragging it down his abs to his bellybutton. Riley sucked in a breath, his back bowing as he struggled not to come just from the heady growl in Lennox's voice.

"I need... God, I need you to touch me," Riley pleaded. His hips moved on their own, seeking to connect with any part of Lennox they could reach. He must be only inches shy of humping the older man's leg like a dog in heat.

"Good boy, telling me what you need. Now tell me...how much do you care about these pretty panties?" Lennox purred.

"Wreck them. Rip them off if that's what you want, just *please*, Len—Mr. Nakayama, please just touch me," Riley begged.

Suddenly, Lennox gripped his dick over the lace, his hand dripping with paint. Riley squeezed his eyes closed and shuddered, thrusting his hips into the pressure.

"Can you come like this?" Lennox asked, but it wasn't really a question. It was a demand, his paint-sticky fingers slipping over Riley's shaft slow but steady. Like a tightrope walker being slowly pulled off balance, he tipped toward climax.

Riley nodded frantically. "Yes, I can, yes, just...please don't stop."

Lennox hummed. "I want you to come for me, like this. Make a mess of yourself in these panties. I want to see you blissed out and boneless, then I want you to let me photograph you. Be my masterpiece. Come on, baby. Come for me."

Riley cried out, cum spilling from him like a flood. He felt it soaking the lace, ruining them just like Lennox had asked.

"Perfect, don't move." Lennox sounded rushed. Riley didn't have the energy to open his eyes, let alone move. He heard the click of a shutter, then again, before he heard Lennox drop down in front of him again.

Then, he was being pulled into the other man's lap, hands — still sticky with paint — roaming over his back. Riley, no longer worried about smearing the 'masterpiece,' pressed his face to the curve of Lennox's neck and moaned. His body was sated, worn out and drained, but heat still coiled in his body. He could feel Lennox's erection under his ass, hard and throbbing.

"Fuck me?" Riley asked, squirming against the bulge. Lennox hadn't even undressed yet, and that was even hotter.

"We don't have to," Lennox said, though his fingertips pressed harder into Riley's skin. He wanted to, Riley could tell, and Riley wanted it to.

"Please? I want you to *use* me." Riley's voice was quiet, almost broken, as he admitted something he would never say to anyone else. He didn't know why he trusted Lennox like this.

"Mm, I can give you that," Lennox said, a rasp to his voice that finally compelled Riley to open his eyes. He wanted to see him. Lennox's face was drawn but not with pain. Lust filled every line and divot. Riley wanted to lick the little dimple by Lennox's mouth, so he did.

Lennox laughed, the tension broken, then shoved Riley onto his back, somehow still managing to cradle his head so it didn't hit the floor. It was just another small way Lennox was taking care of him.

"We're going to get paint on the carpet, Mr. Nakayama," Riley said with a breathy moan.

Lennox laughed again. "You've seen my studio. Wouldn't be the first time. Now be a good boy and lift your hips for me."

Riley did.

Lennox slid the ruined scrap of lace down Riley's thighs, smearing paint and cum along his skin. Lennox's gaze grew even more heated as he saw the results of his earlier play. "Beautiful boy. I don't have a condom, so we're going to have to get creative."

"I hid one in here earlier," Riley admitted, since he'd hoped for this outcome. Well, he'd anticipated that *he* would be the one using the condom, but he was more than fine with the change. "Over by the mannequin." He waved toward the poseable doll thing Lennox sometimes used for drawing.

"Smart boy," Lennox purred. He gripped Riley's thighs and forced them apart, spreading him wide for his viewing pleasure. "Stay just like this, precious."

He felt split open, vulnerable…exposed, but in the best way. Goosebumps pebbled his flesh, even though he'd turned the heat up to prevent just that. He watched Lennox fiddle with the things on the desk until he lifted the little foil with a grin.

"Now I just need…hm." Lennox looked around the studio for…something. His grin widened and Riley watched him cross back to the shelf with the paintbrushes, lifting a jar of safflower oil up and inspecting it. "That'll work."

Riley flushed, heat flooding him, strong enough to make his sated dick twitch. Lennox slipped on the condom and coated his fingers in the oil. By the time he had two planted firmly in Riley's ass, he was hard again, his dick waving a greeting.

"Well, hello there," Lennox smirked down at him.

"Please, Mr. Nakayama," Riley rocked back on the probing fingers, enjoying the stretch, the burn, but needing more. "Another."

Instead, Lennox stilled. "Are you in charge right now, boy?"

Riley shook his head, apologies streaming from his lips. Lennox grinned and resumed his torture, stretching Riley out with all the speed of a sloth until Riley was keening again.

Finally, *finally*, when he thought he was going to die, Lennox gave him another finger. It was fire and stretch and *perfect*.

"I'm ready. Please, Mr. Nakayama, give me your dick," Riley begged, his hips twitching and gyrating against Lennox's hand. His voice broke and he sounded strung out, like a junkie pleading for a hit — like an alcoholic, which he was. No liquor had ever held him like *this*.

"I think you can take another. I bet you could take my whole hand…" Lennox had a rasp in his throat that spoke of his own arousal.

"Why aren't you naked yet?" Riley whined, unwilling to admit, maybe even to himself, that the idea of holding Lennox's entire fist inside his body was nearly enough to make him come again.

"Patience, brat." Lennox smirked and smacked his hip, only hard enough to pinken the skin and leave a sting.

"Shit, shit..." Riley cursed, hole clamping on Lennox's fingers. "Too close, *please* Lennox, please fuck me."

Finally, Lennox pulled his fingers free and lined up his sheathed dick. Riley felt the pressure of the bulbous head against his winking hole and tried to shove himself back on it, wanting it—*needing* it—inside. But Lennox denied him, gripping his hips and pinning them to the carpet, teasing him instead with just the pressure of his tip against him.

"Asshole," Riley cursed, straining against him.

Lennox rewarded him with another swat, on the opposite hip this time. It pulled another whine from his throat. "Such a dirty mouth. Maybe I should stuff that instead?"

A whole body shiver had him quaking. If he wasn't so needy, the idea of swallowing Lennox down would be perfect—but not now, not when his ass was begging to be filled. He shook his head, "Please, I'll be good. Need you in my ass. I'm so empty. *Please*, Mr. Nakayama."

Lennox's smirk softened. "Don't worry, baby. I'll give you what you need." He lined up his dick again and, with a smooth push, slowly filled him to the hilt. He waited just long enough for Riley to soften for him, then started to thrust.

Not roughly, not at first. Just gentle, rolling movements, like riding a wave at sea. But, the closer he grew to the crest, the faster Lennox moved, his dick pegging Riley's prostate with unerring accuracy.

Riley was pleading, the words coming out without thought or planning, just a stream of "*so good*" and "*more*" and "*harder*." He wanted to become one with

Lennox's body, to not know where he ended and Lennox began.

To stay in this moment for an eternity.

The pleasure spiked higher, and he spilled again, pearly seed drenching his abs a second time. Lennox wasn't far behind, his voice deepening to grunts as his movements grew erratic. His whole body shuddered as he collapsed atop Riley with a curse.

Suddenly, Lennox stilled.

"What's wrong?" Riley asked, anxiety breaking the brief moment of calm.

"I... You're leaking," Lennox said, an apology on his face. "I think the condom broke."

Chapter Eighteen

Below him, Riley turned milk-white—pale as the semen leaking from his still-gaping hole. "Don't worry," Lennox hurried to reassure him, running his fingers over the younger man's cheeks. "I'm clean. I haven't been with anyone since the last time I was tested."

"Having an STI doesn't make you dirty," Riley snapped, his body tensing like a bow. Lennox took his hands in an attempt to soothe him. "But...I've had one—before. Not now, I mean, but..." Riley yanked his hands away, covering his face. "I used to... I was a prostitute...before." Riley cringed away like he thought the admission would in some way change how Lennox was already beginning to feel about him.

"Sex work is nothing to be ashamed of, sweetheart. It doesn't change anything for me, okay? I still think you're perfect." Lennox tugged Riley's hands down so he could meet his eyes, repeating, "Perfect."

"I didn't want to," Riley admitted, turning his head away to avoid Lennox's gaze. "My dad was... Well, he was a real sick bastard, and I ran away when I was almost thirteen. I didn't realize it was going to be so hard, and everything cost money, and...and I could only make so much begging, especially when I'd been on the streets a few weeks and was starting to smell real bad. And I was so hungry. And I had this friend who did it first, but then he..." Riley visibly swallowed. "But some guy offered me twenty bucks if I'd just...just watch him jack off. Didn't have to touch him or nothing, just watch. And...and it was easy, and it was so nice not to be hungry. So I did it a few more times, but...then he wanted me to touch him, too, and..."

Lennox watched Riley shrug, tears pooling in his eyes and over his cheeks. "If someone hadn't decided to do their good deed for the day and taken pity on me by passing along the address to the Rainbow Center, I..." Riley choked off his words, drawing in a shuddering breath before continuing. Lennox gripped his hand again. "I wouldn't be here. If the STI hadn't killed me, or a john...I think I'd have drunk myself to death. I was heading to hell in the bottom of a bottle, and some days, I think I still am."

Riley clenched his eyes shut. Lennox leaned forward, unwilling to watch him in pain any longer. He pressed his lips to the younger man's forehead, then each of his eyelids, before he planted a chaste one on his soft lips. "I promise that I won't ever let you fall that low. If you need me, I'm here, every step of the way. And we'll go to the clinic and get tested together, okay?"

Riley's nod was jerky, but his relief was written all over his face. "You wouldn't mind?"

"Of course not. I want you to feel safe with me, and if a little bit of blood and a swab up my ass is all it takes,

I'll do it in a heartbeat." Lennox grinned at the laugh that barked out of Riley's throat before he smothered it with his palm.

"Oh, come on, baby. You know you want to watch me. Don't you think I'll look hot with Nurse Ratchet putting a Q-tip up my hole?" Lennox teased, hoping for another chuckle. He wasn't disappointed. Even with Riley's palm in the way, Lennox could hear it escaping.

"Come on, Nurse. Stick me, won't ya? I've been a real bad boy..." He continued joking, rocking his ass over Riley's dick. It was still soft, but the motion seemed to make it perk up. "I think I need a shot."

Lennox pouted out his lip.

Riley finally pulled his hands down, eyes glinting even through the dampness. "You're such a fucking dork."

Lennox feigned a gasp. "Doctor! Such a dirty mouth! Maybe we better go wash it out."

Riley bucked his hips up against Lennox's ass with a grin. "We should go wash *something* out." For a second, the grin wobbled at the reminder of what was leaking from his ass, but he recovered before Lennox could say anything. "Take a shower with me?"

"Hm-m, anytime you ask, dirty boy." Lennox stood with a wink, tugging Riley up with him and swatting him playfully on the ass. "Lead the way to the shower, Doctor."

"Gonna make me all clean again?" Riley walked ahead of him, hips swaying as he stared back over his shoulder. "Because I think I'd rather you dirty me up more."

"Shower tiles are hard on the knees," Lennox pointed out, pouting at the admission.

"Let me have your ass and I promise to keep your knees out of it." Riley winked. "I'll make sure to grab the water-based lube this time."

"Oh! Is *that* why it broke?" Lennox flushed, embarrassed. So the condom breaking *was* his fault and not a fluke. Riley had every right to hate him.

Riley stopped immediately and spun around. "Hey, don't worry. I know that I freaked out, but it is what it is. We'll go get tested and probably everything will be fine, yeah? Maybe it broke because you're a beast in the sack."

"A beast, huh?" Lennox perked up. "Want me to ravish you again?"

"My hole needs a break, but I'd love a go at yours." Riley reached around to grab Lennox by the ass, squeezing the soft flesh. Cool air hit his hole, and Lennox moaned.

"Whatever you want, Doctor," Lennox replied, his voice breathy.

Riley chuckled. "We need to wash up before we go to the operating room. Will you be a good patient? Let the doctor give you a full check-up in the shower?"

"Ooh, yes, Doctor. Can you check my hole? I think it hurts."

"Aw, do you need the doctor to give it a kiss?" Riley teased.

"Yes please, Doctor."

"I won't even complain about my knees."

* * * *

Riley had bruises blossoming on his knees, but it was worth it to hear Lennox cry out his name as he spilled his seed into the shower drain. Riley almost regretted the waste, but he wasn't willing to give up the taste of Lennox's ass to save it. He loved the way the muscles clenched around his tongue.

"Baby, you gotta—oh God, Riley—you gotta stop. I'm going to— Damn it! God," Lennox babbled, words nearly unintelligible. Riley knew he should stop, knew how sensitive *his* ass was after coming, but he couldn't help it. He savored the sound of Lennox's pleasure, drawing it out as long as possible.

By the time Riley pulled back, pressing one last kiss to the furled pucker, Lennox was sobbing and hard as a rock again. "Gonna let me in here?" Riley asked.

"Need it," Lennox begged.

"Pass me the lube and a condom," Riley ordered, reaching around Lennox to accept it. He sheathed himself quickly, then coated his fingers in lube.

He probed Lennox's hole with the tip of his forefinger. He was loose and wet with spit, but Riley still slicked him with lube. First one finger then two, and by three, Lennox was begging again.

God, Riley loved that sound.

He stood up, holding back his wince when his knees cracked as they straightened, then lined himself up with Lennox's hole. "Hands on the wall, Mr. Nakayama. Be a good patient while I give you your shot."

"Is it going to hurt?" Lennox panted, not a trace of fear in his voice. He arched his back, shifting his ass even closer.

"You might feel a lit—big prick," Riley hurried to correct himself, his cheeks burning.

Lennox snickered, but before the sound could get all the way out, Riley surged forward, trusting his prep and the massive amount of lube to ease the way.

Lennox's laugh broke off into a loud moan, and he sank forward, elbows to the tile. The water beating down on them was by now only barely lukewarm, but the heat swirling between them was enough to steam the glass.

And Lennox's hole was so hot and tight... Riley wasn't going to last long.

He surged forward again, groaning into Lennox's neck, his front plastered to the man's back. Art must take more muscles than he thought, because Lennox was *ripped.*

"So fucking good," Lennox panted. While Riley couldn't see his face, he could see the whiteness of his knuckles as he pressed his hands to the tile harder. Riley curled one hand around Lennox's hip to hold him close then leaned even closer, planting his hand on top of Lennox's. He threaded their fingers together as he pistoned his hips deeper into him.

"You're so damn tight, Lennox baby. Squeezing me like a glove, *fuck* I love y—this." Riley mouthed the other man's shoulder, sucking bruises along the curve. He wanted to mark him up and claim him. Anyone else who dared try to get where he was now would see them and know that Lennox was *his.*

His to kiss, to touch, to fuck.

Despite practically just coming, he felt his balls drawing up tight to his body. "God, sweetheart, I'm so close. You gotta get there, I can't—I can't hold back much longer. You're so perfect."

"Already there, baby," Lennox panted. He curled his fingers tight around Riley's, almost painful. Riley reached his other hand around, gripping Lennox's dick and stroking until his sticky release coated his palm.

Riley groaned, finally allowing himself to spill into the condom. His hips stuttered as he tried to bury himself as deep in his lover as he could get. He dropped his forehead to Lennox's shoulder as he stilled, his breath ragged.

Now that they weren't moving, he felt the chill of the water. Shivering, he finally let go of Lennox's dick to spin off the water. "I'll grab you a towel as soon as my knees start working," Riley promised.

Lennox laughed. "Thought you weren't going to complain about them?"

Riley gave him a half-hearted swat.

Chapter Nineteen

The world was a shitty place sometimes.

As he swept the cement floor in the animal shelter, Riley felt guilt swelling in his chest. Everything at home was going so perfectly. He and Lennox had gone to get tested and everything had come back clear. He'd given Lennox a rule about eating lunch *and* a rule about bringing his dishes to the sink—and he'd gotten to spank the older man twice already.

Which, of course, had led to more rounds of amazing sex. *And* Lennox had turned *his* ass red yesterday for a photoshoot.

He shouldn't be this happy when he was two days away from being out of his main source of income, and these poor animals were two days away from euthanasia.

The other shelter had taken almost two-thirds of them. That left them nineteen dogs and fourteen cats with nowhere to go. A 'Free Adoption! All Fees Waived' event five days ago had brought the number down to twelve animals—two dogs, ten cats.

The dogs were both elderly, with rheumy eyes and creaking joints. It didn't make it better, but it made it *easier* for him to accept. They were being put down, but they'd lived long lives, and…and maybe the end of their suffering was better? In the long run? He didn't believe it, but he was trying to convince himself.

The cats, though…

The next day, one day until doors closing, there were eight remaining.

An hour before the doors would close for good, Riley forged adoption papers for the six remaining cats, and 'borrowed' three cat carriers. He didn't realize how hard it would be to smuggle them onto the bus — or how expensive, since the driver required a Jackson to ignore the presence of animals on a 'no pets allowed' bus — and made him pay for an extra ticket to account for the seat the carriers took up. Then he had to do it all over again to bring back the last three.

Not to mention the cost of the fan he'd bought from the supermarket to cool down the storage shed behind Lennox's house. He didn't know how he was going to explain the presence of the cats to Lennox when the man found out — because he would, eventually, even if Riley had yet to see Lennox use the shed.

No matter how unobservant Lennox could be, at some point he'd notice the empty litter tubs in the trash and start questioning.

He knew he would struggle to buy the food and litter, but he couldn't let them just…die. He promised himself — and silently Lennox — that he would keep looking for new owners to rehome them.

He wasn't going to keep them.

Even if he'd already named them.

The little orange one was Princess Murder Bitch, named so because she'd, while still purring, left a scratch mark on his neck from chin to collarbone. And there was Mysterio, the all-white cat who acted like no one could see her while she was hiding in plain sight. But it wasn't her fault she was blind. And of course, there was Fuzzy Bottom, whose butt he had to keep cleaning and brushing because she had way more hair than any cat needed.

Simba was a Maine Coon that came nearly to his knee and had balls the size of a dinner plate, or so it appeared when he kept sticking his ass in Riley's face, and there was Sphinx, the hairless cat who wasn't supposed to be hairless but came into the shelter so matted and smelly that they'd had no choice but to shave it.

The last one was Damsel.

"Oh, sweetheart," Riley cooed at the pretty kitty. She was old and gray, though he thought from the little bit of color she had left that she'd started out black, and her one eye never stopped weeping. But she purred like a fire engine and wanted nothing more than to sit on his lap when he perched awkwardly on top of a broken weight bench right next to the foul-smelling litter box.

One of his precious little fuzzy-wuzzies had diarrhea.

He strongly suspected it was Simba.

Simba yowled at him like he was offended that Riley even dared to think the accusation. But when he turned around and stuck his tail indignantly in the air, there was a small clump of poop hardened around his furry butt.

How in the *hell* was he supposed to give six cats a bath? In a toolshed? Without Lennox finding out?

Damsel let out a loud fart.

Riley sighed. *Make that two cats with diarrhea.*

He reached awkwardly up behind him, dragging down an old, stained rag. Just the edge had been hanging over the shelf and he was lucky there was nothing sitting on it, he realized as it slipped into his lap. Considering it was Lennox's toolshed, there was no telling what weird things could have been sitting up there.

As he wiped the liquidy poop off his pant leg as good as he could, he found himself wondering how he'd gotten here. Not literally here, because he knew how he ended up in the toolshed, but...here in a...pseudo relationship? With his landlord.

As if his position in the house wasn't precarious enough with his strained income, now he had six illegal cats and the risk that he and Lennox would get in a fight on top of it. He knew better — or *thought* he knew better — than to get in a relationship with someone in a position of power over him.

He'd seen it too many times on the streets. Girls who started sleeping with their pimps and paid the price — or girls who moved in with johns, thinking they were in love. Inevitably, it ended with them back on the streets again or worse. Men who paid for sex rarely wanted to find a wife. Most wanted a punching bag or sex toy.

There'd been a few clients who hadn't been horrible — shy guys who were too embarrassed to tell their wives they wanted anal or lonely men who lamented why they couldn't get a date and this was just a one-time thing, *promise*. It rarely was.

Considering the shitty experiences with sex that he'd had up until now, he was surprised at his reaction to Lennox. Not once had he felt fear or disgust. It had felt...right.

If they kept playing around, would that continue? Or would he stumble on a trigger he didn't realize he had? If that happened...would Lennox get angry? Would he tell him to find another place to live?

Immediately, Riley's heart said no. It was stupid to trust it, after all the ways it had let him down in his life, but...he wanted to. Something inside told him that Lennox was different.

He slid Damsel off his lap and stood, taking a steadying breath. Maybe Lennox would prove him wrong. Maybe Lennox would reaffirm everything that life had hammered into him. But...

Maybe he wouldn't.

Maybe it was time Riley tried to trust again.

* * * *

There was a cat in his toolshed.

Lennox stared through the screen door, staring at the little orange face peering out at the lawn from the small window. Had it snuck in to get out of the heat and gotten trapped? He doubted it, since cats were intuitive. Maybe it was just sleeping somewhere that wasn't an alley.

Still, he should go out and check on it, make sure it wasn't hurt. He took a side trip to the kitchen and grabbed a bottle of water and a little bowl to put it in, carrying them out to the shed.

It was a pity Riley was at work. Lennox was sure he'd love to go out and pet the poor thing. He could just picture the younger man cooing and cuddling it. Maybe he could bring it inside? Set it up in the den with a scratching post and a litter box. Maybe a little bed.

He juggled the water bottle and the bowl as he wrenched open the shed door. He really needed to oil the hinges. They were rusted from disuse because he couldn't honestly remember the last time he'd used it — probably well before Mike moved out, if he had to guess. He'd hired a landscaper to do the yardwork after the first week of living here, caving to the obvious realization that if it was left to him, it would never get done.

And since the landscaper brought his own tools and supplies, he didn't have to worry about getting them in and out.

He slipped into the toolshed and shut the door quickly behind him, just in case the poor creature decided to try to run. The last thing he wanted to do was chase it around the yard or, worse, for it to injure itself further. At least his lawn was fenced in, but he was pretty sure cats were good jumpers.

However, when he pulled the chain to turn on the single bulb light, he saw...cats. Plural. Multiple cats of varying colors and sizes. A giant tabby was sprawled on top of his old work bench, grooming his belly with his leg cocked up. The little orange one was making itself even smaller on the windowsill, its long tail curled up over its shoulder.

He started to count. Four...five...six?

How on earth had *six* cats made their way into the toolshed?

Not on their own, he realized when he spotted the litter box tucked into the corner, a pooper scooper propped up beside it. He snickered.

He'd been right.

Riley *would* love the cat, since they *had* to be his. Unless Mike had adopted a herd...cluster? Pack? Of cats and abandoned them when he moved out. Since that had been over a year ago, though, he doubted they'd made the food stretch that long.

Which left either a roving vagabond stowing cats in his toolshed in the dead of night...or Riley.

He wondered if he should bring it up. If he did, then they could bring the cats inside, where they'd have more room to wander. There was plenty of room in the laundry room to set up some litter boxes.

Lennox would try to remember to talk to him about it after Riley got home. Until then, he settled down on the old weight bench. Immediately, one of them leapt into his lap.

She was graying, her fur soft under his fingers, and her purr stuttered and revved like the engine of an old car. *Poor girl.* He swiped his pinky over the crusty corner of her eye.

"Hello, Darling."

Lennox stayed out with them until the sky started to darken, then headed in to start on dinner, thoroughly washing his hands first, of course, after handling the cats. There was no way he was going to be able to bring the poor babies in on his own, not without a carrier. He'd scoured the toolshed—which wasn't that hard since it wasn't very big—but he hadn't found anything he could use.

He was worried if he carried them in one at a time, he'd lose one halfway into the yard and the poor thing would run off. When Riley got home, he'd ask for help, but until then, dinner was the next best thing to work on.

He wished he was a better cook, but the only things he could reliably cook in the kitchen was mac and cheese and grilled cheese, and even that was hit or miss.

By the time Riley came inside, his face lined and worn, Lennox had only slightly blackened sandwiches waiting on the table. His plans to ask Riley for help with the cats were forgotten as soon as he saw the drawn expression on the younger man's face. He'd clearly had a rough day.

"Ditch your shoes, and I'll get you something to drink. Want water? Milk? I think I have some tea…"

* * * *

For the third day in a row, Riley stared at the full food bowl in the shed. Six cats should be eating more. He hadn't had to fill it since Monday. He quickly inspected each of the cats, lifting them up and feeling their bellies, checking their teeth and mouths for sores.

They all *looked* fine, but…why weren't they eating?

Riley swiped his palms over his eyes, his breath ragged as he let it out. He didn't have money for a vet bill, not for one cat let alone six. None of them *looked* sick, but none of them were eating. They'd all have to go.

But his boss's nephew, who had walked out of his shift without notice a few weeks ago, had just begged for his job back—and got it, since apparently not showing up for most of your shifts wasn't a big deal if you were related to the person who made the schedules—so not only had he lost his work at the shelter, but his hours at the restaurant kept getting cut, too. He was a hundred dollars short for rent this month still, and it was due by Friday.

He was going to have to visit his old corner.

And, even *if* he managed to earn enough money for the vet bill, he couldn't take six cats on the bus. It had taken him three trips to get them all to the house from the shelter and he'd had to bring the carriers back to avoid getting the cost deducted from his last paycheck.

"Shit," he cursed, realizing what he was going to have to do.

He gathered the last shreds of his courage, scritched Damsel one last time behind her ears and headed into the house. He followed the sound of whistling to track down Lennox. He was in his studio, the door open. Riley fidgeted as he leaned against the doorframe.

"Um…Lennox? Could I borrow your car maybe?" Riley asked, his voice shaky.

Lennox looked up from the canvas he was painting. "Hm? Oh, yeah. Sure. Why, everything okay?"

"I…" Shit, this was harder than he expected. His heart was beating wildly in his chest. He could lie, say he wanted to grab groceries or something, but…he didn't want to lie to Lennox. "I have to go to the vet."

Lennox dropped his brush, eyes widening. "Oh, are you sick? Do you need me to drive you?"

"No, I…" Riley stopped, head tilting. "Wait! Why…" He pressed his lips together against a smile. "Lennox, if I was sick, I'd go to a doctor."

"Oh. Yeah. Oops? Wasn't thinking, I guess." Lennox giggled. "Um…so, a vet?" He looked confused before his face cleared. "Oh, the cats! Are they okay? Did one of them get hurt? I keep forgetting to ask if you'll help me bring them in."

"They're not eating. I haven't had to fill their bowl for— Wait, you know about the cats?" Riley abruptly switched topics.

"Oh, yeah, I forgot. I found six cats in the toolshed, and I assumed they were yours. I didn't think I couldn't bring them in alone, but I've been filling their bowl every afternoon though because they eat a *lot*." Lennox paused. "Which would explain why you haven't had to fill their bowl lately, I guess."

The tension weighing his shoulders down like a boulder slipped away. "You're not angry?"

"Hm? About the cats? No, they're adorable! I've named them all. Want to go meet them?" Lennox smiled brightly.

"Uh...I...yeah, sure." Riley decided not to point out that, since he brought them home himself, he'd already met them. He was curious what Lennox had decided to call them.

Apparently, the cats liked Lennox's names better.

Lennox called them when he opened the door, and they all came running, rubbing up against his shins and yowling for scritches. Riley couldn't help but laugh when Lennox called Simba, though. Apparently, they both had *Lion King* on the mind.

"You really wouldn't mind if we brought them inside?" Riley asked. He scratched behind Mysterio's — or as Lennox was now calling her, Snowball's — ears. She purred and butted her head against his palm.

"I think they'd like having more room. Although, I think I want to get them a friend. They look lonely. Don't you think they look lonely?" Lennox gave him puppy-dog eyes, batting his lashes.

Riley looked at the clowder of cats. He highly doubted *any* of them were lonely. "Yeah, sure."

What could he say?

He loved cats.

And maybe, Lennox, too.

Chapter Twenty

"Let me send you some money," Tweety said on the other end of the phone, his voice filled with sympathy. To Riley's ears, it sounded way too much like pity.

"Nuh-uh, no way. No charity," Riley refused.

"Dude. It's not charity when you're my *best* friend. Besides, I'm making decent money now. You'd be saving me from wasting it on video games. I've run out of places to store them," Tweety whined. "I just bought the new *EverQuiet* expansion. You know the one? Where they open up that whole section in the Enchanted Woods behind the oval arch?"

Riley settled back on his bed, leaning against the pillows, to listen to his friend. If he was lucky, Tweety would forget what they were talking about in the first place. He hated the idea of sponging off his friend now that the boy was finally starting to make a comfortable living.

He wasn't going to be that person.

"And there's this treasure chest filled with gold and diamonds and rubies and—Oh, shit. Why did you let me prattle on like that?" Tweety said, his voice accusatory. "We were talking about you. Anyway, I'm really sorry the shelter shut down. I know how much you liked it there. You should get your vet tech license. Is that what it's called? Whatever... You know what I mean."

"It costs too much," Riley sighed. "I looked into it with Ms. Ally, and there's a few scholarships out there, but I'd still have to drop a lot of money and short of winning the lottery..."

"You *know* I'll lend it to you."

"I want to do it on my own. I've been thinking..." Riley hesitated. Tweety was the only person who knew everything—who Riley's father was, how he'd ended up on the street. What he had to do to *survive* on the street.

"Of? Oh, *hell* no! You are *not* going back out there. Nu-uh, I won't let you. I'll call Ms. Ally," Tweety threatened, panic leaking through the phone.

"Not *that*. Not unless I get really desperate," Riley clarified. "But there's a few clubs that do amateur nights? I guess you can make a couple of hundred dollars just for an hour or two of stripping. And I found this website. You can cam and make a bunch in tips if you're good enough. Do you...I mean, would you judge me? If I tried something like that?"

He didn't want to let anyone else's opinions color his decisions but...Tweety was his best friend, and even though he could be scatterbrained at times, Riley trusted his opinion more than anything.

Tweety didn't say anything for the longest time, and Riley's heart fell. He'd spent over an hour this morning filling out his profile on the camming site, finding the best angle for his profile picture before he broke down and used one of the kinky ones Lennox had taken for inspiration with his art.

Riley was about to retract his statements when Tweety finally spoke. "I don't think you should go to the clubs. Not alone. If you want to try your hand at it, wait until I'm between seasons or take someone with you. Your roommate seems laid back, so he might go? Just in case something triggers you or the audience gets too frisky... You know you're hot," Tweety's voice lightened at the tease. "But the camming might be okay? You'd have the control to shut the computer down if it got to be too much."

"Yeah, you got a point," Riley admitted, turning his gaze to the desk where his laptop rested. He'd been going back and forth on pawning it. The little bit of money he got would be enough to make up the rent he was missing, but he'd need a computer if he ever managed to start his studies. Ms. Ally had given it to him and said exactly that.

Mind made up, he relaxed, turning the conversation back to Tweety's new quest on *EverQuiet,* at least until a cat started scratching on the door. He briefly put the phone down to let Pumpkin in. The little orange creature prowled inside, her whiskers twitching as she darted under Riley's bed.

Riley rolled his eyes but wasn't actually angry. He dropped back on his bed in front of his laptop and picked his phone back up. "Okay, sorry. Where were we?"

He sank back into the game, losing himself to the quest until a throat cleared in the doorway. "Riley?" Lennox asked.

Riley jerked, darting his focus to the clock then the window, the sky dark. "Shit, what time is it?"

"Eight?" Lennox's voice rose, like he was nervous, and guilt filled Riley's chest. It was becoming a familiar feeling.

Him and Lennox were *supposed* to eat dinner together.

"I'm *so* sorry!" Riley practically hung up on Tweety in his haste to shut down the computer. "I lost track of time. Did I miss dinner? You didn't wait, did you?"

Lennox sucked his lower lip into his mouth for a second before speaking. "Um…I tried to keep it warm but…I might have burnt it? So I ordered takeout. I hope you like Chinese?"

"I'm a *terrible* person," Riley admitted as he rolled off the bed to hurry to Lennox. "I can't believe I did that, and you have every right to hate me."

"I don't. Hate you, I mean. I lose track of time, too, so it would be rather hypocritical!" Lennox gave a self-deprecating laugh and swiped a hand through his hair. "Next time I'll be late, guarantee it. So, Chinese is okay?"

"Yeah, I eat pretty much anything, if you haven't guessed," Riley agreed, scanning Lennox's face for signs of anger he just wasn't admitting to. He didn't see any, so he felt some of the tension flee.

"Good. That's…good. I'm glad." Lennox's cheeks turned a pretty pink. "Chinese is my favorite, and I know that's ironic, but don't make fun of me 'cause it's *nothing* like traditional Japanese cuisine. It's really—" Lennox rambled.

"Good?" Riley finished for him with a grin, relishing the deepening of Lennox's blush.

"Yeah," Lennox chuckled. "Wanna eat in the living room? We can turn a movie on or something?"

"Sure, but I have one condition. You pick the movie."

Later, Riley decided he shouldn't have bothered with the ultimatum, since it hadn't mattered anyway. The end credits were still rolling on the TV, but Lennox hadn't even made it halfway through the movie he chose, some new superhero film, before he was snoring. It was cute, a snuffling noise that barely counted, reminding Riley somehow of a puppy.

He had to resist the urge to pet Lennox's hair as he carefully covered him with one of the throw blankets off the back of the couch. As much as he wanted to drape himself over Lennox and cuddle-cling, he had plans that would be easier to follow through with if he knew Lennox was out here sleeping.

His heart thudded quickly as he went back to his bedroom, double checking the door was locked behind him. He opened his laptop and reopened his browser. It routed him back to the camming site he'd researched earlier. His thumb hovered over the *Finalize Profile* button.

At the last minute, he backspaced out his previous username — @GlitterAngel69 — and typed something new.

Something daring.

For the first time since he was thirteen, he typed his real name.

@RylandEmersonScottIII.

He doubted more than ten or fifteen people would ever stumble on his profile, since he was nothing special to look at and had no intention of filming any longer than it took to pay his rent and get a new job, but it felt like a big "Fuck you" to his father.

His father, Senator Ryland Emerson Scott II, self-proclaimed holy man on a crusade to spread the Word of God to all the non-believers.

Senator Ryland Emerson Scott II, currently running for Governor of Texas.

And also currently under fire for his participation in a child sex trafficking ring, not that his followers seemed to care.

It would serve him right for *someone* to recognize Riley and ask the senator what his son, the same one who was allegedly cloistered in a high brow religious monastery in Europe like a vestal virgin or some other bullshit, was doing filming gay porn.

Even if it was just jacking off while shoving a dildo up his ass.

Chapter Twenty-One

Three months later

Mike slapped Lennox's thigh for the eight billionth time. "Lennox, Lennox. Lenny. Hey, Lenny, Dude. Lennox. What the fuck? What the *fuck?* How the... *Lennox!*"

"What, man? I'm trying to *eat*," Lennox whined, glaring at the barbecue now staining his white skinny jeans, thanks to his best friend's elbow.

"Yeah, *my* food, at *my* bachelor party, which you somehow roped a famous *gay porn star* into coming to. Like...is this a joke? A hidden camera show? Did Wendy put you up to this?" Mike's jaw was still hanging open as he stared with wide eyes toward the bookcase.

Lennox stared as well, trying to figure out which one of the dozen guests was moonlighting as a porn star. Somehow, he didn't think it was Mike's dad, who was standing beside Riley, but there was no one else in that corner of Mike's living room.

"Are you talking about your dad? I just texted him. It was super easy..." Lennox said to clarify. He was pretty sure Mike's dad was an estuary, but careers changed.

"No. Ew, *gross*. No, the hot little piece *talking* to my dad. Dude, he's like...the biggest name at OnlyStiXXX Studios. Only does solo videos but his dad's some famous conservative politician dude."

"Uh..." Lennox stared at his roommate-with-fucktastic-benefits with new eyes, wondering when Riley had started porn and, more importantly, why. And also whether it would be inappropriate to *find* those videos. "Why do you know so much about him? You're straight!"

"Bro, how do you *not* know anything about him? You're gay! And also...you invited him. Dude, I'm so confused right now."

Lennox could tell. Mike was doing that thing with his nose that he always did when he tried to figure out difficult math problems — or whose turn it was to take out the trash.

"That's my roommate, Riley. I told you about him," Lennox said, though he wasn't positive.

"No shit, you say his name in every other sentence, but you *didn't* say that your new roommate-with-benefits was hot and did *porn*. Like...dude. I know all about how cute his eyes are, and how you love his rainbow nails, and that it's just adorable how he sneezes whenever Princess Peach sticks her butt in his face, but you didn't share *that*? I thought we were friends!" Mike wailed.

"Okay, but like…you still haven't clarified why you're watching gay porn?" Lennox decided to worry about the important questions first. "Are you trying to come out to me? You *know* I won't judge. This is a safe place. I'm a safe person. You're safe here. We're safe together." He patted Mike on the shoulder. "Are you and Wendy being safe?"

Mike rolled his eyes. "Yes, everything is safe. Don't worry, we still use condoms with all our bed buddies. But Wendy is the one who found him. She says that gay porn seems less demeaning. And sometimes she likes to stick things up my ass with it playing in the background for like…research and shit."

"You shouldn't say 'shit' when talking about butt stuff. Also, TMI, dude." Lennox scrunched his nose.

"Hey, you told *me* about that guy who had a fetish for kneecaps," Mike protested.

"I only told you that he liked to lick them. That has nothing to do with sticking shi—*stuff* up your ass."

"Like I don't know that after he got done licking them, he stuck shi—*stuff* up *your* ass." Mike rolled his eyes.

"You don't know that! Maybe he just jerked off on them then crawled his pert little ass back out on the street to find the next set of knees to worship. *Maybe* he didn't like my knees. *Maybe* he said my knees were knobby and you *assuming* he liked them is bringing up bad memories. *Maybe*—" Lennox's voice grew louder as he protested.

"Your knees are perfect," Riley's amused voice interrupted Lennox's monologue. "So even *I* know whoever you're talking about didn't leave you…*knee-dy.*"

"Hot *and* punny." Mike elbowed Lennox while smiling at Riley. "I'm this lonely bastard's best friend. You should drag him out of the studio more often."

"I don't know. I rather like putting him on his *knees* in there." Riley smirked, but his eyes were dark with lust as he stared down at Lennox. "Maybe I *knee-d* to do it more often if he still remembers fetish-dude."

"To be fair," Lennox protested, "it would be hard for *anyone* to forget someone wanting to jack off onto your joints."

Riley narrowed his eyes, but Lennox could tell there was no real anger in them. And like always, all he'd have to do is tell Riley to 'stop' and everything would. Instead, Lennox grinned and tipped his head back a bit to better meet Riley's gaze. "Maybe you should spank me. Remind me who I belong to?"

Mike cleared his throat. "It's *my* bachelor party, Lenny. Doesn't that mean *I* should get all the spankings?"

Riley carded his fingers through Lennox's hair, their eyes still locked together. He tugged on the strands, yanking almost to the point of pain before relaxing. "How long until the bachelor party really kicks off?"

Lennox could hardly think, though as the best man he knew he should have the answer. Instead, it was Mike who responded, "Mine and Wendy's parents are leaving in a few minutes, and after that, we can migrate to a club."

"Hm-m," Riley hummed, and it was a low and dangerous threat—one that had Lennox rock-solid in his jeans. If he wasn't careful, there would be more than barbecue staining them.

"I'll let you have your best man for one hour. After that..." Riley turned his gaze to Mike, dominance bleeding from his pores that had even the larger man leaning back with approval on his face. "He's mine."

* * * *

True to his word, once they hit the club, Riley stayed back, letting Lennox ply Mike with drinks. Lennox tried hard to make sure that Mike was having a good time, but his attention kept getting drawn away from the dance floor — to the elegantly curved mahogany bar where Riley was leaning.

Riley gave him a smoldering look as he lifted the glass of bottom-shelf bourbon — that he should have been carded to buy — up to his lips. Riley's mauve jeans clung to every line of his hips and thighs like a second skin, and his mulberry crop top left a handspan of pale flesh exposed, begging to be worshiped.

Lennox wasn't the only one watching. He'd seen Riley turn away half-a-dozen leather daddies. Each one that approached had jealousy burning in Lennox's chest, and each time Riley turned one away, Lennox breathed a new sigh of relief.

Also true to his word, exactly an hour after they arrived at Envy, Riley abandoned his glass and strutted out onto the dancefloor. The crowd parted like the Red Sea. Every step Riley took resounded in Lennox's chest like a drum, drawing him closer until they met. Lennox said a hasty goodbye to Mike before following Riley deeper onto the dance floor.

Riley snaked his arms around Lennox's waist and yanked him forward, plastering their chests together. He was hard, Lennox could feel it. Then Riley slid his thigh between Lennox's, bringing them even closer.

"Did you like watching me dance, Sir?" Lennox breathed, submitting instantly to the dominance oozing off the younger man like musk.

"You're pure sex out here, Kitten," Riley purred, sliding his hands down Lennox's back to cup his ass. He rocked them slowly in a sensual dance, a facsimile of lovemaking.

Lennox moaned, arching into the touch. "I hear the bathroom stalls are quite...roomy..."

"I'm not fucking you in a bathroom," Riley promised, the words barely more than a growl. "We're going to dance, and I'm going to tease you. And you...are...*not*...going to come. I want you begging and hard and so goddamn needy that I'm the *only* one you think of. The *only* one whose name dances on your lips while you're throbbing."

"You already are, Sir."

"Goddamn right." Riley let go of Lennox's ass and he was disappointed — until Riley brought it back down in a *smack!*

"Shit," Lennox cursed, only the sheer tightness of his jeans enough to keep him from coming. "Damn, you can't... Sir, too much!"

The music shifted to something more upbeat, but Riley stayed aching slow, increasing the pressure on his trapped cock. It throbbed — either from his heartbeat or the bass. It was the best kind of pain.

"Sir! *Riley*, please..."

"Tell me what you want, Kitten. Want me to let you make a mess in your jeans? In those pretty panties I *know* you're wearing?" Riley teased. His glossy lips turned up in a smirk.

"Yes," Lennox whined, impulsively pressing up on his toes to steal a kiss. Riley allowed it, groaning into his mouth. Lennox could taste the bourbon, the oaky vanilla more bitter than he preferred, but on Riley...on Riley's tongue it was a thousand-dollar vintage.

"Hmm-m." Riley broke away with a sigh. "You make me want to put you on your knees right here on the floor, where everyone can see what a good boy you are." Riley ran his fingers over Lennox's lips, then slipped them inside. Lennox sucked, flicking his tongue over the tips. Riley tasted of salt and sweat.

"Oh, I think you like that."

Lennox wished Riley would do it, put him on his knees right here, but this wasn't *that* kind of club. Instead, he reluctantly allowed Riley to remove his fingers.

"How long do we have to stay?" Lennox asked, voice breathy.

"As long as I want," Riley grinned. "And guess what, darlin'?"

"Yes, Sir?" Oh, Lennox *loved* the way Riley's tongue curled around the pet name, the way it rolled off like butter.

"Tonight's amateur night, and I want to see you dance." Riley worked his hands under Lennox's shirt. "Dance for me? Show everyone how sexy my little kitten is?"

"Up *there*?" Lennox blanched, glancing toward the platforms, but he didn't say stop, and he didn't remove Riley's hands from his heated skin.

Riley gripped the hem of his shirt and slowly started sliding it up, exposing him inch by inch. "Yes, Kitten. On the platform, in just your pretty panties. Show everyone this perfect ass." Riley yanked the shirt over Lennox's head before sliding his hand beneath the waistband of his jeans and under his panties.

Lennox arched into his palm. Riley cupped his ass perfectly, holding him tight. His touch chased away every thought, every worry. He would do anything Riley asked. Riley's hands circled around to his front, popping the button on his jeans.

"Let's see what you're hiding under these," Riley purred, slowly working them down his thighs.

Lennox had picked out one of his favorites, a pair of cheeky blue scraps of lace that cupped him nicely and left him with only the illusion of modesty. Riley's eyes darkened as he exposed them. "Perfect, Kitten. Goddamn, look at you. I changed my mind. We're going home *now*."

Riley grabbed for his hand but Lennox just laughed, stepping back and out of his jeans. It was a trick to work the tight fabric over his Chucks, but he managed. He tossed them at Riley and shook his head.

"Nope. You wanted to see me dance, Sir. I intend to make sure you always get...*everything* you want."

Riley cursed himself as he watched Lennox strut away. His attempt to tease Lennox had backfired spectacularly and now, it was *him* who was paying the price.

If his jeans got any tighter, he was going to lose feeling in his feet.

Men catcalled and whistled as Lennox passed, and several hands reached out to touch, but Lennox brushed them all off as he made his way to the nearest empty platform. Riley followed a few steps behind, watching as Lennox leaned forward to have a few words with the bouncer.

Riley knew—from the same way he knew it was amateur night—that the bouncers screened the amateurs hoping to dance. Not everyone made the cut to get up there, but Riley had no doubt Lennox would.

He was right. A quick up and down from the tattooed bouncer and Lennox was allowed to scramble up onto the slick podium. He looked skittish, uncertain—until the song changed. The opening notes to Nickelback's *Next Contestant* started playing and Lennox lit up.

He was still awkward. Riley couldn't deny it. He was no professional. But what he lacked in skill, he made up for in exuberance. And the way the blue lace cupped his obvious erection was obscene. Riley adjusted his own with little success. The neon club lights strobed against Lennox's smooth flesh in an erotic dance.

Riley wasn't the only one entranced by him—though he suspected the audience was captivated more by Lennox's near nudity and sexy body than the way he was moving it. And just like in the lyrics of the song, when a burly man stretched to grab Lennox's ankle, holding on for just a second before the bouncer removed his grip, fury flared in Riley. He wanted to see that man limp out—preferably with a broken hand.

Nobody touched what belonged to Riley. He was a possessive bastard, and Lennox was *his*.

Riley strutted closer to the podium, Lennox's clothing thrown over his shoulder. He stopped just in front of it to stare up at Lennox with *fuck-me* eyes. He crooked a finger and, even though the song wasn't over, Lennox scrambled down, his cheeks flushed and bare skin damp with sweat.

Riley couldn't stop himself from grabbing Lennox by the neck, forcing him to lift his chin so Riley could catch a salty bead as it trailed down the column of the man's throat. He took his time, teasing Lennox as much as himself.

"Such a good boy," Riley finally said as he pulled back. "I'm going to take you home and fuck you over the back of the couch. Wanna spread you out and break you for anyone else."

Lennox whimpered, plastering their chests together. Riley didn't even care when it left his shirt damp. "Now? We can go *now*?"

"Not like this, Kitten," Riley slid his fingers along the waistband of the pretty briefs. "The quicker you get dressed, the sooner we can leave." Riley winked.

Lennox yanked his clothes off Riley's shoulder, dropping his jeans in his haste to tug on the shirt. Riley laughed and crouched down, letting him use his shoulder to lean on as he helped him step into the pants. Riley tugged them up his legs, only taking a *few* extra moments to linger, entranced by the view.

Reluctantly, he tugged up the zipper and closed the button, blocking the lace from view before he stood back up. "Ready?"

Lennox grabbed his hand and practically sprinted toward the exit. Riley laughed.

Apparently, he was.

Chapter Twenty-Two

Lennox barely remembered the cab ride home. All he knew was that Riley had dragged him into his lap and they'd made out *so* hard, roaming his hands everywhere *except* where Lennox needed them. By the time the cab stopped outside his house, he was ready to burn the torture device someone called jeans. He popped the button while Riley fumbled with the front door key.

"Shit, Kitten, wait." Riley pulled away from the heated kiss with a curse. "Gotta get us inside first," he added, mostly to himself. Lennox almost didn't care that they were still standing on the front porch. If Riley didn't touch his dick soon, he was going to explode.

Riley shoved the front door open. It banged against the wall and bounced back hard, but Riley caught it with his foot. Then, he dragged Lennox inside.

Lennox's breath caught on a gasp as Riley kicked the door closed behind him, backing Lennox against the wood.

Lennox barely had a second to appreciate the needy look on Riley's face before the younger man cradled his face with gentle hands. Too gentle to prepare him for the heat of the kiss that followed — the way Riley stole the breath from his lips.

Then they were moving, though Lennox refused to break their kiss to see where. He remembered Lennox's threat — promise? — just before Riley yanked away, spinning Lennox around and pressing against his shoulders, draping him over the back of the couch.

"I'm going to fuck you here, like this, unless you tell me to stop." Riley's voice was deeper than usual. He didn't wait for a reply, trusting Lennox to tell him if he went too far, just like Lennox trusted him to stop if he asked. Instead, he worked his fingers into Lennox's jeans, stroking his dick through the lace before shoving everything down — baring Lennox to his greedy eyes.

Cool air kissed his ass when Riley pried his cheeks apart. "Such a pretty hole, Kitten. You should see it begging for me. I want you to be a good boy and feed it your fingers while I grab supplies. Can you do that for me?"

Lennox frantically nodded, already reaching around to sink a finger into himself. The angle was awkward, and the stretch burned without lube. He couldn't go deep like this. Still, it was the hottest thing they'd done together yet. More than anything, it was his thoughts that got to him, the knowledge of what he must look like, bent over the back of his couch with his own fingers buried in his ass just because his roommate told him to.

It made him feel like such a slut, and he *loved* it.

Cool lube dripped over his fingers before he even realized that Riley was back. The young man could be so quiet when he wished, moving like a shadow. That, or Lennox's moans had just drowned him out.

"There you go, Kitten. Look at you. I bet you feel so tight," Riley teased. Lennox whined when Riley slid in a finger alongside his, probing deeper and making the stretch just that much more intense. "Clench around me, baby. Strangle our fingers with this tight little hole. I wanna feel you work yourself open."

Lennox tried to clamp down on the invading fingers, the ring of muscle tightening him up even further. "Fuck, fuck..." he cursed. It wasn't enough. He tried to angle his fingers or hips to get deeper, to reach that needy little button inside him just begging to be touched, but it was impossible.

Lennox laughed. "Again, Kitten."

Crying out, Lennox obeyed. "Not enough, Sir, need you. Please, want your cock. I *need* it."

Instead, Riley pulled out his finger, dragging Lennox's hand away as well, leaving him empty and gaping, desperate. A pitiful whine spilled from Lennox's throat. "No, wait! Sir, I'll be good, I promise I will. *Please* fuck me. I need it. Give me your cock, and I'll...I'll—"

Before he could decide what he'd be willing to do, he felt it. The latex-sheathed crown of Riley's cock pressed against his hole, popping through the ring easily as he sank inside, slow but steady.

Lennox moaned at the stretch, unable to breathe until he felt Riley's balls strike his just under where their hips were joined. "Fuck." He let out a slew of curses as Riley withdrew before slamming back into him, hard enough to make the couch squeak forward on the hardwood.

Lennox gripped it tighter to hold himself steady as Riley began to pound into him like an animal. He couldn't let go to take himself in hand, but he didn't need to. Every thrust struck his prostate with the force of a hammer, shoving him toward his climax like he was clinging to a cliffside. He couldn't hold back much longer.

"Sir, I'm close. I can't—"

"You can," Riley growled, fingers clamping down on Lennox's hips to hold him still. "Hold on for me, Kitten. I want you to come down my throat. God, *fuck*, I'm almost there. Hold on. You can do it..."

Lennox felt tears burn his eyes as he struggled not to come, to be a good boy and hold out. He didn't think he was going to make it but then, *just* as it got to be too much, Riley's hips stuttered and he yelled, spilling into the latex between them. Riley's chest shuddered against Lennox's back for just a moment before he tightened his grip again, spinning Lennox around until he leaned against the couch.

Riley dropped to his knees, and that was it. Lennox cried out as he came. Riley barely had time to wrap his pretty lips around the head of Lennox's dick before the first spurt.

It felt like forever until it stopped. Lennox felt boneless, sinking down against the back of the couch for support. He winced when his tender ass touched the floor, but he couldn't have moved if he tried.

Riley slid down beside him, tangling their fingers together against his thigh, breath coming out in pants. "I swear, you get hotter every time we do this," Riley muttered.

"You fucked my bones out," Lennox said, his own breath shaky.

It drew a snicker from Riley.

"Hey," Lennox started, abruptly realizing that he'd gotten so caught up in the heat of the moment he'd never asked about what Mike told him. "Are you really doing porn?"

Chapter Twenty-Three

Lennox was just curious, but Riley turned white as a sheet and cursed. "Did you—have you—oh God…" Riley started to scramble up, but Lennox refused to let go of his hand, tugging him back down.

"Hey, don't go. You don't have to tell me if you don't want to. I didn't mean to upset you. Don't be mad. I was really just curious…" Lennox tried to reassure, squeezing his fingers. Simba strolled out of the kitchen, took one look at Riley, then trotted over, trying to curl up in his lap.

Lennox winced when he saw the cat's claws dig into Riley's naked thigh. Riley just shifted Simba to the side and tugged his jeans up, stripping the condom off and tying it. Lennox reluctantly pulled up his pants as well, though he left them unbuttoned.

"I just… I should have known you'd find out eventually. I just…didn't think the videos would blow up like they did. I needed some extra cash a few months ago and thought camming would be a better alternative to hooking." Riley sounded embarrassed, and Lennox hated that he felt that way.

"There's nothing wrong with camming," he said, shifting up on his knees to better meet Riley's eyes. "I'm not going to judge you, if you're worried about that. I mean, you've seen the nude paintings I've done. Pretty much the whole Texas art scene has seen my schlong at one point or another. Besides, you *know* you're fucking hot, right? I'm not surprised at all that they blew up."

"Did you watch them?" Riley finally asked, after several seconds of silence.

"No," Lennox pouted. "Mike told me about them today at the party. Trust me, there ain't *no* way I'd have been able to watch you have sex on screen and not rub my dick raw."

"I mean, I don't have sex with other people…just solo videos," Riley said quickly, like he was in a hurry to explain in case Lennox was worried—which he wasn't, though maybe he should be. They'd never clarified their relationship, never talked about an expectation for exclusivity, even if Lennox hadn't been sleeping with anyone else since they'd started anyway.

So Lennox could only shrug. "I wouldn't have been angry, even if you did. I don't know what this is between us yet"—he gestured between the two of them— "but I can't hold you to a rule we've never discussed."

Riley grew quiet, glancing away for a long moment. When he turned back, his eyes were wide and sad. "Have you been sleeping with other people?"

"No," Lennox answered quickly. "Just you. Trust me, I'm more than satisfied with your dick." He winked in an attempt to lighten the mood, and it might have been his imagination, but it looked like Riley relaxed.

"Honestly, though, I've never seen the need to have more than one partner at a time, even if it's pretty casual, but I don't judge people who do. If you *don't* want exclusivity, I won't be angry. It's your body. If you want to share it with others, the only thing I ask is that you communicate with me, that way I know to continue getting regularly tested and we can keep everyone involved safe."

"I don't," Riley blurted, his face turning red, "want to sleep with others, I mean. Being exclusive sounds…nice." He dropped his gaze to his lap, and Lennox itched to tip his chin back up. "Do you want me to stop making the videos, though? I never got a call back on most of the jobs I applied for after the shelter closed, but I can keep putting out applications."

"Honestly, if you like camming, then I don't want you to stop. If you're just doing it for the money, though, I can help you get out of it. I don't need the rent money, if you need a break for a few months, and I'm more than willing to help you with other bills, too, if you need it." Lennox detested the thought of Riley forced into something that he hated, especially over something so stupid as rent money Lennox didn't need.

"I… You know, I didn't think I was going to like camming. I was only doing it for the cash, but I don't think I want to stop. It was really stressful at first, but now that I'm working with OnlyStiXXX, it's a lot more fun. They pay me a decent cut and"—Riley's cheeks turned even redder— "it's nice seeing the comments sometimes."

"You know what I'd like?" Lennox decided to take a risk and moved to straddle Riley's lap. Riley's eyelashes fluttered and his lips parted, slipping his tongue out to wet them, but he didn't shove Lennox off.

"I'd like to watch one with you. Sprawl out on my mattress beside you and put on a show for you...while *you* put on a show for me. Oh" — Lennox shifted against the hard length he felt growing again under his ass — "you like that."

Riley nodded, his eyes still wide but no longer sad. Instead, lust steamed the air between them.

Lennox stood, holding his hand out to tug Riley up. He swatted the younger man on the ass, grinning when Riley yelped. "Go on. Take my laptop into the bedroom and log in. Pull up your favorite video, then I want you, naked, on my bed waiting for me."

"What are you going to do?" Riley asked but he was already moving toward the bedroom, staring back at him over his shoulder.

"You'll see," Lennox promised. He waited for Riley to go into the bedroom before he revised his plan. He was just thinking of them jacking off together, but something told him that Riley needed to see how sexy he was and how much Lennox still desired him.

So instead of following right away, he detoured into the bathroom, grabbing a bottle of massage oil from the cabinet and carrying it back with him.

Riley was on his back, naked, his legs spread. His dick, despite just unloading in Lennox's ass, was standing, hard and proud, toward his well-toned abs. Even with his obvious arousal, Riley still looked nervous.

Well...we can't have that.

Riley met Lennox's gaze, struggling to not show his nerves. He wanted to think that Lennox meant what he said, that he didn't judge him. But Riley had judged himself for the things he did with his body for so long that he couldn't convince himself that today he'd get that lucky.

Then Lennox smiled, soft and gentle. "Don't worry, Bunny."

Riley jerked at the nickname. It wasn't the first he'd been given, but something about *this* one left him breathless. Maybe it was just because of how Lennox said it.

Lennox didn't seem to notice his reaction, though. He continued, "By the time I'm done with you, there won't be any doubt left in your mind about how I feel." He winked, then tossed a bottle of something on the bed.

Riley wanted to know what it was, but not enough to tear his gaze away from Lennox as the other man started to strip, leaving his clothes in a trail behind him as he approached the bed. He was nude when he climbed on the mattress, his dick dangling erect between his legs as he crawled.

"I want you on your stomach, Riley baby, facing the TV," Lennox clarified, grabbing a pillow and dropping it near the foot of the bed, clearly where he wanted Riley's head.

Curious, Riley obediently laid down as directed. The position was a little awkward, but with the pillow, he could still see the screen. It was frozen on the opening credits—the OnlyStiXXX logo brilliant blue against a black screen.

He felt an unfamiliar tingling in his stomach— something like nerves but far more pleasant. He had a strange anticipation at the thought of Lennox watching him. Goosebumps rose on his skin.

He didn't think his dick could get any harder but then Lennox straddled him, cradling his dick in the crevice of Riley's ass. A *snick* sounded as he popped open the lid of the mystery bottle.

Riley tensed, anticipating the cold, but the oil that landed on his skin was room temperature. Then, Lennox dug his strong fingers into his back. "Push play, Bunny," Lennox ordered.

Fumbling for the remote, he finally managed to press the button. He flinched at the volume of the title screen, obscene moans and panted breaths, but knew not to turn it down. The actual video was never as loud.

Heat flooded Riley's body as the title faded and he appeared on screen. This had been the first video he'd filmed on set instead of at home in his bed. He'd had to take a day trip to San Antonio to get there, but it had been worth it in the end to be able to use their props and costumes.

He'd brought his own toys.

"Oh, sexy librarian," Lennox purred, continuing to work his hands over Riley's muscles as they both watched him on screen. He'd been dressed in corduroys and a blue button-down, complete with a sweater vest and glasses. The set they'd led him to had been made up like a library. They'd even found a library cart.

"You look so strait-laced there, Bunny," Lennox teased. "I just want to muss you all up." Riley could tell he wasn't lying, not with the way his hips shifted, sliding his dick back and forth between Riley's ass cheeks. It was hard — Riley snickered at the unintended pun as it crossed his mind — *hard* proof that Lennox really was turned on.

"Oh, fuck," Lennox cursed a few minutes later as they watched on-screen Riley, now half-naked, his button-down shirt open but draped half off his shoulders, reach into the library cart and pull out a large purple dildo.

Riley's hole clenched at the memory of it invading him. Even with all the prep he'd done before filming, that thing was a monster. It had stretched him past what he'd thought he could take.

It definitely wasn't a toy he'd want to use often, but once in a blue moon? Well...he'd be open to using it again.

Lennox's hands stilled on his body, and Riley craned his neck around to see why. He didn't need to worry, he realized. Lennox was staring, his eyes heated and tongue peeking through his lips, at the screen, watching Riley's ass swallow the purple toy inch by inch.

He stared like he was watching someone perform a miracle, or like what Riley was doing on screen was a magic trick, not like he was disgusted.

Riley arched up his hips and clenched his ass cheeks around Lennox's shaft as much as he could. "You know, I still have it," he said, "if you ever want a...*private* demonstration."

Lennox blinked, tearing his gaze from the television with obvious reluctance. "Later, Bunny. The only thing going in this hole tonight" — he slid a slippery finger down Riley's spine to tap his pucker — "is me."

Riley moaned, trying to press back against the finger.

Lennox removed it and swatted his ass. "Patience, Bunny. I'm not ready to fuck you, yet. Not until we watch you come." He cupped Riley's cheeks, massaging them as he squeezed them around his dick, pausing only once to slide on a condom and coat it with lube before he re-buried himself.

Not, of course, where Riley *needed* him.

Riley reluctantly turned back to the porn, trying to remember how long it took him to come in this one. "Shit," he cursed, squirming against the mattress. "I changed my mind, this one *isn't* my favorite anymore." If he remembered right, the director wanted him to tease himself for it, edge the viewers for at least twenty minutes.

Riley didn't think he could hold out that long without Lennox's dick in his ass.

Lennox just laughed, the *fucker*.

It was worth the wait.

As soon as on-screen Riley painted the library carpet with his seed, Lennox sheathed his dick and pressed the crown against Riley's hole. "Tell me to stop," Lennox warned, holding it there but not entering.

Riley shook his head.

"Can you take me like this? No prep, just me?"

"Go slow?" Riley pleaded, not willing to wait for Lennox to open him, not even if it meant the initial burn would be worse.

And it was, but he relished it, knowing that he'd be even tighter for Lennox, wrapped around his dick like a glove. Despite the burn, he clenched down. Lennox's answering groan made Riley grow even harder.

Lennox's entry into his body was a torturous crawl. He slid in only a fraction before pulling out, then entered him again, just a bit farther. He repeated the agonizing tease until Riley was a whining, whimpering mess beneath him. Finally, he had enough. Gathering his strength, Riley pushed up on his knees and back, giving Lennox no time to do anything but sink his dick in farther, all the way to the hilt.

It burned like a motherfucker, and he hissed, but it was worth it to feel Lennox's hips pressed to his, and to hear the groan spill unbidden from the man's throat.

"Brat," Lennox finally moaned, when he was able to speak again, landing a stinging swat to Riley's hip. Riley hissed but shook his head, refusing to apologize. Lennox's grip on his other hip held him steady. "I'm in charge now, Bunny. You'll take what I give you."

Riley shuddered, planting his forehead on the mattress and canting his hips up farther in a silent plea. Lennox held steady for several more seconds, long enough that Riley thought he was going to lose his mind.

Finally, Lennox began to move. Still slow, but the smooth drag against his inner walls had Riley whining. "So fucking good," he cursed, struggling not to push back against him.

As he fucked him, Lennox spoke. "Wanna watch all your videos, every one of them. Going to have to buy more lube, baby. God, you're so fucking hot. Wanna watch everything. God, wanna see us on screen together, show the world who you belong to—who *I* belong to. You can use me like your living dildo if you want. Just push me down and ride me right on set. Fuck," Lennox shuddered and pressed Riley down until he was flush with the mattress, the comforter rubbing against his dick to give him the perfect amount of friction.

Riley had never been a screamer, but his cries were loud now. Everything, from the way Lennox felt inside him to the way he gripped his hips to the fantasy he was spinning was *perfect*, drawing Riley closer.

"Gonna come," Riley admitted, curling his fingers in the bedspread and gripping tight.

"Do it. Come for me. Milk my cock, Bunny. You're so...fucking...perfect. Fuck!" Lennox panted in Riley's ear.

Riley let go of the single thread of control that had kept him from spilling. He didn't even care that he was now lying in the wet spot, not when Lennox's thrusts grew rougher, his voice practically a growl in Riley's ears as he thrusted into his body, spilling only moments later.

Lennox shuddered, plastering himself to Riley's back for several long seconds. His ragged breath tickled Riley's hair until he finally groaned and rolled off, pulling Riley with him. Lennox arranged him until they were lying chest to chest, their legs tangled. Riley was sticky from his release and now so was Lennox, the condom leaking pearly fluid down his thighs where they touched Riley, but neither of them moved to clean up.

"Did you mean it?" Riley asked, tilting his head to stare up at Lennox. "That you want to make a video with me?" The studio had been hinting that they would eventually need more than solo videos, but he'd been stalling as long as he could. As long as the solo videos were still doing well, which they were, he knew they wouldn't press, but he'd been dreading the day when they weren't.

Lennox smiled, eyes twinkling. "Bunny, I'd do *anything* with you."

Chapter Twenty-Four

Riley let Lennox's half-hard dick slip from his lips, laughter making his shoulders shake as he buried his face against Lennox's iliac crest — the sharp, sexy curve of his hip that Riley longed to lick and nip.

Only Lennox would be halfway through getting a blow job and start chatting to the cameraman about the type of lights they were using to illuminate the set.

"Lennox, baby..." Riley finally said once he got control of his breathing. "As glad as I am that you're making friends, it's hard to give you a sexy blow job when you're only...half hard." Riley turned his head and kissed the not-quite flaccid dick he'd hoped would be pummeling his throat right about now.

"Hm? Oh, sorry, Bunny, I just... These lights are so bright, look how pretty they make your skin look. Would be great for painting." Lennox ran his fingertips over Riley's cheek, drawing out a shudder.

Unlike Lennox — who thankfully was already plumping back up again — Riley was hard as a rock. He didn't need to look down to know the bright lights would be catching on the sticky pre-cum and illuminating it, leaving no way to hide it from the cameras.

Or, apparently, Lennox. "For someone who's sad I'm talking to the cameraman, your dick is leaking like a faucet. I think you like me ignoring you a little."

Riley felt his cheeks heat, surprised to find that…yeah, he kind of did. Mostly because he knew Lennox would never *really* ignore him, not in a way he found painful. All he needed to do to get Lennox's attention was ask. Sometimes, it only took a look…or a subtle touch.

Now, Lennox was fully hard, and he wasted no time guiding Riley's head back onto his dick. "Look so pretty with your mouth full, sweetheart. Now be a good boy and keep my cock warm while I talk to my new friend."

Riley froze at the order, his heart beating rapidly. It was hot—*so* hot—and his dick was throbbing, but surely the director wouldn't let it continue. The older man had outlined the scene as a simple exchange of blow jobs, not…whatever this was.

Surely he would be angry about the amount of editing he'd be forced to do, cutting out Lennox's conversation—was he talking about *camera angles* now?—and somehow making it all look natural.

But to Riley, the fact that his boyfriend was carrying on such a casual conversation, like it was just an everyday thing to be standing on a porn set getting your dick sucked…Fuck. The only sign that Lennox was struggling to hold onto his control was the tight grip he had in Riley's hair, the little twitches of his hips and, occasionally, an indrawn breath that had his words catching in his throat, causing a little stutter.

Riley almost made it. He was getting pretty good at staving off orgasm until the director asked for a cumshot, but then he looked up—just in time to see Lennox grin at the camera. "See how much he's leaking?"

Riley wasn't prepared for Lennox to shove him off his dick, and he landed on his ass with a shocked "*ooph!*" Lennox just chuckled and straddled his thighs, forcing Riley to lean back on his hands to avoid toppling over. Lennox swiped his thumb over Riley's slit, and as good as it felt, the visual was better.

"I don't have a paintbrush," Lennox mused, "but I'm still pretty good at fingerpainting." With his thumb sticky with pre-cum, he raised it to Riley's lips, smearing the liquid around like lip gloss.

"Such a good little slut," Lennox said quietly, soft enough Riley wasn't even sure it would be heard on camera, but *Riley* heard it.

Untouched, he cried out, cum painting Lennox's abs in spurts.

From off camera, he heard the director curse and the camera man rush forward in an attempt to catch it on film, but Riley barely noticed, his whole body shaking as Lennox grinned at him. Gently, Lennox pushed him down onto his back, running his palms through the pearly fluid.

With Lennox, the cumshot was never the end…just a happy place to pause.

* * * *

"An escape room?" Riley's lips twitched as they stood outside the brick-face building less than an hour after finishing their showers in the OnlyStiXXX studio locker room. Lennox had said he wanted to do something fun, and Riley must have still had dick on the brain because he'd expected a heavy make-out session in a dark movie theater or...or a trip 'stargazing' in an empty field.

"It'll be fun! I've always wanted to do one!" Lennox grinned, so much child-like enthusiasm leaking from his pores that Riley felt...*uncomfortable* about the erection pressing into his zipper.

He shouldn't have decided on skinny jeans.

Lennox's smile wobbled when Riley was too slow to answer, distracted by the sunlight lighting on Lennox's cheekbones. "We can go somewhere else. I just thought..."

"No! I mean...no, this is fine. It sounds fun. I want to do you — *with* you. Do it with you," Riley rambled.

"Bunny, you can do me *any* time." Lennox winked.

Riley smirked, sidling up to Lennox and fiddling with one of the little buttons on his salmon shirt. "How about we make a — hang on, are these *flamingos*?" Diverted from his train of thought, he squinted down at them.

"Yeah. Cute, right?" Lennox said. "How about we *what*?"

"Oh, right." Riley gave the button one last look, then buried his smirk. "How about we make a little bet?"

"Mm? What are the stakes?" Lennox grinned, twisting around until he was pressed chest to chest with Riley. He gripped Riley's hips, yanking him closer still.

"How about…whichever one of us finds the final clue first gets to top tonight?" Riley suggested.

"You're on." Lennox winked, reaching around to squeeze Riley's ass.

"Ah," Riley tsked, pulling away. "No playing with the merchandise until you've won, Mr. Nakayama."

"Bunny, top or bottom, I'm gonna feel like a winner either way." Lennox stepped back, his eyes glinting as he readjusted himself in his pants.

"Tease." Riley stuck his tongue out and headed inside.

* * * *

"Come on, come on…" Riley could hear the clock ticking down—literally, since the old-school grandfather clock on the wall was ominously loud – as he rapidly flipped through the leather notebook that he'd found under the false bottom of the desk drawer. There had to be a password somewhere, since why else would there be an old-school box monitor computer with a login screen already loaded up?

Just as he found a string of numbers, Lennox yelled, "Ah-ha!"

"No!" Riley cursed and spun around, just in time to see the bookshelf creaking open and Lennox releasing what must have been a faux book.

He ran toward the newly revealed opening. Maybe he could get there before Lennox—which might be cheating, but all's fair in love and war—but Lennox elbowed him out of the way, racing around the bookshelf just seconds before Riley.

And immediately bouncing off a brick wall with a large shiny safe.

"Oh, shit!" Riley yelped, leaping backward as Lennox stumbled, dropping down to his knee and holding his head. "Oh *shit*, you're bleeding!"

"Are you sure?" Lennox dropped his hand and—yep, definitely bleeding.

Riley gagged, feeling his skin go hot as the world spun. "Oh...shit..."

Then *his* knees buckled.

He didn't remember hitting the floor, but he definitely remembered the two hours he and Lennox had spent side by side in the ER, waiting for brain scans to rule out concussions. The taxi ride home was a bit of a blur though.

"They're never going to let us come back," Riley moaned, holding an ice pack to his head.

"Some couples share food. We share ambulances," Lennox said so dryly from behind *his* ice pack that Riley burst out laughing.

Then he winced, holding his free hand to his forehead. "Ouch! Wait. Don't make me laugh."

"Okay, so no comedy clubs, got it."

"Our date options are getting slimmer than a spokesman for Jenny Craig," Riley teased.

"Oooh, now I want ice cream!"

"Room service?" Riley suggested.

Lennox, forehead wrapped in gauze, nodded. "Yeah. But you have to call 'cause I can't reach the phone, and when I move, my head feels like a bowling pin."

"Oh, we could go bowling!"

Chapter Twenty-Five

"Seriously, Lenny? Gay porn? How on earth did you think they wouldn't notice?" Ally said. Lennox could hear her rolling her eyes through the phone.

"Uh, well...since it's *gay* porn, I didn't think our *conservative* parents would find out. Because, you know...it's gay and porn. Gay porn. Honestly, I didn't think they even knew what porn was, let alone...gay porn." Maybe, if he said 'gay porn' enough, she'd understand why he was...surprised, to say the least, that their parents had seen it.

And wasn't *that* just a boner killer.

Who wanted to think of their parents watching porn?

Lennox still wouldn't change anything. Filming that scene with Riley, even if so far they'd only exchanged a super-hot blow job on camera, was the sexiest thing they'd done yet. He loved watching the video they'd made and could hardly wait to do another. Apparently, he was an exhibitionist. Who knew?

"You know they're planning to fly out and read you the riot act," Ally said. Lennox grimaced at the thought. "They've even called and lectured *me*, like it's somehow *my* fault you exposed yourself on camera, and you know how pissed they must have been if they had to dig out my phone number from whatever hole they'd buried it in."

Lennox shrugged before remembering she couldn't see him through the phone. "I'm not worried. I already paid them back for the house — with interest — and they can't touch my trust fund anymore, so what are they going to do? Cut me off?"

Ally didn't say anything because really, there wasn't anything to say. Except for Christmas and birthday cards, and the random Mother's Day flowers he sent when he remembered, they hadn't been in contact since his dreaded graduation.

Not that he'd outed himself on purpose... He just hadn't realized that his father would decide to use the same bathroom he was in. At least him and Robby Sanders were only making out.

"I'm not worried," Lennox decided. "They'll either come and yell before leaving like their pants are on fire, which will be exactly what they did the last time we spoke, or they'll actually listen to me for the first time in their lives and maybe, we can move past it. Either way, no skin off my nose."

"It's your funeral," Ally said bitterly.

Lennox felt guilty. Mama and Papa hadn't even bothered coming to Ally's wedding. As soon as they realized she was dating a woman, they'd cut ties. Not a word of warning, no explanation, just...dead air.

Until now, when suddenly they were pissed at Lennox and took it out on Ally, like it was somehow her fault that he was dabbling in porn. Granted, they still thought he was actively practicing law, so he supposed he could understand their concern.

Of course, he was sure they were actually more worried about *their* reputation than his.

"Kitten? Did you forget something this morning?" Riley's amused voice sounded from the hallway and Lennox flinched, fumbling the phone and nearly dropping it. He glanced at the clock on his nightstand. It was…several hours later than he thought.

"Shit," he cursed. "Ally, I gotta go. I forgot to start the laundry."

"Since when do you do la—" Ally said but Lennox hung up before she could finish. Riley had taken to giving him chores a few months ago, rotating them out each week for Lennox to work on.

This week, Riley had even reminded him before he'd headed off to the studio. Lennox couldn't wait until the new film studio opened in Austin in a few months because, while San Antonio might not be as far as Houston or Dallas, it was still quite a trek. He worried about Riley driving it—not because he cared about his car, which Riley was borrowing, but because almost two hours in the car after an intensive masturbation scene had to be hell on his ass. Especially since Riley never lingered, always hurrying to get back to Lennox.

Lennox raced out to the living room, wringing his hands as he stared at the baskets of clothes he'd abandoned by the couch. He'd had every intention to carry them to the washer and dryer in the garage but halfway there, he'd realized he forgot to grab the bathroom towels. Once he'd made it to the bathroom, though, he'd thought it would be a good idea to take a shower *before* he ran the washer, and he'd gotten distracted shaving his legs and pits.

And freshly shaved legs meant he needed the right pair of silk panties, and it was all downhill from there.

"I forgot to finish it," Lennox admitted, biting his lip.

Riley looked more amused than angry. "Why don't you go take it in now and start a load, then we'll talk about your consequence."

Lennox hardened in his jeans but knew better than to acknowledge it. "Yes, Sir." He scurried to grab the first basket and get it loaded into the washer, adding a bit too much soap in his haste. Oh well, it would probably be fine.

He slammed the lid closed and turned to head out, but Riley was blocking the doorway. He'd stripped off his shirt but left the black fitted jeans and was leaning against the doorframe with his arms crossed.

He looked...hot. And intimidating, despite the smile on his face. It was an expression Lennox recognized, and a shiver spread down his spine, arousal tingling in his gut.

"You have a choice to make," Riley said, his voice loud in the silence.

"Yes, Sir?" Lennox asked, his knees threatening to buckle at the dominance Riley exuded.

"A spanking, now. If you don't come, I'll bend you over the washer and get you off tonight. If you *do,* then no more until Sunday. You can just be my little cock warmer." Riley smirked.

Three days? He thought Lennox would be able to make it *three* days? Then again, he might not have a choice, hard as he was. There was no way he was going to keep from coming during a spanking. "And," Riley added, "no matter which one you choose, you'll need to add your lines to the notebook."

Lennox shivered. As much as he hated writing lines, especially something as boring as "I will do my chores when asked," he *loved* the way it made him feel, just like he loved the rest of the punishments Riley devised. Or, 'funishments' more like, since none of them were ever meant to *actually* discipline him.

"I...I don't think I can stop myself," Lennox admitted, already squirming in his jeans.

Riley's answering smile was deadly. "Strip, Kitten, and bend over the washer. Show me that pretty ass I'll be leaving my handprints all over."

Lennox whined, shoving his jeans and panties down in one go, his dick bobbing free. Pre-cum seeped down his length. He turned around and bent over the washing machine. It vibrated under him as it spun. *Damn, what would it feel like to be fucked on this?*

Soon, he'd get the chance to find out.

Riley's footsteps echoed as he approached behind him, pressing against him. His jeans were rough where they dug into Lennox's ass. "You look perfect like this, Kitten. Bent over like a little slut. If only I didn't have to punish you, I'd give you the ride of your life."

"Don't *sound* sorry," Lennox made the mistake of muttering.

Crack!

Riley's palm smacked over his ass, and Lennox's breath caught on a moan. "Mouthy little brat." Riley rubbed away the sting, but just when Lennox relaxed, he swatted him again. A flurry of blows — none too hard, just enough to burn — landed on his ass.

He almost made it, but then Riley gripped his cheeks and spread him, and the cool air against his hole was all it took. Lennox cried out, covering the front of the washer in his cum. He'd have to clean it later.

For now, he collapsed onto the lid with a whimper.

"Poor Kitten, you were so close," Riley teased, and Lennox could tell from the dark humor in his voice that there was never a chance he was going to be able to hold out. Riley had *wanted* him to come — wanted him to be hard and wanting until Sunday.

Fucker.

* * * *

Lennox needed something to distract him from the stress of his parents' upcoming visit, so Riley thought a few days of edging was the perfect prescription. He couldn't deny that seeing Lennox pout was a bonus. By Saturday morning, Lennox looked pathetic — in the best way.

Riley couldn't stop staring at the obscene erection tenting Lennox's sleep pants as he poured himself a coffee. Then, he laughed, realizing he didn't have to resort to just *perving*. He gripped his dick through his boxers and strutted over.

"Kitten," Riley said, jutting his hips out as he leaned against the counter.

Lennox glared over his coffee cup. "Yes?"

"Oh, Kitty sounds grouchy," Riley teased, hopping onto the countertop and spreading his thighs, leaving his erection on display. "I guess that means you don't want to help me with this, then."

Lennox looked torn. His gaze dropped to Riley's dick, then back up, and though he tried to maintain his glare, Riley saw past it.

"If I get you off, will you let me come?" Lennox asked, his voice hopeful. Riley almost hated to disappoint him.

"Sure I will," Riley promised, then grinned. "First thing tomorrow morning."

"Sadist," Lennox accused, but something on his face made Riley certain he enjoyed it.

"Sadist, *Sir*," Riley corrected with a cocky grin. "And I think you have better things to do with your mouth than run it, don't you, Kitten?"

Lennox groaned, setting his coffee aside as he stepped forward, into the cradle of Riley's thighs. His hands were steady and quick to lower Riley's briefs, freeing him into the chilly, air-conditioned kitchen.

Heat swirled between them as Lennox bent forward to suck on his crown, teasing him with the tip of his tongue. Riley moaned and carded his fingers through Lennox's soft hair. For once, it was free of paint, though Riley suspected that wouldn't last the day.

"Such a good boy," Riley praised as Lennox worked his length with a single-minded determination.

He was so involved in the blow job — they *both* were — that neither of them heard the front door open.

"Oh, for *Christ's* sake!" a woman's voice shrieked in the entryway, startling them both. Riley cursed as Lennox accidentally clamped down on his dick, his teeth grazing the tender flesh as he yanked away in surprise.

Lennox looked apologetic, meeting his eyes for a second before he turned to glare at the woman. "Mama, don't you know how to knock?"

Riley fumbled to shove his aching dick back under his boxers as he slid off the counter to the floor.

"I bought this house. Why would I knock?" The woman *tsk*ed, staring at them with disapproval. She had hair bleached to white — the roots were growing in dark — and it was pulled back in a tight bun. She had on a skirt suit that couldn't have been comfortable to travel in and white stockings on her feet.

"And I bought it from you as soon as I passed the Bar, remember? So *technically*, you're trespassing," Lennox pointed out, and Riley was surprised by how cross he sounded. He knew there was some distance between Lennox and his family, but this seemed like more.

"Oh, *psh*. Honey, I'm your mother, even if you never make time to call anymore. I suppose that's *his* fault." She glared at Riley as she said it, making it easy to guess who the 'his' was.

"No, it's the fact that you caught me kissing a boy and suddenly realized you had more important things to do than watch me get my diploma." Riley watched Lennox curl his hands into fists and decided it was time to step in. He reached out and clasped one of the fists in his, prying Lennox's fingers apart to intertwine their hands.

"You must be Mrs. Nakayama." Riley smiled politely and reached out his hand.

She ignored it with a sneer. "Nakayama-*san*."

"Sorry, Nakayama-*san*," Riley corrected, his smile only slightly more tense.

Lennox huffed beside him. "Mama, you haven't used that since *Baba* passed."

"How would you know? You barely speak with us anymore." She pursed her lips, reminding Riley of the stern tutor he once had, the woman who liked to smack his knuckles with a ruler when he dozed off.

"We thought you'd be stopping by tomorrow," Riley jumped in, hoping to defuse the tension.

"Not that it's any of *your* business, but we flew in early." She sniffed, nose jutting into the air as she turned away. "Lennox dear, I don't suppose you can ask your little...*friend* to go home? Your father will be bringing in the bags any moment, and it would be best if he didn't have to be reminded of your... eccentricities."

Riley stiffened, anger flaring. He didn't know what pissed him off more, being called Lennox's 'little friend' or being expected to leave so they could continue pretending Lennox was straight.

"No," Lennox snapped before Riley could find his voice—or a polite way to decline something he had no right to say no to. "I told you when you called not to bother flying out. Besides, Riley has the guest room, so I don't have a bed for you anyway. You're going to have to find a hotel or something."

"A...a *hotel?* You'd rather let some...some...some *floozy* stay with you instead of your parents?" she screeched, hand pressing to her chest.

Riley snorted at being called a floozy, struggling to stay quiet instead of saying what was running through his mind.

Lennox shrugged. "Riley's my boyfriend, but even if he *didn't* live with me, I don't want you here. You and Papa made your beds. Go lie in them."

"We gave you *everything*. How *dare* you—"

"No," Lennox interrupted, and Riley was so proud of him, of the way he straightened his back and spoke his mind. "You gave me *things,* but not what I really needed—not two parents who loved me and Ally for who we are, the way we deserved. You only cared about me when I was following *your* rules and *your* script for me. Guess what? I *hate* law. I've been making my living off art, just like the pair of you always said I couldn't, and I've never been happier."

"What's going on here, Haruka?" A slim-shouldered man with perpetual frown lines stepped into the doorway, looking between the three of them with a scowl.

"Taiyo, your son says we can't stay here. He'd rather let this...this...boy-slut stay instead." Haruka's high-pitched voice grew nearly shrill.

Riley knew he should be insulted, but he fought the urge to laugh. *Boy-slut?* That was the worst she could come up with?

The older man's scowl deepened, tugging furrows into his face. "I thought you said he outgrew that shit?"

"That *shit*?" Riley blurted, finally angry enough to break the vow of silence he'd made after the woman's rudeness only minutes before. "Sir, it's called being gay, and it's nothing to be ashamed of."

Lennox gripped his hand tighter. "I think you both should leave. Clearly, you're not here to visit or mend fences. If you want a straight son, you're going to have to look elsewhere. Maybe try popping out another kid. I've always heard third one's the charm."

Lennox's mother looked aghast, stuttering out something that sounded like, "Can you believe the *nerve*, talking to your mother that way," but his father just grabbed her by the arm and practically dragged her out of the kitchen. A moment later, they heard the front door slam.

Lennox winced at the noise. Riley half-smothered him with a hug, squeezing him tight around the middle. Lennox allowed it for several long seconds but too soon, pulled away. He shook his head, planting on a wry smile that Riley could easily tell was fake.

"I suppose that went better than I expected," Lennox said, his voice upbeat, like his parents' behavior hadn't hurt him, when Riley knew damn well it had.

"You don't need them," Riley decided. "You have your sister and her wife, and you have Mike and his fiancé. And...you have me." He reached out and squeezed Lennox's hand. "Your...boyfriend?" His voice raised in question, his heart beating fast. Had Lennox just said that to piss off his parents, or did he really mean it?

Lennox's cheeks bloomed pink. "If you want. I mean, *I* want, but...only if you want, too?"

"I really do," Riley agreed, a wide grin spreading over his face. He'd been calling Lennox his boyfriend in his head for weeks. It was only a matter of time before it had slipped out. He was glad Lennox said it first.

Chapter Twenty-Six

"You know, right about now I'm *really* glad we never got that other one," Riley muttered as he stared up at the pair of cats. Somehow, Pumpkin and Fuzzy-Butt had figured out how to climb on top of the cupboards.

Which, you know, was great and all, until Pumpkin realized that she still needed to come down, and apparently the two-foot jump from the cupboard to the fridge to the counter was just too much. Overdramatic little fucker, she might as well be a teenager.

She was curled in the back corner, yowling. Fuzzy-Butt *could* get down. He'd watched her do so twice, but then she'd hopped right back up.

Probably because she was having a grand old time knocking down all the napkins stored up there. It looked like it was raining paper.

He'd finally given up and pulled the rest of the package down, shoving it under the cupboard beneath the sink, but now she was flopped up there on her belly, grooming her paws.

Conveniently blocking him from reaching Pumpkin, even though he was currently kneeling on the counter just in front of the coffee pot.

"You know," Lennox said, his voice seeming to come out of nowhere, "I've made some pretty bad decisions in my life, but that doesn't seem safe."

Riley flinched, nearly tumbling off the counter before he caught himself on the edge of the fridge, knocking the door open with his elbow.

"Shit," Lennox cursed then his hands were on Riley's ass, holding him up even though he'd already stabilized himself. "I should spank you for that."

"Go ahead," Riley grinned, looking back over his shoulder at him.

Lennox narrowed his eyes, then he landed a hard spank on Riley's left ass cheek. "Get down, now, before you fall and break your neck, you little idiot."

"But Pumpkin is stuck," Riley pointed out, pouting his lips.

"She's a cat. She'll get down when she wants to. *You'll* get down now." Lennox scowled, clearly not amused.

Riley smirked and rolled his eyes. "Yes, Daddy. Whatever you say, Daddy."

Lennox's lips twitched but he stepped back, seemingly reluctantly. He kept his hands spread like his plan was to catch Riley if he slipped. Like getting down off a waist high counter was any sort of challenge—

Riley's knee slid off the edge and he tumbled, landing against Lennox with an *"Oof,"* and windmilling arms. Lennox barely caught him, his breath escaping in a loud gasp as they both stumbled back.

"Oops?" Riley said as soon as he caught his breath again. He gave what he hoped was a cute enough grin to keep him out of trouble.

Lennox's scowl deepened. "There went one of my nine lives."

"How about a kiss? Will that make it better?" Riley offered.

Lennox shifted until Riley was standing chest to chest with him, their noses only inches apart. "Please don't do that again," he said seriously, clearly not in the mood to joke.

Riley sobered, realizing that Lennox had truly been scared, and nodded. "Okay, I'll be more careful."

"I wasn't joking when I said you deserve a spanking," Lennox added.

"I wasn't joking when I said, '*go ahead*'."

And by God, Lennox did. When he was finished tanning Riley's hide, he felt floaty and detached, halfway to subspace without even coming. He wasn't sure if spankings would end up being a good deterrent for him, but he'd point that out to Lennox...later.

When he was done cuddling.

They fell into a nice routine after that. It wasn't what Riley thought having a boyfriend would be like, since very little changed. They still cuddled on the couch like they did before, still teased each other about the amount of hair products they had between the two of them. Riley still did Lennox's nails, and Lennox still routinely asked Riley to help him unglue himself from various objects.

Riley had, for some reason, thought that dating— officially dating—would change everything—like in the romance movies Lennox secretly enjoyed, where the characters' lives revolved around each other, and they became the 'center of each other's universe'.

He wasn't willing to give up his daily shower jerk or his weekly *EverQuiet* session with Tweety. And Lennox still stowed himself away in his study at God-awful early in the morning.

Except for the sheer *amount* of sex, not much had really changed.

A few days after the Great Counter Fall of 2023, Riley's ass was still pleasantly pink. He stood, humming, in the kitchen, stirring a metric ton of sugar into Lennox's coffee with a smile. Excitement swirled in his belly. He'd made plans for the day. He didn't have another shoot for a few days, and Lennox had said the night before that he was between projects. He'd just finished up the last painting for this set of kink portraits and wasn't due to start another one until tomorrow.

It was the perfect day for a date.

Riley carried the coffee into Lennox's bedroom — though they spent more nights curled up together here than apart — and set it on the nightstand. Then, he climbed onto the mattress and straddled his sleeping boyfriend's hips.

Lennox shifted but didn't wake. He just tugged at the blankets with little success, his eyes scrunching even more tightly closed and mouth pouting. Riley trailed his fingertip over them before leaning down and brushing his lips over Lennox's.

Lennox stayed soft and pliant, until Riley was just about to pull away. Then, a hand curled in Riley's hair to tug them closer together. "Morning," Lennox murmured, his voice raspy.

"Morning," Riley whispered back, his breath mingling with Lennox's. "I made you coffee, and breakfast is waiting on the table."

"Hm-m," Lennox groaned, finally blinking open his pretty brown eyes. "What's the special occasion?"

Riley shrugged. "I want to take you out."

"Out? Like...*out*-out? On a date? Out in Austin?" Lennox stumbled over his words, blinking away sleep to prop himself up on his elbow.

"Yeah. There's a festival going on, over on Sixth Street," Riley grinned. "You ever been?"

"That's uh...the Pecan Street Festival? Is it September already?" Lennox twisted to stare at the window, like the small gap between the curtains and the glass would somehow turn into a calendar.

Riley laughed and sat back, resting his weight fully on Lennox's thighs. "Yep. Comes after August every year. God, I used to *love* this festival. Haven't gone since I lived on the streets, though."

"Why not?" Lennox asked, finally turning back to him.

Riley shrugged. "Always felt like I should save my money. Before the Rainbow House, I'd go down to beg. People were always in a good mood, and sometimes they'd give me cotton candy or hot dogs or something. Might not make much money that week but I'd eat like a king."

"Mike and I went in college a few times, but it's been years. I always say I want to get a booth there, sell some of my art heavily discounted just for fun," Lennox mused, eyes going distant. "But I always seem to forget when the time comes."

"Well, maybe next year I can help you remember," Riley promised. Lennox was right, though. Since his paintings were selling for thousands of dollars apiece, sometimes even higher, he'd definitely have to do a heavy markdown. "You should bring your sketch book and some colored pencils. I'm sure there will be places to sit, and maybe you'll find a new muse while we're there."

"Doubt it," Lennox chuckled, running his hands up Riley's thigh and dipping under his shirt to brush over his skin. "*You're* my muse."

"Such a flatterer," Riley said, but his breath caught on the last word when Lennox reached into the waistband of his sleep pants to squeeze his dick. He jerked, thrusting into Lennox's palm without warning. "No time for that if we want to walk around before the bands start."

Lennox, apparently, cared less about the bands than the music he drew out from Riley's lips as he came.

They left the house later than Riley planned, both sated and showered. At Riley's insistence, they took a rideshare. Lennox had insisted he was fine to drive but Riley didn't want to deal with parking.

He also held out a small hope that Lennox would let him steal a few sips of whatever drink he ended up with, since he was fairly certain the vendors would be a lot stricter about carding than the bars Riley frequented when he felt the urge to drink away his worries.

Which, now that he thought about it, hadn't been for a while, not since just after the shelter shut down and he was worried about cash. Still…not having to worry about being the designated driver was probably a good idea.

The ride share driver refused to go closer than two streets over, worried about being able to get back out, but the weather was great for walking. Mid-eighties, already several degrees cooler than the past few weeks, and sunny. The sidewalks bustled with activity, most people heading in the same direction they were.

Like them, everyone was dressed for the heat, bright colors abounding. Lennox had on a pair of sexy white shorts that barely reached mid-thigh and an off-the-shoulder tie-dye shirt that only clashed a little with his neon green Chucks and rainbow fanny pack. Riley's shorts were just as tiny but hot pink, a bright flash of color under his flowy white blouse. He'd stuck with his shit kickers.

It took twice as long to reach the festival as it normally would, but the wait was worth it. Lennox gripped his hand tight, dragging them toward the first booth. The woman behind it looked surprised. She was tucked in the corner by a row of port-a-potties, so maybe she hadn't expected customers so quickly. Or, maybe it was the near-manic grin on Lennox's face.

Then she opened her mouth and Riley realized the real reason for her surprise. "Oh my, you're Lennox Nakayama!" Her eyes glinted and she was clearly starstruck as she stared, open mouthed, at Riley's boyfriend. "Nobody will believe me when I say you stopped by my booth. I've seen *all* your work!"

Riley grinned when his boyfriend blushed. He looked so pretty, all pink and flushed, like a porcelain doll with his perfect rosy cheeks. Lennox stuttered out some words of gratitude to the woman and they walked away from the table twenty dollars poorer, with an eight-by-ten print of a rundown building, grayscale and shuttered. It had a vague familiarity, like Riley had passed it on the street and not given it a second look.

More often than not, Lennox was recognized at the artist booths. And, each time someone's eyes widened and they started to gush, Lennox blushed and ended up buying at least one thing.

Pretty soon, they were both juggling a handful of canvases with nowhere to put them. "Maybe we should have gone to the booths last," Riley mused.

"Here, hold this. I'll call Ally." Lennox shoved another three canvases into Riley's hands so he could pull his phone out of his pocket. Riley cursed, grappling one that nearly slid to the sidewalk. Thankfully, he caught it with the tip of his finger, sweat beading on his forehead.

Lennox rambled on the phone with his sister for several long, uncomfortable minutes before he hung up, beaming at Riley as he helped grab the art back. "She said she'll come and pick them up from us as soon as she gets done helping the kids clean up from breakfast."

Riley groaned. "So, like…another half an hour."

"Exactly!" Lennox grinned, far too happy. "Oh, tacos!" Then Lennox was off, heading toward a taco vendor as if his arms weren't overladen. Riley shook his head and followed.

Three tacos apiece later, they were able to pass the art off to Ms. Ally—he didn't care that it was weird, he couldn't *not* call her Ms., not even when she asked—who gave Riley a lingering look before a soft smile crossed her face. She didn't say anything, but her wink implied she approved. Or, at least, didn't *disapprove*. Or maybe her eye was just itchy.

Riley was surprised at the next booth when it was *him* who was recognized. After years of no one giving him a second look—unless it was in disgust that some dirty homeless kid was digging through their trash bins—he still wasn't used to the way someone's eyes would widen, or the way their cheeks would turn pink before they stuttered their way through a greeting.

Which, of course, would lead *him* to flushing as he realized the man—or sometimes woman—had seen him naked. They knew his come face, and how many freckles he had on his ass.

After the initial burst of embarrassment, it would fade, quicker each time.

Now, when the man in the booth selling rainbow dragon sculptures blinked at him with scarlet cheeks, he barely flinched. The man was older than him and Lennox, his hair dark but streaked with silver near his ears. He was attractive in his own way, though not Riley's type.

Clearly though...Riley and Lennox were *his* type, because his cheeks turned pinker the longer he looked between them. "Y-you're Ryland! And...and you're his..."

"I'm his boyfriend. Do you guys know each other?" Lennox smiled brightly.

"No," Riley and the man both said at the same time.

"Oh. Oh! You saw the video then?" Lennox asked, not embarrassed at all. "It was so much fun."

Riley chuckled. Only Lennox would have no problem talking about his porn debut with a random stranger on the street. Even the stranger was beet red.

"Ooh, look at this." Lennox pointed at one of the little sculptures, already moving on from the conversation. Riley obediently peered over Lennox's shoulder, listening to his boyfriend coo at the little pink-and-purple cat dragon sleeping in a wine glass.

"It's so cute," Riley agreed, curling his fingers into Lennox's shirt to avoid touching. It looked... "Fragile, though," he added.

"I... Um, I don't normally offer, but I can hold it for you? And you can come back um...and grab it later? I'll be here until three, but if I'm already gone, you can tell my assistant that Adrian put it aside for you?" Adrian offered, fidgeting with the tablecloth.

"Really? That would be awesome! Can I get that one, too?" Lennox indicated one sitting on a folding table near the back of the tent. It was blue, but one of the wings was missing.

"Oh, I'm not selling that one. It needs fixed," Adrian said.

"I think it's perfect the way it is." Riley could tell Lennox meant it, because his eyes were wide and fixed on the little sculpture.

"Are you sure? I mean, yeah, you can have it I guess, if you really want it. I can keep it with the other one."

Lennox made grabby hands. "Nah, I want to bring him with me. He looks lonely." Lennox snagged it quick when the man handed it over, spending several long seconds cooing over it, until Riley chuckled and led him away. "More booths or do you wanna head toward the music?"

"Hm? Oh, we can go see who's playing. I don't think I brought enough money." Lennox grinned and carefully tucked the little sculpture into his fanny pack, zipping it closed and patting the outside softly.

Riley snickered. "You realize it kind of looks like you're patting your dick, right?"

"In public?" Lennox faux gasped, lips twitching. "What kind of boy do you take me for, Mr. Scott?"

Riley stepped forward, curling his fingers around Lennox's neck to drag him closer. He nipped Lennox's lower lip. "The kind I want to take home with me."

Lennox slipped a finger into Riley's belt loop and tugged. "Say the word, baby."

Riley sighed, stealing another kiss before stepping back. "One hour, Mr. Nakayama, then your ass is mine."

Lennox's eyes darkened but whatever he started to say was drowned out by a lady's high-pitched voice. "Ryland! Mr. Emerson Scott, just a moment of your time." The woman shoved her way through the crowd to push between them. She had a voice recorder in her hand, shoved up in front of his mouth. A little red light blinked at the top.

He was too shocked to say anything, and by the time he found his voice, she was speaking again. "What are your thoughts on the allegations against your father, Senator Ryland Emerson Scott II? Should voters lend them any credibility while voting in the upcoming gubernatorial race?"

Riley flinched, his gaze dragged down to the sidewalk with the weight of his memories — of the hands, the shame and fear and pain, of telling his mother and her urging him to stay silent, voiceless. The names his sister Anna called him because her fiancé, the rich man 'Daddy' set her up with, would *never* have touched him if Riley hadn't been a tease.

Deciding to run away because it would fix everything but selling his ass a few months later to afford something to eat.

"That man," Riley snapped, hands shaking, "may be my sperm donor, but he is no father of mine. And all these people in this state who claim to care about children and God, should ask themselves how they can justify continuing to support a man who not only has been credibly accused of involvement with a cartel dealing in drugs, arms and human beings, but repeatedly raped his own child for years. The only children Senator Scott cares about are the ones he can stick his dick into." Riley was shaking as he spoke the words out loud for the first time in years.

He couldn't take them back, swallow them down with a bottle of brandy. They were out there now, his truth that he'd struggled to bury for years.

Maybe, it was time to shine a light on them.

Lennox entwined their fingers and squeezed. When Riley met his gaze, he didn't see pity or shame. No accusation, either…just support.

It gave Riley the strength to draw in a shaky breath and turn back to the stunned reporter. "I'm on a date with my boyfriend now, but if you want my story, I'll share it. We can set up a time."

The reporter hurried to scribble down Riley's number, her eyes blazing, likely at the thought of the interview to come.

Riley watched her walk away, the surge of energy he'd got from speaking out against his father dissipating. His shoulders sagged.

Lennox drew him in close to his chest, cupping the back of Riley's head until Riley let his forehead fall onto his strong shoulder. "That was so brave, sweetheart."

"Can…can we just go home?"

"Yeah. We can go home."

After a quick stop to pick up Lennox's purchases, they called for a rideshare. It dropped them off at home less than an hour later.

Riley went straight to bed.

Chapter Twenty-Seven

Lennox was worried about Riley.

It had been four days since their aborted trip to the Pecan Street Festival, and except for trips to the bathroom and far too few voyages to the kitchen for food—which he only picked at—Riley stayed entrenched in the bed.

Lennox hovered in the shadowed doorway, a war waging inside. The loving boyfriend wanted to climb in bed and hold him, wallow together until Riley felt better. The concerned friend, though...? He wondered if he should call Ally for advice, wondered if Riley should see someone.

A therapist...or a counselor.

He'd always suspected that Riley's childhood hadn't been pleasant. No one ended up at the Rainbow House without *some* tragedy. Sure, some of the kids who used the Drop-in Center had great, supportive families who let them come to spend time with other LGBTQ youth, but they were few and far between. And none of those kids *lived* there.

He hated knowing that his young boyfriend had suffered so much — and at the hands of someone who should have protected him, should have kept him safe.

The more he thought of it, his mind unable to block the images of a young, battered Riley from his head, the more he thought maybe *he* needed therapy, too.

"You're staring," Riley mumbled from under the comforter. Only the tips of his fingers, clutching the coverlet, and the curls on top of his head were visible. With his back turned to Lennox, he shouldn't have known.

But Riley always seemed to know, some sixth sense betraying Lennox's eyes.

"Should I stop?"

Riley's curls bounced as he shook his head. "Come to bed."

"It's only four," Lennox said, but obediently crawled onto the mattress and wiggled his way under the blankets. He snaked his arms around Riley, wincing as he felt the sweat-clammy skin.

He refused to pull away.

Riley clasped his wrist and pulled Lennox's arm even tighter around him, snuggling back against his chest. It wasn't sexual, even when his ass butted against Lennox's flaccid dick.

"Whenever you're ready to talk, I'm here," Lennox murmured, pressing his lips to the back of Riley's neck. His caramel curls tickled Lennox's face.

Riley stayed silent and Lennox sighed.

"Are you mad at me?" Riley's voice was quiet.

"No, never. Sweetheart, I'm only worried." Lennox fumbled for Riley's hand. "I just want to help."

"I... God, I just need a fucking drink," Riley cried, voice pitched high and dripping pain. "Every time I think I'm happy, that fucking *bastard* rears his head. Even when I ignore the news and the stupid political yard signs, he's always fucking *there*."

Lennox's face fell. He knew about Riley's drinking problem, though they'd never brought it up. Ally had warned him before Riley moved in that he needed to keep the alcohol in the house to a minimum, just in case Riley relapsed. He hadn't said anything when he found the empty bottle of bourbon a few months ago, or when he tasted the whiskey on Riley's breath a few weeks later.

"Sweetheart..." Lennox started to say but hesitated, not sure what words he could use that wouldn't be an accusation or a platitude.

"I *know*, okay?" Riley shuddered in his arms. "I know it's not the answer. I know I'm not old enough to drink for another month, and I *know* that it's an addiction. I know, but it doesn't help. I just...don't want to think anymore."

"Then let me help you," Lennox shoved the covers off and sat up, forcing Riley to roll to his back and meet his eyes. "You don't have to think, just *feel*."

Lennox was a casual kinkster. A just-in-the-bedroom, just-for-fun fetishist with no real desire to be more than that. *Before.* Before Riley, and his pain-filled admission.

If Riley needed to shut his brain off, to not think, then Lennox would take him out of his head and make him fly, until the only thing he could think of was Lennox, the only thing he could *feel*...was Lennox.

Riley's eyes were wide, his mouth parted on a trembling breath.

Lennox waited.

Then, Riley nodded. "Please, yes."

Lennox gripped Riley's hands and pinned them to the bed. "Yes, *Sir*."

"Yes, Sir," Riley corrected, then he wet his lips with his tongue, his pupils blown wide as Lennox straddled him but didn't release his hands.

"Your safeword is 'pecan'. I expect you to use it." Lennox would hate himself if he pushed Riley too far, especially now, when he was vulnerable…fragile as sea glass. For today, at least, he wanted more than *stop*.

"I won't," Riley promised. "I trust you, Sir."

"Keep your hands here," Lennox ordered. "I'm going to break you, sweetheart. But just like the art of Kintsugi, I promise to put you back together better at the end. I'm going to find all your cracks" — Lennox trailed his hands down Riley's chest to the hem of his pajama top, stripping it off to leave Riley bare from the waist up — "and make them shine."

Riley shivered, a moan sliding from his mouth like honey.

Lennox couldn't resist capturing the taste of it on his lips. He could drink down the sound for the rest of his life, especially when Riley whined, needy and desperate. But his dick pressed painfully against his shorts, and Riley was equally hard beneath him.

Lennox carelessly shucked his clothes but took his time removing Riley's, lowering the pajama bottoms down inch by glacial inch. Riley's dick strained against the waistband before springing free, no underwear to contain it. Lennox ignored it for now, with every intention of circling back.

Riley, though, was impatient. He jerked his hips up in protest, the weeping tip of his dick drawing a line down Lennox's cheek before he backed away. He tutted, shaking his head in faux disappointment. Inwardly, though, his dominant side crowed. "Naughty boy, maybe I should tie you up."

It was a jest, until Riley's eyes widened and his dick visibly twitched, hardening even further than Lennox thought possible. "Oh, look at that," Lennox breathed, dragging his fingernail gently along the sticky trail of pre-cum sliding along the thick cock down to the base.

Stubble prickled against his fingertip as he dragged it over Riley's balls and the young man twitched, a whimper sounding. "Poor baby, I bet that's itchy." Lennox shook his head, trying to keep his voice sympathetic instead of excited. "I'll make it all better."

"What...what are you going to do?" Riley asked, blinking up at him with wide, innocent eyes. So trusting, his hands still fisted around the headboard.

"Don't worry, sweetheart, I'll take care of you. Tie you up nice and tight so you don't have to worry about being naughty anymore, then I'll clean you right up." Not for long, though, since Lennox had every intention of dirtying him again.

Riley was quivering, his eyes drifting half-closed as he bit his lip. His erection stood tall and proud. Begging for attention, but Lennox refused to cave.

By the time Lennox was through with him, he wanted Riley soaring, so far in subspace he couldn't find the ground with either foot.

Lennox crawled off the bed and walked to the door, pausing only to say, "I'll be back with the rope, sweetheart. Best get your wiggles out now." He winked, waiting until he was out of sight to sprint to his studio, only tripping once on the way. He was sure Riley heard the clatter of the end table and its contents, but when he got back to the bedroom, yellow safety scissors and a coil of rope in hand — and only mildly out of breath — Riley didn't comment or tease.

Instead, he licked his lower lip, his gaze glued to the blue rope wound around Lennox's wrist. Eight meters of hand-dyed and treated jute.

"Have you heard of kinbaku?" Lennox spoke quietly, refusing to yell just to feel powerful.

Riley shook his head, his dark hair flopping over his eyes. Lennox dropped the supplies on the bed to brush it away, then ran his fingertips over Riley's forehead and down his nose, lingering over the fullness of his soft lips. "It means *'tight bondage'* in Japanese."

"Like…like shibari?" Riley asked, and Lennox could see his hands tighten on the headboard, his knuckles stripped of color.

"It's funny. Shibari is bondage tying and was always used, traditionally, for binding prisoners. Not for pleasure… Most people, when they say shibari, are *actually* thinking of traditional kinbaku. Western cultures just appropriated the wrong name and it stuck." Lennox spoke calmly, but the whole time, he was running his hands over Riley's body, mapping him out again by touch as he planned where to lay the ropes.

Nothing too extreme, he decided. He didn't want to push Riley's limits by accident, not their first time playing and not when Riley was already vulnerable. Besides, Lennox might have trained under a professional Dom at the *Lighthouse,* the BDSM club down on Sixth Street, but this was his first time playing in his own house, without a dungeon monitor on site.

Hence the safety scissors.

"Tell me now, sweetheart." Lennox tweaked Riley's nipple, enjoying the way the younger man arched below him. "Can I tie you up like a little present?"

Riley nodded, his pupils blown. "Yes, please."

Lennox grabbed the rope and dropped the bundle on Riley's chest. He whimpered as it landed and Lennox grinned. "Tell me your safeword, sweetheart."

"Pecan," Riley answered, shaking his head back and forth. "I'm not using it."

"Good boy," Lennox purred, uncoiling the rope with ease. He hummed as he laid the first knot along Riley's wrist, binding the slender joints together with an elegant twist of his fingers. He worked slowly, stretching over Riley's prone body to make the ladder down his arms, the blue vivid against the boy's pale skin.

While he artfully made the pattern of jute down Riley's arms, Lennox made sure to grind his ass against Riley's erection, keeping him stiff and keening. He loved seeing Riley's muscles strain against the ropes, the way the knots dug into his tender flesh but held strong.

Lennox tied the final knot around Riley's biceps. The jute rope stretched between his arms, under his head like a pillow, forcing him to keep his neck arched and his head angled up. Carefully, Lennox examined each knot and binding, checking the tightness, before he reached up and felt the man's fingers. They were warm, no sign of circulation loss.

"There you go, my pretty little Rope Bunny," Lennox purred, crawling up to straddle Riley's chest.

His boyfriend's eyes were hooded and dark, mouth open in a pant. Lennox took a moment to stroke along Riley's neck and up his chin, tracing the line of his jaw.

"Next time, I'll add a chest harness — maybe bind your thighs, keep you open and exposed for me. Would you like that, Bunny?"

Riley keened.

"Open your mouth again, Bunny. Want to see you suck my cock." Lennox ran the crown of his dick over Riley's lips then Riley parted them obediently, allowing Lennox to slip inside his wet heat.

It was sloppy and imperfect. Riley was clearly too blissed out for his usual technique, and that made it all the better. Lennox ran his hands over the ropes as Riley sucked him, feeling the knots against his palm. Every time he pressed down, Riley moaned, the sound vibrating along his dick, and Lennox was quickly too close to coming.

He pulled out, groaning as he watched the string of pre-cum connecting his tip to Riley's mouth until it snapped. Riley slipped his tongue out to taste the remnants.

"Goddamn, baby, your mouth is too good," Lennox complained. He squeezed the base of his dick to forestall his orgasm, then yanked down on his balls as he breathed through his nose at the sight of Riley pulling at the ropes. "I want to come in your hole, sweetheart. Can I take your ass while you're all tied up?"

Riley's eyelids fluttered shut and he clamped his teeth down on his lips, nodding frantically.

"You like being my little Rope Bunny?" Lennox asked as he moved down Riley's body, planting kisses as he went, until he was nestled between the boy's splayed thighs. His pretty pink hole was tightly furled and, like his jaw, newly stubbled with pale fuzz.

It reminded Lennox of his original plan and he chuckled. "Oops, baby. I made you a promise, didn't I?"

"Huh?" Riley whimpered, hips twitching.

He pressed a kiss to Lennox's hole, then another to his straining dick, enjoying the way Riley twitched below him. Then, he sat back. "Will you be okay like this for two minutes if I run to the bathroom?"

Riley blinked slowly but eventually nodded.

Lennox shifted forward and pried Riley's hands off the headboard. He let them rest on the pillow, then carefully placed the scissors in his palms. "If you need to, cut yourself free, but I promise I'll be quick."

Riley nodded, gripping the scissors. Lennox waited just a second to be sure, then left the room. He gathered the razor, shaving cream, a towel and a little bowl of water, then carried them back to the bedroom. He spread the towel on the comforter by Riley's left hip, placing everything but the water on top of it. Gently, he took away the scissors and put them on the nightstand.

The bowl, he nestled in the hollow of Riley's lower abdomen, between the defined V that Lennox could never resist licking. "I need you to hold nice and still, sweetheart," Lennox said. "We don't want to spill it, do we?" Also, he wouldn't want to accidentally nick him when he was trying to be sexy.

Riley froze, barely seeming to breathe. The water in the bowl rippled. "Good boy," Lennox praised, then reached for the shaving cream. He squirted it in his hands, working it around the base and down over his hole. "Okay, sweetheart. Ready or not..."

He ran the razor carefully over the stubble, leaving behind a strip of smooth skin. Slowly, methodically, he stripped Riley of the days of regrowth. He saved his hole for last, prying Riley's cheeks apart with one hand and shaving with the other, until the winking hole was bare, begging to be licked.

He dropped the razor on the towel and leaned forward. The few white dollops still streaking Riley's skin looked enough like whipped cream that he wasn't worried.

Not until he swiped his tongue over the puckered hole and the bitter foam stuck to his mouth. "Gah." He sat up abruptly, wiping his tongue on his arm to try to get the taste out. He gagged. "Oh, gross…"

Riley snorted, which turned into laughter after Lennox pouted at him. "Your face!" Riley crowed, chest shaking enough he dislodged the bowl onto his belly. Lennox jerked forward to grab it but did nothing more than tip it over, soaking the mattress and comforter.

"Oops?" Lennox grinned, the seriousness of the previous moments abandoned to ridiculousness. But that was who they were, he realized. They were a pair of semi-functional mostly adults and expecting anything else was a joke.

"Well, it rinsed away the rest, I'm sure," Riley pointed out, staring down at his sopping wet dick. It was, somehow, still hard.

"Don't worry. I'll clean you all up, nice and slow like," Lennox teased, winking as he fought to bring back the sensuality of the moment. Riley swallowed a chuckle, the sound coming out strangled, and his eyes twinkled with humor, but he didn't protest.

Lennox snagged the towel and, nice and slowly, started drying up the water and remnants of shaving cream. "Mm, how's that feel, baby?" he asked, stroking the fabric over Riley's dick an extra time.

"Kinda weird, if I'm honest," Riley answered, his lips twitching.

Lennox chucked the towel at Riley's head then bent down while Riley's vision was obscured, taking his cock into his mouth and sinking down to the root in one move. His thick crown pressed against Lennox's throat, and he swallowed around it, moaning at the feel of it blocking his airway.

He wasn't into breath play, except like *this*, when he was in control—when he could pin Riley's hips down and the boy's hands were unable to grab his head. Pre-cum, thin and salty, leaked from Riley's slit like a sieve, coating the back of Lennox's tongue.

"Oh God, oh fuck," Riley cried, a slew of nonsense spilling from his mouth as Lennox teased him, bobbing his head and massaging his frenulum with the tip of his tongue on every pass. He barely caught the pulsing of Riley's dick in time to pull off.

"You *fucker!*" Riley cursed, hips straining as he fucked the air, his orgasm thwarted.

"Oh, naughty." Lennox laughed, leaning over the edge of the bed to grab the lube and a condom from the nightstand. He lost his balance, only a last-second grab to the edge of the mattress keeping him from tumbling, but he made it.

"Um, Lennox?" Riley stuttered, his face pink when Lennox turned to look at him.

"Yeah, sweetheart?" he asked, pausing to make sure that the younger man was okay.

"Do we have to use that? The condom, I mean? I think...I think I want to go without." Riley's voice was shaky but not, Lennox thought, with fear.

"Only if you're sure, sweetheart. I don't mind wearing one if it makes you more comfortable," Lennox promised.

"I trust you," Riley said.

Three words, but it was enough to pull on Lennox's heartstrings. "Thank you, sweetheart. You don't know how much that means to me." He shifted up to press his lips to Riley's in a kiss that, while not chaste, was filled with more emotion than lust.

He didn't hold it nearly as long as he wanted, distracted by the erection Riley kept thrusting up against his belly, a not-so-subtle attempt at getting himself off.

Lennox tutted against Riley's lips before pulling back. "Not until I'm buried in you so deep you don't know where you start and I end, Bunny. Wanna fill you with my cum, mark you from the inside out."

"Then what are you waiting for?" Riley asked through gritted teeth, his eyes flashing dangerously.

"You're all tied up and at my mercy," Lennox didn't hesitate to remind him. "I can make you wait all day if I want." He lined up their dicks and gripped them with one hand but refused to move. "Ask me nicely, pretty Bunny."

"I… But…" Riley whined, his face falling. "*Please* don't make me wait. It *hurts*…"

"Closer, sweetheart. Keep going. I love hearing you beg so prettily." He gave them one single stroke, teasing himself as much as Riley, to reward the boy's attempt.

"Mr. Nakayama!" Riley cried, face flushing red, "Please mark me. I want you to come in my ass. It'll be nice and tight, and…and just for you! Please, Sir!"

"There you go, pretty Bunny," Lennox coated his fingers in lube and slid them between them, working Riley's ass open until he could take three fingers easily. Reluctantly, he moved lower, releasing Riley's dick so he could watch the boy take his digits like a pro. He pulled them out once to watch the pretty pink hole gape.

"God, look at *that*," Lennox murmured, replacing his fingers again, loving the way the tight ring clamped around his knuckles. "Someday, I'm going to put my whole hand in here."

"Not today. I want your dick, *please*, Mr. Nakayama!" Riley cried, his body twitching like an Energizer Bunny on the mattress, not seeming to notice or care about the water he was still lying in.

Lennox finally slathered the remaining lube on his dick and lined himself up. "Since you asked so nicely," he praised, sliding just his tip inside. He groaned, dropping down over Riley's body like a blanket. He pumped his hips slowly, in and out, claiming the boy inch by inch.

His bare dick didn't feel much different without the condom. It was a bit hotter, the walls of Riley's ass just that little bit tighter, but the *thought* of it had him close to coming already. There was nothing separating them, and they were truly joined, skin to skin.

Riley panted, leaking whimpers from his mouth and sticky pre-cum from the slit of his dick. It painted Lennox's abs with every thrust.

He didn't last long. He'd be embarrassed if it didn't feel so good. Riley's ass pulsed around him as he hit his climax, and Lennox followed him over the edge, crying out as he filled Riley's ass with his seed.

"I'm coming, Bunny," Lennox groaned, burying his face into the curve of Riley's neck. "Feel me filling you? You're mine now, sweetheart. I'm not letting you go."

"Yours," Riley agreed, his breath ragged. His body was drenched in sweat below him, and Lennox took a few seconds to enjoy the moment before he forced himself to sit up and cut Riley free. He pressed kisses to each of the red marks that remained on Riley's arms, a shadow of the ropes, rubbing his fingers to make sure the blood was still flowing.

"Let me clean you up?" Lennox asked, but Riley shook his head.

"Wanna take a bath with you," Riley murmured, voice hoarse.

"With oil? Or bubbles?" Lennox was fine with either, and he had no problems with the idea of holding Riley tight in the bathtub. The second best thing about sex, after the orgasm, was the cuddling after.

"Oil," Riley said, then shook his head. "No... bubbles."

"How about both?" Lennox compromised.

Riley perked up, all traces of his previous depression gone.

For now, at least.

Chapter Twenty-Eight

The next day, Riley perched — albeit uncomfortably, due to the twinging of his ass — in the center of the round table tucked in the corner of Lennox's art studio, wishing he'd thought to grab a pillow. The marks on his arms had mostly faded, little more than a memory he couldn't wait to relive.

Until he was able to, he was chilling in here, watching Lennox work on his newest painting. "Do you always sell portraits?" Riley asked, tilting slightly to better see the image. It was still mostly a rough sketch, but he could already tell it was based on one of the photos from their mini-modeling session. A man on his knees, his head tilted back out of frame.

"Depends how you mean," Lennox said, his tongue sticking out from his lips as he stared at the canvas. "If you're asking if all my portraits sell, yes. Normally before the gallery can get them hung on the wall, actually. They told me there's a waiting list. But, if you mean do I only *paint* portraits...I dabble in more eccentric things—"

"Like the duck lamp?" Riley interrupted, his dick hardening in his basketball shorts as he remembered the scene that followed.

Lennox grinned. "Yeah. The whole attic is full of things like that. I do them mostly for fun, an outlet to get away from the more serious paintings."

"Why don't you sell them?" Riley asked.

"My first agent suggested I stick to what would guarantee to sell. She was worried that it would detract from my 'serious painter' image." He used finger quotes around the words and Riley frowned, sensing that the agent's words still impacted Lennox today.

"What if you sold them under a different name? People do that, right? Like...authors use pen names?" Riley honestly wasn't big on art, except for when it was Lennox's. And...honestly, he liked that so much because he loved watching those long, slender fingers grip the paintbrush and make such gentle strokes on the canvas.

And, sometimes, Riley's skin.

Goosebumps erupted on his arms at the memory.

"I haven't thought about it," Lennox said, his eyes zoning out as he stared toward the window. "Hmm. I guess it's something to think on, isn't it?" Lennox brightened back up and turned to the painting again. Nothing seemed to keep him down for long. "I don't hate making paintings. It was worse when people expected like...*here's a painting of an apple. Here's a tree, isn't it pretty?* But I love the portraits."

"You should, they're super-hot," Riley put his hands in his pockets, purposefully stretching the fabric of his shorts over his erection with a grin.

"Horny little thing," Lennox teased but wiped his own hands free of paint—on his jeans, of course, but Riley was coming to love Lennox's eccentricities, even if it did mean more cleaning up after.

"Just for you," Riley admitted. He'd never liked sex before, not really. Even when he'd fooled around with Tweety back at the Rainbow House—just as friends, curious what it was like with someone you trusted, even if they didn't have feelings beyond friendship for each other—it had only been okay.

Never like this, never like he was going to erupt into flames if Lennox didn't take him in hand.

"Top or bottom?" Lennox asked as he swaggered over, bold as a peacock and just as colorful with the paint streaking his arms and clothing.

Riley didn't care, as long as they both got off, but something about the arrogance of Lennox's swagger made him want to put him on his knees, so he grinned. Riley stood abruptly and grabbed Lennox by the throat. Not hard but demanding. "Top," he answered. "Get on your knees, Kitten."

Lennox's pupils dilated as he dropped so fast Riley lost his grip. Instead, Riley carded his fingers through Lennox's hair, forcing him to tilt his head back and look up at him.

"What are your thoughts on pet play, Kitten?" Riley asked, suddenly struck by the thought of Lennox with a collar and leash, following after him on all fours—a horny little kitten clawing Riley's thighs or a dirty dog humping his foot...

Lennox shivered. "Never done it. Why, you wanna pet me?"

Riley grinned at the slew of dirty images flooding his head, sliding his hands down Lennox's spine to cup his sexy bubble butt. "I want to put you in a collar. Make you crawl for me...stick your ass in the air like a dog in heat." Riley dropped down to his knees and worked his thigh between Lennox's, yanking him closer. "Wanna fuck you like an animal."

Lennox's moan was sudden and loud. Riley leaned in, biting Lennox's earlobe before licking it in apology. His breath skimmed the damp skin as he murmured in Lennox's ear, "You have a fenced-in backyard... Could chase you around after dark. You'd have to be quiet..."

"Fuck," Lennox cried, hips thrusting against Riley's thigh. "Don't tease me."

"But I love hearing you whine. So needy, Kitten. Makes me think you like me." Riley tightened his grip on Lennox's ass, urging the older man to rock against him. "But I'll tell you what. You can get yourself off just like this, humping my thigh like a dog...or you can hold off until this evening and I'll fuck you in the grass."

"Shit, shit..." Lennox cursed, clamping his jaws down on Riley's shoulder in a bite so unexpected Riley couldn't even flinch. "Tonight. In the grass..." Lennox finally let go to whine, his face shiny and beaded with sweat. His breath came out in pants, ragged and feral.

"Oh, such a good Kitten, waiting patiently. I think you've earned a treat. Want some cream, little Kitty?" Riley stood, shoving his basketball shorts down to his thighs. He wasn't wearing briefs, so his dick just bobbed free, hard and leaking.

Fuck, he looked so pretty on his knees, staring up at Riley with his mouth open, the tip of his pink tongue sticking out. Riley couldn't wait to dirty him up. "Meow for me, pretty Kitty."

Lennox turned red so fast that Riley worried about his heart, but then the cutest sound crept from his throat, a soft and tentative, *"Meow..."*

Riley's grin gentled and he ran his hands through Lennox's hair, pausing to stroke behind his ears the way he would a *real* cat.

He also firmly ignored the *actual* meow from the other side of the door, loud and confused. Lennox, however, turned even redder.

"Ignore them, pretty Kitty," Riley said, angling his hips so just the tip of his dick rested on Lennox's lower lip. It was soft and plush, beckoning him in farther, so he gave in. Slowly, he sank into Lennox's mouth. "So good, sweetheart, your mouth — God, so fucking perfect. Go ahead and get your treat, baby. Suck out all the cream. I made it just for you..."

He fisted his hand in Lennox's hair, not pulling but holding tight. By now, he'd learned that Lennox liked a bit of pain, just enough to keep him centered.

Lennox's groan vibrated the underside of Riley's dick and he twitched, accidentally burying himself in the other man's throat. Lennox gagged but curled his hand around Riley's hip, keeping him from pulling out until he'd swallowed around him — drawing a moan from *Riley's* mouth this time.

"God*damn*, Kitten," he cursed, barely holding back his orgasm.

Then Lennox blinked his pretty brown eyes up at him and he lost it, spilling his 'cream' down Lennox's throat in spurts. Lennox didn't release him until Riley whined, his dick oversensitive to the point of pain. His lips unlocked with a pop as he pulled away, a single string of cummy spit connecting them until it broke.

Riley ran his thumb over the sticky mixture, cleaning it off Lennox's mouth by licking it into his own, instead. "Thank you for sharing, Kitten."

Lennox whined, pressing the heel of his hand into his still hard, likely throbbing dick. "Still okay to wait?" Riley asked sympathetically, inwardly more than a little smug when Lennox nodded.

"Good boy," Riley purred, leaning down to kiss Lennox's forehead.

He couldn't wait for nightfall.

Chapter Twenty-Nine

Riley was putting the finishing touches on dinner — slicing radishes to garnish the salad — when his phone rang. He set the knife down and glanced at the screen. *Unknown Number.*

But it was an Austin area code, so he answered it, just in case.

"Good afternoon, am I speaking with Ryland?" A bright, vaguely familiar voice came over the line.

"Riley, yeah," he answered, frowning down at the bowl of greens as he tried to place her.

"This is Lindsey King, a reporter with channel twenty-seven. We spoke at the Pecan Street Festival last week? I got clearance from the producers to run with the segment, and I'd like to set up a time to do an interview. Over coffee, maybe?" She spoke quickly, like she thought if she didn't, he would hang up.

Honestly, it was a valid fear.

"Oh, um...Yeah. Yeah, I can do that. Not tomorrow, though." He had already agreed to go with Lennox to some gallery opening. "Oh, and um…probably not Friday, either. I have a…thing." By which he meant, he had to drive to San Antonio to sit through a boring award show with a bunch of other porn stars to possibly accept an award he was pretty sure he had no chance of winning.

"What about next week?" she asked, not deterred by his busy schedule. If she was frustrated, at least she didn't sound like it.

"Um…I could maybe do Tuesday? I can't Monday." He bit his lip, hoping she didn't ask why. He already had a job lined up to film his next solo session for OnlyStiXXX, though Lennox had hinted he'd be willing to join him.

He could hear the tapping of her keyboard through the phone. "Hmm. Well, I have a few meetings, but nothing I can't move around to fit your schedule. I think I can make Tuesday work. In the morning?"

"Yeah. Yeah, I can do Tuesday morning, sure," Riley stammered, his heart thudding in his chest. He was really doing this.

"How about nine, at that little coffee shop down on Springdale? Sa-tén? It's Japanese, and you can bring your boyfriend."

Riley rolled his eyes, but at least it cut through his nerves. Lennox would go with him anyway, and it seemed insulting — and vaguely racist — to pick a coffee shop based purely on Lennox's ancestry. "How about Fleet? It's on Webberville. My boyfriend loves their lattes." Well, his boyfriend had tried them at least once, since Riley remembered throwing away one of the to-go cups Lennox had left in the shower. Close enough.

"Yep, I can make that work!"

"Do I...need to bring anything?" Riley fidgeted with the salad tongs.

"Just yourself and your story. See you at nine!" She hung up before he could reply and he pulled the phone away, staring at the screen long enough it shut off.

"Was that the reporter?" Lennox asked, his voice startling Riley into dropping his phone into the salad bowl.

"Shit," he cursed and fished it out, grateful he hadn't added dressing yet.

"Don't worry. I'm not concerned about catching your germs." Lennox laughed, walking over to wrap his arm around Riley's waist. He rested his chin on Riley's shoulder and urged him to lean back. "I am, however, worried about *you*. Are you okay?"

"Yeah, just...nervous, I guess. I've not really ever talked about it. A bit in therapy, but I didn't use any names, because I didn't want to risk my family being able to track me down. I told my mom and she said talking about...*it*...was disgusting. My sister said I asked for it because I was...you know, gay." Riley bit his lip. "If she wouldn't believe me, why will anyone else?"

"*I* believe you," Lennox promised, and Riley felt his lips brush the skin of his neck.

Riley gripped his arm tight. "Thank you."

"Don't thank me, Bunny. There's nothing special about what I'm doing. You deserve to have people listen to you, to believe you." He squeezed Riley tight, and the comfort it gave almost made Riley cry.

He cleared his throat and shook the melancholy free. "Come on. Let's eat." He plastered on a smile that grew real as he looked over his shoulder and met Lennox's soft eyes. "Lennox?" he said, twisting in the other man's arms so he could press closer.

"Yeah?"

"Would it freak you out if I say that I might have feelings for you?" Riley asked, fidgeting with the hem of Lennox's shirt to avoid meeting his eyes.

"No. Would it freak *you* out if I say that I *definitely* have feelings for *you*?" Lennox grinned, dropping his forehead gently against Riley's.

"No...no it wouldn't," Riley admitted, a warm flush spreading through his chest and out.

"Good. Because I *definitely* have feelings for you, too." Lennox said the words like a promise.

Riley didn't want to let him go. He could stay wrapped in his arms all night, but then Lennox's belly rumbled loud and clear. He laughed and stepped back. "Dinner."

"Dinner," Lennox agreed, reaching around him to snag the bowl. "You set the table. I'll bring the food."

"You're just worried about dropping the plates," Riley teased.

"Again."

"Well, don't drop the salad, or we'll be reheating pizza."

"Again," Lennox repeated with a grin.

* * * *

Hunting Lennox down in the backyard to fuck him like an animal was *not* as fun as it sounded. He'd thought it would be super-hot...and it was, because it was hot out. Also, he hadn't factored in the vast amount of exposed flesh that would quickly become a feasting ground for mosquitoes.

And just as he'd managed to tackle Lennox, he'd landed on a scorpion and screamed like a little girl. They'd had to *nope* the fuck back inside.

Instead, they decided to stay in the safety of the living room, cuddling on the couch. It was funny how much he was enjoying them rubbing calamine lotion on each other's bug bites while an old season of *Glitter Nation* played in the background. Riley had seen most of the early season back at the Rainbow House, where it had basically become a cult classic.

He supposed it was an okay show, but he always felt a bit too much like the main character Adan to be comfortable watching it for long. He wasn't *technically* raised in a cult—unless you count fundamentalist Christianity, which he did—but the character's so-called prophet of a father reminded him far too much of his own—outwardly charismatic but a liar to his bones.

Lennox loved the show, though, and Riley didn't *dislike* it enough to protest whenever he turned it on, especially not when the show turned *Lennox* on, and Riley could only benefit from that.

Even now, covered in bites and chalky pink lotion, Lennox was hard. And since he was still naked, it meant easy access for Riley. He was draped over Lennox's chest like a blanket, their legs entwined. The cool breeze from the central air left a chill on Riley's exposed ass that felt, somehow, both erotic and awkward.

Even though there was no one else in the house, he felt embarrassed, like he was flashing someone...and that humiliation tangled with his arousal in a way that left him flush and needy. It was a newly developing kink...one he was more and more curious about exploring.

Slowly, he slipped his left hand between their bodies, wrapping his fingers around Lennox's dick. Lennox jerked at the touch, then moaned when Riley started to jerk him off, his eyes fixed on the screen.

"Bunny," Lennox moaned, but Riley shushed him.

"Gotta be quiet," Riley whispered, concocting a scenario in his head on the spot. "Wouldn't want your parents to know what we're up to..." He peeked up at Lennox through his lashes, wondering if he was pushing too far.

Lennox turned pink, then a sly grin tipped his lips up. With the hand not currently holding Lennox's dick, Riley dragged the blanket off the back of the couch and draped it over them both.

"Don't you think they'll wonder why we aren't wearing shirts?" Lennox asked, his voice pitched higher. Riley imagined him younger, his high school sweetheart, if he'd been allowed to go to high school.

"We'll just tell them we're hot..." Riley whispered.

"And under the blanket?" Lennox's smirk grew bigger.

Riley huffed and let go of Lennox's dick with a pout. "Jeez, you're no fun."

"Aw, baby don't be like that," Lennox whined and sat up, dislodging Riley. He fell backward, sprawled on the couch in a position that felt awkward, until Lennox planted his hands on Riley's thighs and pinned them in place, splayed open and exposed.

"Lennox!" Riley yelped, cheeks heating.

"Shh, don't want to wake them up. But I won't have you under a blanket, Bunny," Lennox purred.

"But...what if they hear us? They'll know what we're doing!" Riley protested, getting back into the role.

"I'm not ashamed, Bunny." Lennox didn't wait for a reply. With the flexibility of a cat, he almost folded himself in half to suck Riley's dick into his mouth, swallowing all of him in one go. Riley bit his knuckle hard to avoid crying out.

His plan for a fumbled, secretive hand job went out of the window as Lennox quickly worked him up. "Shit, shit...God, I can't... *Fuck!*"

"Don't hold back, Bunny. I know you can come twice," Lennox pulled off him just long enough to order. Then, he swallowed Riley down again and it was too much, the feel of Lennox humming against his crown.

After his climax waned, he sagged against the couch with a shudder. "You're far too good at that." He hadn't wanted to come so quickly, but Lennox had a magic tongue.

"Don't worry. We're not done yet." Lennox had a glint in his eye, a promise that, with anyone else, would have left Riley a strung-out bundle of nerves.

And he was, but now the nerves were exciting, fueling his curiosity instead of panic.

Lennox grabbed his thighs again, folding him in half until his knees touched his chest. Then, he angled his hips so Lennox's dick was tucked in the cradle of Riley's thighs.

"Are we frotting?" Riley asked, wetting his lips with his tongue as he peered down. Lennox's hard, leaking tip looked even larger next to Riley's flaccid cock, though he knew it wouldn't stay soft for long.

Lennox slid his hands down the back of Riley's thighs with reverence. "No, I'm not losing my chance at sinking in your tight little hole, Bunny. I just want to take a moment to worship you. You're so fucking pretty."

It was the best kind of embarrassing, lying here while Lennox looked at him like *that*, stroking over his skin like a prayer.

"If you lived in the Renaissance, Michelangelo would have made you his masterpiece," Lennox murmured. "Fuck David."

"No...no fucking David!" Riley protested, straining against Lennox's hands, trying to move his hips, *anything* to get friction on his quickly hardening dick.

Lennox rolled his hips in a maddening tease. "Are you jealous, Bunny?"

"I'm not...good at sharing," Riley panted. "Fuck, can you just fuck me already?"

"Impatient little brat," Lennox chuckled and swatted his hip. "I'm not done worshiping you yet."

"You're the devil!" Riley wasn't sure he had the patience for teasing. Even though he'd just come, he wanted to feel Lennox inside him more than he wanted to breathe. He didn't care that he was itchy or that he could still see flecks of dirt on his scraped-up knees.

"You were calling me 'God' a minute ago," Lennox said dryly, moving his fingers up to tweak Riley's nipples one at a time.

"Fucker!" Riley cursed, back arching. Not that he could move much, he was pinned by his own knees.

"You love me," Lennox grinned.

"Still a fucker!"

"Ah, but you don't deny it."

Riley let go of his thigh, reaching up to grab Lennox by the back of his neck and drag him down. He planted a violent kiss on Lennox's mouth, biting into his lip as he released. "I'm not going to deny the truth, but if you don't put your dick in my ass right now, Kitten, I'll put you on your back and ride you like a fucking bronco."

Lennox paused, something changing on his face. "You know, I think I'll wait." His lips twitched, and Riley saw through his words.

He dropped his legs down and wrapped them around Lennox's hips, using the movement as leverage to do exactly what he promised—put Lennox on his back. Lennox landed with an "*oof*," his eyes widening in surprise—like he thought Riley either couldn't, or wouldn't, do it.

But Riley had taken self-defense classes at the Rainbow House. Putting Lennox on his back was easy, especially since Lennox wasn't fighting him. "Stay, Kitty," Riley ordered, leaning over to fumble with the coffee table drawer. Finally, it came unstuck, and he was able to grab the lube.

When he was done slicking Lennox up, leaving him a slippery, shiny mess, it was *Lennox* cursing.

This was fun.

Chapter Thirty

"It's a teacup," Lennox said, his hands shoved deep into his back pockets to forestall his inclination to touch. He was dying to pick it up and see if there was something on the underside that explained how it could be classified as —

"Art, Lennox. It's art." Riley sniffed, tipping up his chin in a highbrow way that made Lennox shudder. It reminded him too much of his parents.

"Maybe, if they'd painted it," Lennox scoffed, rolling his eyes and walking away from the plain white table setting. "As is, it looks like someone just forgot they had a gallery to curate and grabbed the first thing they found in the bin."

"The *bin*? Are you British now? Oh ho, you've been reading those romances again, haven't you?" Riley laughed.

"Shut up." Lennox didn't need a mirror to know he'd turned beet red. "They're…they're research?"

"Oh sure, *research*. Uh-huh. What are you researching, Kitten?" Riley stopped walking to the next exhibit and moved close to Lennox instead. He backed Lennox up against the brick pillar near the wall, narrowly avoiding the painting hanging just over Lennox's shoulder.

"Uh..." Lennox stammered, words lost somewhere in his throat as he got caught in Riley's gaze. Fuck, it shouldn't be legal for him to look at him like that in public.

"Hm? Go ahead and tell me, Kitten. Tell me what you're researching." Riley leaned in even closer, his voice a purr.

"I...I just...okay I know you think you know what I'm researching, but Milo might be adorable, and Oz is sassy AF, but I just feel really bad for the ghost, and I want him to get his happily ever after but he's *dead*, so I don't think—" Lennox stammered out a convoluted explanation.

Riley's laughter boomed out then he was kissing him, his mouth soft and warm.

Until a woman clearing her voice had them springing apart, anyway. "Mr. Nakayama?" she said, her voice shaking with what sounded like fear, which made absolutely no sense. He wasn't intimidating and didn't have a reputation for being quick to anger.

"Yes, dear?" Lennox asked when he finally found the ability to respond.

"The... The artist says he appreciates your desire to see the exhibit but...but wonders if you could refrain from such public displays of affection until after the show?" Her voice grew high and squeaky, and Lennox struggled not to laugh.

"Of course," Riley said while Lennox struggled to keep his composure. "Tell the artist we apologize."

She stammered her gratitude and left, just in time for Lennox to break out in a snicker. "The *artist* is probably worried our public display of affection will just distract from the lackluster pieces on display. Wanna get out of here? I'm hungry."

"Kitten, who knew you had claws?" Riley faux gasped, but he obediently took Lennox's extended hand and dragged him out onto the sidewalk. Lennox held in his laughter, but only barely. It burst out of him before they made it around the corner.

"You should. I use them on you often enough," Lennox replied, punctuating his grin with a snap of his fingers.

"Tease." Riley pouted his glossy lips.

"I could be." A quick glance up and down the sidewalk reassured Lennox that no one was paying them any attention, so he grinned and stalked toward Riley, until he had him backed into the mouth of an alley. Lennox shoved Riley just enough to pin him to the wall. "But you're one to talk, Bunny, kissing me like that in there. You were practically begging for a spanking."

Lennox watched Riley's cheeks flush, and a suspicion formed in his mind. He couldn't say it was the first time he'd wondered but now...well, he was confident enough in their relationship to ask. "Bunny, I think you've got an exhibitionist streak."

Riley's skin grew darker, he flushed fire-engine red and his chest heaved with quick breaths. "I... What?" His focus skirted farther down the alley, then back to the sidewalk.

Lennox grabbed Riley's dick through his chinos, not stroking but just keeping a nice steady pressure. Even through the fabric, Lennox could feel how hard he was. "I'm not going to blow you in the alley, Bunny, so you can stop looking around like the police are going to show up any second."

"Then..." Riley blinked, face falling. The disappointment was easy to read.

"Do you trust me?" Lennox asked.

* * * *

"What is this place?" Riley asked, staring up at the black steeple. It had the bones of a church. The comparison sent phantom shivers down his spine. But there was something not quite right about it and it went beyond the non-traditional color.

Lennox, though, just smirked and took Riley's hand, pulling him along behind him into the chapel. Riley instinctively shifted closer but felt silly once they stepped inside. The walls, like the exterior, were black, satin curtains blocking the little light that might have filtered in through the windows. Instead, the small entryway was lit by red sconces along the wall, leaving the desk in the center of the floor — and in the same token, the tiny man behind it — cast in flickering ruby shadows.

"Mr. Nakayama, it's been a while." The small man's voice was deeper than Riley expected and his eyes sharp.

"Jasper," Lennox greeted as he pulled Riley in under his arm. "I want you to meet my boyfriend, Riley. He's my guest tonight."

"Ah." Jasper smiled, and it was like looking at the sun. It almost made Riley uncomfortable. "He's a cute one. I see why you've stayed away."

"Lennox," Riley interrupted. "Seriously, where are we?"

"You didn't tell him?" Jasper lifted a brow, smile fading slightly. "You know the rules here at the Lighthouse. Informed consent is key."

Lennox's shoulders dropped as his face fell. "I guess I wasn't thinking about it like that." He shot Riley an apologetic look. "It's a BDSM club. I thought you'd like getting to play in public but somewhere safe. I'm sorry. I should have asked. We can go—"

"No," Riley interrupted, grabbing Lennox's arm tight to keep him from walking out. "No, you're right. I...I think I want to try. I know you'll take me home if it's too much. I trust you."

"Thank you," Lennox's voice was soft as he gripped Riley's hand, squeezing it gently.

Riley didn't know how long they got lost staring in each other's eyes like lovesick idiots, but he was startled from the moment by Jasper giggling. "You two are too cute. Here, take your bands before I get jealous." He held out a basket full of multicolored silicone bracelets and shook them.

"Green is if you're open to playing with others, yellow means everyone will leave the first move to you, in case you're not certain. Red is if you just want to watch, purple is if you are here and exclusive with a partner—"

Riley snagged that one without waiting for the rest of the list. He wasn't sharing Lennox with anyone. Maybe, *someday*, if Lennox wanted to play with someone else, they could discuss it, but Riley didn't see that happening anytime soon, if ever.

He couldn't stand the thought of someone else's hands on Lennox...or someone besides Lennox's hands on him... It was enough to have him seeing red.

Lennox laughed and grabbed a purple one as well, slipping it on his slender wrist.

"The House safeword is 'red'," Jasper said to them both. "We have four Dungeon Monitors tonight, and they'll be walking through all the rooms and listening. Lennox, I will remind you that while scarlet and ruby and sangria are all shades of red, please make sure to actually say *red* if you need it."

The man's lips were twitching as he said it and Riley grinned, turning to Lennox with a smirk. "Have you been causing trouble, Kitten?"

"Always." Lennox tossed his hair and winked. "Let's go play."

Riley stepped out of the changing room in just his black lace briefs. If he'd realized they'd end up here, he'd have worn something...more. Whether more daring or more covering, he wasn't sure. His skin felt hot, despite the fact that the room they entered was no warmer than he was used to. It was the feeling of eyes on his bare skin.

Lennox stepped up against his back, equally undressed. His lace panties were smaller than Riley's, doing little to stop Riley from feeling his erection, hard as steel against his ass.

"We can just look around," Lennox murmured, breath tickling Riley's ear. "We don't have to do anything if you don't want to."

Riley relaxed at the reminder of what he already knew—that Lennox would never make him do anything. He shouldn't need it, but the reassurance was enough to convince him to keep walking.

At some point, this had probably been the Sanctuary, and it was still called that—he could see the black sign with scarlet writing hanging in front of the stained-glass window. Riley almost looked over it, until— "Is that Jesus on a St. Andrew's cross?"

Lennox laughed. "Don't worry. From the outside, no one can tell." He brushed his fingertips over Riley's lower back, scant centimeters over the band of his briefs. If he dipped lower... Riley shuddered, pressing in closer to Lennox.

"I'm..." He swallowed and tried again. "I'm not worried."

"Not yet," Lennox said, his gaze intent on Riley, enough that Riley, for just a second, wondered if he *should* be worried. Not that Lennox would hurt him, never that, but that he was in over his head— swimming in the deep end when he'd barely left the kiddy pool.

Riley cleared his throat and looked away, taking in the room. What was supposed to be just a few seconds to pull himself back together turned into wide-eyed wonder. It was an eclectic mix of naughty and nice. Whoever started this place had left the stage, but instead of choirboys and podiums, it was filled with spanking benches, a Sybian-style chair, and of course, a St. Anthony's cross at the center.

They'd even kept the pews, though they were padded with black leather.

"Oh, look!" Lennox grabbed Riley's arm and dragged him toward the stage. "They're going to have a sounding demonstration!"

"Sounding? Is that the ASMR thing where people talk really quiet, and it's supposed to get you hot?" Riley asked, not entirely sure he was into that and reluctant to waste time figuring it out if there were other, hotter things they could be doing.

Lennox laughed as he pulled Riley down into a pew beside him. "Sweetheart, that's a different thing entirely, but I think I'll let you see for yourself."

Sounding, apparently, involved a thin rod being shoved into a part of his body he'd always thought of as an *out* hole only. At first, watching the glass rod get slowly inserted into the sub on stage's body made him cringe, but then he saw the rapture on the young man's face and the way the Dom looked at him — a soft, gentle look that nonetheless reeked of ownership.

The rod was thin, narrow — but not when compared to the size of the sub's piss slit. Riley didn't know whether to be afraid for him or jealous *of* him. But with each lube-slick plunge of the rod, the sub moaned, and his face was filled with so much rapture that he looked…well, like Riley should definitely be jealous.

"I want that," Riley said as the Dom hustled his sub off stage for aftercare. "Can we do that?" Riley turned to Lennox before the lights had even fully come back on, dim though they may be. He wasn't even sure if it was the sounding he wanted this bad or for Lennox to look at *him* the way that Dom was looking at his sub.

But, when Riley met Lennox's eyes, he found that he already was.

"Come on." Lennox took his hand and squeezed it. "I know someone who might be able to help us."

"I don't want a stranger doing it. I want you," Riley immediately protested.

"I can't do it alone. I promise I won't let him touch you, but if you *really* want to try, I'd feel more comfortable with an expert in the room."

* * * *

Lennox convinced Master Ede to help him with their scene—not that it took much convincing. He simply asked if the man was busy, and he said he'd be more than happy to help assist. He even let Lennox borrow his sounding kit—a new one he hadn't been able to use yet, that Lennox could buy from him if they liked it. If not, Master Ede promised he'd be able to take it to his clinic and sterilize it to be as good as new.

Rather than the Sanctuary, where the demonstrations were given, or the Fellowship Hall— essentially an orgy room—Lennox had booked one of the smaller, more intimate Sunday School rooms instead. They were still open for people to flit in and out, watching if they wished, unlike the Confessional and the Baptismal Font, but wouldn't be *so* open that Riley might get nervous.

As it was, Riley was sprawled on the leather top of a double cage bondage table. His panties were stretched tight around his thighs, leaving his flushed cock exposed, bobbing and leaking pre-cum, to the scattered voyeurs holding up the wall. Lennox didn't mind them watching, as long as they stayed quiet and out of the way.

Master Ede was a large man, due mainly Lennox was guessing to a love of sweets rather than the gym, but he had a steadying presence and a gentle voice as he talked Lennox through how to sterilize the rods in the future to prep them for insertion.

Then, Master Ede held out a box. "Do either of you kids have a latex allergy?"

"No, sir." Lennox chuckled as the honorific slid from his mouth, feeling far too toppy to attach any sort of meaning to it, and Riley was staring so hard at the blue surgical gloves—his eyes wide and breath coming out fast—that Lennox doubted he even noticed.

But Master Ede's lips twitched, clearly able to see the humor in it. "Glove up, doctor."

"Is that a club rule or..."

"Best practices," Master Ede finished for him. "It's not required, but I always suggest to novices that you wear them, at least until you get in the habit. The lube can get slippery, but you also don't want to introduce any pesky germs into your sub's body."

Lennox took the gloves, pulling them on with a snap. At the sound, Riley shivered, his pupils blown wide. "Ah, you like that, Bunny?"

Riley nodded, his teeth leaving dents in his lower lip. Lennox reached up to free it but Master Ede caught his wrist in a gentle grip. "You'll have to change your gloves."

Lennox reluctantly pulled his arm back as soon as Master Ede let it go. Instead, he took the alcohol wipe the man passed him with a frown. "What's this for?"

"I know it doesn't seem sexy, but you're going to wipe his slit with it, just to be extra certain everything is sterile," Master Ede explained.

Lennox hesitated, but after a quick glance at Riley, he obediently opened the wipe and cleaned the head of Riley's dick. "Losing battle, this," he murmured as he tried to gather the pre-cum just for more to seep free. He watched the clear bead form then fall.

"I think your sub here has a humiliation kink," Master Ede said, and when Lennox looked up at Riley's face, he had to agree.

Riley looked blissed out, and Lennox had barely touched him. His skin was pink and glistening, his chest heaving and all they'd really done so far was talk over him. But much like at the porn studio when Lennox had chatted with the cameraman, something about that really seemed to get Riley going.

"He's such a good little slut," Lennox said softly, his eyes locked on Riley's as he tested the waters. He was rewarded with Riley's moan, and it was sweeter than any candy Lennox had ever tasted.

"Please, Mr. Nakayama," Riley panted, his dick bobbing as his hips twitched under Lennox's gaze.

Lennox tried to hide his smirk as he flicked — gently but enough to sting — the head of Riley's dick. "Hush, Bunny. The men are speaking."

Riley sucked in a sharp breath but stayed silent. Lennox waited for a safeword that didn't come.

" — ube." Master Ede's voice filtered in between the sounds of Riley breathing.

"Hm?" Lennox said, finally turning back to the older man.

He was met with a smirk as Master Ede waved another packet, this one purple, at him. "I said, "*now use plenty of lube*." Pull apart the slit a bit and pour it right in. There you go, just like that. A bit more..."

"It seems like a lot..."

"Never enough lube." Master Ede leaned closer, and Lennox barely held back his growl. Thankfully, the older man chose not to take offense. He just smirked and stopped leaning in. "Now you're going to choose a rod. I'd recommend this one to start."

"Isn't that a bit big?" Lennox asked, staring at the slightly less than medium-sized rod Master Ede was pointing at, careful not to touch.

"A too-small sounding rod is just as dangerous as one that's too big. Don't worry. You're submissive here is larger than average, so this rod is perfect."

Lennox picked up the rod. "How dangerous is a shaky hand?"

Master Ede laughed. "Again, *don't worry*. This is very safe if done right, and you're going to be letting gravity do all the work."

"Someone better do *something*," Riley interrupted, his voice a plaintive whine.

"Bunny, what did I say?" Lennox sighed, shaking his head at his poor, needy boyfriend. "Would you prefer a spanking instead?"

Riley shook his head, his dark hair flopping over his scrunched-closed eyes.

"Then try to be a good boy for me. We wouldn't want to waste Master Ede's valuable time, would we?" Lennox added another layer of sterile lube to the rod, just to be safe, then hovered it over Riley's slit. He loved watching the goosebumps beading up on Riley's skin, the way his body shook, but more than that, he loved the desperation leaking off him in waves.

Just as Riley shook his head again, Lennox, after a quick glance at Master Ede, inserted the tip of the rod into the tiny hole and let it fall slowly. It sank inexorably down, and Lennox couldn't help but stare, fascinated, at the way Riley's slit stretched around it.

"God, Bunny, so fucking hot. Can you feel it? Don't come, not until I say. Be a good boy for me." Lennox continued blathering on as he let the rod fall all the way down, leaving it in place for a few seconds so Riley could get accustomed. The young man was taut as a bowstring, digging his teeth so hard into his pink lips that they were nearly white, his hands fisted at his side.

And when he pulled it back up, Riley keened. "No, leave it in, please," he begged, his hips twitching as Lennox worked, bringing the steel rod almost all the way to the end.

Then, just as it was almost out, he let it drop. "Oops," he grinned as Riley cried out. "Sorry, Bunny. Looks like your dick wants to keep it."

Riley threw his head back, the cords of his neck like violin strings, desperate to be plucked. "So fucking perfect for me," Lennox murmured, working the sound in and out, in much the way he wanted to sink into Riley's body. "Tell me when you're close."

"Almost there, I can't... Lennox, I can't hold it, I'm *so* close. Fuck!" Riley screamed.

Lennox knew as soon as his name slipped from his lips that he was too far gone to wait. He yanked the sound out just in time for Riley to spill, pearly seed shooting from his stretched, reddened slit to coat the young man's abs and Lennox's hands.

It was, by far, the most intimate experience of his life.

Then, Master Ede cleared his throat. "He's gonna need to piss soon." Lennox choked on a laugh. Riley, though, didn't notice. He was boneless, wrung out from his orgasm.

Lennox climbed up onto the bondage table and snuggled up to Riley's side, burying his nose into the younger man's neck. He breathed in deep, relishing the scent of his sweat. He barely noticed Master Ede guiding the voyeurs out of the room and closing the door behind them, signaling that the scene was over to give them time for aftercare.

Riley's breath was slow, steady and his eyes were glossy, but Lennox was in no hurry. They lay together for several long moments until Riley shivered, tightening his arms around Lennox's shoulders.

"Lennox?" Riley finally murmured, his voice plaintive.

"Welcome back, Bunny." Lennox brushed a kiss over his sharp collarbones, then sat up. "Time to pee."

Riley scrunched his nose. "It's cold."

"The sooner you get up, the sooner you get warm," Lennox promised, rolling off the table and pulling Riley up after him.

Riley allowed Lennox to help him back into his panties and lead him to the bathroom, but he did not, unfortunately, allow Lennox to help him pee. Instead, Lennox lingered just outside the door until he heard the toilet flush and the sink run. Finally, Riley rejoined him in the hall, slipping right back under Lennox's waiting arm.

Once they were dressed—Lennox lent Riley his cashmere scarf, draping it around his neck and shoulders—they walked, languid and content, onto the sidewalk. Lennox didn't even care that he hadn't come. His erection had half-waned, and he suspected it would be gone before they reached home. It was worth so much more to him than an orgasm to have an experience like this with Riley.

"I wanna come back," Riley murmured, his voice slurred. Lennox shifted his grip, wrapping his arm around his trim waist, just in case sub drop kicked in. "We can come back, right?"

"Sure, Bunny. I'd like that." Lennox kissed Riley's forehead, ignoring the hair that tickled his nose. As he straightened up, he thought he saw a strange man in a leather jacket watching them.

When he turned to get a better look, the man was gone—vanished, like he was never there in the first place.

Chapter Thirty-One

"I said, don't touch that!" Riley hissed, itching to swat Lennox's hand but unwilling to do so in public, especially not at a fancy dinner, even if that dinner was being served at the twenty-sixth annual Awards After Midnight ceremony.

The AAMs, not to be confused with the AMAs.

"But it's a dildo, and they have it just sitting there," Lennox whined, his gaze locked on the flamingo-pink silicone dick at the heart of the centerpiece. His index finger hovered a scant centimeter away from the helmet-shaped head.

"I swear to God, I will bite you." Riley broke down and grabbed for Lennox's hand, dragging it down into his lap. He pointedly ignored the snicker from the twink beside him, a dark-haired beauty named Galaxy who was well known for his fisting and double penetration videos.

Riley had spent an awkward amount of time just after taking his seat staring at the guy, because he looked even tinier in person. Riley had no idea how he could take a pair of fingers, let alone a pair of dicks.

Of course, Lennox had been staring, too, and Riley wanted to get jealous, but then he'd just asked Galaxy where he bought his earrings. Riley's jealousy felt rather silly after that.

Lennox squeezed Riley's hand, not seeming to care that Riley had yanked it away from the centerpiece like he was a naughty child. Instead, his smile was playful. "Don't worry, Bunny. I wasn't going to try to use it, I just wanted to see if it was real."

"Of course it's not real, Kitten. It's pink. They didn't chop off an alien dick and glue it to a saucer," Riley teased.

"Imagine if they had, though. I always wondered what would trigger the extra-terrestrial invasion." Lennox wagged his eyebrows, the expression so silly that Riley burst into laughter.

"You two are fricken' adorbs," Galaxy huffed, but his eyes twinkled. "Tell me one of you at least has pimples on your ass or something."

"Will it make you feel better? We can pretend the cameras didn't get a nice close-up view proving otherwise." Riley winked.

At the same time, Lennox grinned and yanked down the collar of his silk blouse. "It's not on my butt, but I have one right here, see? By the collarbone?"

Riley squinted. "That's a freckle, Bunny."

"Oh. Are you sure?" Now Lennox squinted, staring down—or attempting to—at his chest, his neck bent at an angle that was surely uncomfortable.

"Pretty sure," Riley said dryly, letting go of Lennox's hand to skim his fingers over the offending mark. "I kissed it this morning."

"Oh. Well, *if* you're sure." Lennox beamed at the other man. "Sorry... I don't think I have any pimples then."

Galaxy's lips twitched. Then, he turned back to Riley and said, his voice low and teasing, "He's cute. If you ever decide to branch into three-ways..."

"No," Riley replied immediately, his voice sharper than he intended. He swallowed and softened it. "I mean, thank you. It's a kind offer, but I don't play well with others." He plastered on a smile he hoped looked genuine.

Galaxy's smirk widened, a knowing gleam in his famous blue eyes. If Riley had been single, he might have been tempted, but the man—no matter how cute—didn't hold a candle to Lennox.

Before Galaxy could say whatever sly comeback was dancing on his lips, scantily clad waiters in black neoprene G-strings and clunky motorcycle boots began delivering trays of appetizers.

Riley didn't think he was imagining the look of appreciation on Lennox's face as he stared at the nearest, a dark-haired beauty with skin like polished brass and a neatly trimmed Brett beard. He couldn't even be jealous, since he was staring as well.

"Damn," Galaxy said out loud what they all were thinking, practically drooling as the handsome waiter passed out little plates full of cocktail weenies.

"I know..." Lennox breathed. "I can't wait to put one in my mouth..."

"Me either— Wait, what?" Riley blinked, turning to stare at his boyfriend in shock.

"I haven't eaten in ages," Lennox said, except it came out mangled, his mouth stuffed as it was with the little crescent-wrapped hot dog. He shoved a second one in before he'd even swallowed the first.

"Oh. Yeah, I...I was also talking about the weenies..." Riley lied, taking one for himself.

Galaxy snickered. "Sure you were."

"Shut up." Riley glared, but there was no heat behind it.

"What? You were *definitely* talking about that nice... thick...juicy weenie."

Riley cringed, scrunching his nose. "Please don't say it like that."

"Like what? Oh, weenie? Would you prefer di—"

"Good evening, entertainers!" a loud voice boomed through the PA system, interrupting Galaxy's tease before it could finish. Relieved, Riley shoved another pig-in-a- blanket into his mouth and twisted in his chair.

On stage, the event coordinator stood holding the microphone, grinning under the bright lights that made his straight white teeth look too large for his mouth. "I'd like to welcome you all to the twenty-sixth annual Awards After Midnight ceremony. We hope you enjoy the appetizers that our sexy wait staff will be delivering throughout the show—and the lap dances they may be persuaded to offer for dessert." The man gave a booming laugh that seemed to land flat on the crowd, but he didn't let it stop him. He continued as if the awkward moment hadn't happened. "Filming will begin momentarily, and I'll be passing the mic over to our lovely host, who I'm sure you all will recognize. Until then, we have just a few business matters to attend to. I know, I know," he waved off the groans that filtered through the gathering, "but rules are rules, and the only firemen I want showing up are the sexy ones."

That time, he got a bigger laugh, though Riley still didn't find it all that hilarious. But, he conceded to himself, the man hadn't claimed to be a comedian. Riley half-listened to the safety speech pointing out the nearest exits, as well as directions to the bathrooms — just outside the ballroom, down the hall to the left.

Up until this point, Riley hadn't thought much about this evening. He was nominated for 'Best Solo Performance', but he was running against several performers with years of experience under their belt. And he and Lennox had watched the other scenes and *damn*, some of them were hot.

The only reason Riley had gotten as popular as he had was because of who his father was. People liked the idea of watching a famous man's son debase himself on camera. Even the senator's followers watched, out of some morbid combination of twisted curiosity and moral outrage. He knew because they left comments on the videos, things like "your father must be ashamed," and "Jesus still loves you." Riley no longer read them, but they popped up like clockwork whenever a new video dropped.

At first, he'd thrived on it, the knowledge that every scene he shot had to be driving his dad up the wall. That all these supposed, God-fearing Christians were watching him fuck himself on camera. But...

Lately, the only times he enjoyed going to set were when Lennox went with him. Those scenes felt...real and fun, not like he was doing it just to stick it to his dad.

Not like the memory of his dad was even now still somehow controlling his life.

Tonight, sitting at this table filled with other performers, performers who deserved to be here, performers who did their jobs because they loved the work, not just to prove a point—and who got their followers because they'd earned them, not because of their last name—made him feel like fire ants were crawling over his skin.

Absently, he scratched at the skin of his wrist, digging his fingernails into flesh until it burned, red and irritated. The event coordinator wrapped up his speech, passing the microphone over to one of the stage managers, but Riley barely noticed. He twisted in his chair to stare at the glowing red exit sign.

"I'll be right back. Bathroom," he blurted, pushing away from the table and standing abruptly. The air felt thick, heavy around his shoulders and nearly impossible to breathe in.

He snagged a flute of champagne from a passing waiter's tray, downing it in one swallow before grabbing a second. He abandoned the empty flutes in a potted plant just before he exited to the hallway.

Bathroom… *To the right*, he thought, turning down the hallway and hurrying down it until he found the men's room. Thankfully, fancy as it was, it wasn't one that had an attendant waiting to pass you a towel or scented soaps. He went straight to the stall at the end and locked himself in.

The champagne was little more than bubbles in his stomach, and he found himself wishing for brandy or Scotch—even a cheap bottle of whiskey, anything to numb his skin. His hands shook with the desire to grab Lennox's keys out of his pocket and drive to a liquor store. He could already taste the burn on his lips. He so thought he'd licked the problem with alcohol that he'd had earlier, but maybe not.

"Fuck!" Riley cursed, punching the stall door hard enough to split the skin of his knuckles instead. The blinding pain left the world white, and he cursed again, feeling the blood dripping down his fingers. He cradled his hand against his chest and leaned against the wall, sliding down until he was huddled in front of the pristine toilet.

Shame coiled in his stomach as he stared at his bloodied knuckles, warring with anger that he'd let his cravings get the best of him. How many times had his sobriety — so hard won during his stay at the Rainbow Center, bought with years of therapy, Alcoholics Anonymous meetings and late-night sessions with whatever hall monitor caught him trying to sneak out — lapsed because of his weakness?

He couldn't even name on both hands the number of drinks he'd had since leaving. He'd justified some, like the glass of bourbon he'd downed a few months ago at Mike's bachelor party, as no big deal. *A drink among friends, nothing to worry about.* Not a problem and certainly not something that would *become* a problem.

Now, the phantom feel of the drinking glass, chilly in his sweaty palm, haunted him and the taste of liquor teased his lips.

For the first time since leaving the center, Riley did what he should have done months ago.

He slipped his unbloodied hand into his pocket and pulled out his cellphone, his fingers shaking as he tapped out one of the few numbers he knew by memory. It only rang twice before the familiar voice on the other end answered. "Don't worry, Riley," Dean, his sponsor, said gently, needing no prompting or explanation. "Tell me where you are, and I'll be there. We'll get through this together."

* * * *

Something was wrong.

Lennox knew it, but he didn't know what to *do* about it. Riley was not, he reminded himself, a child in need of a chaperone. But there'd been something on his face as he excused himself, something dark that Lennox couldn't quite lay a finger on.

Lennox planned on giving Riley time, but when the first three categories were announced and he still hadn't returned, he gave in to the small voice in the back of his head urging him to go check on him.

The voice grew more insistent as he spotted the abandoned champagne flutes in a flower arrangement by the door. They might not have been Riley's, but Lennox knew better. He remembered the warnings his sister had given him about Riley's struggles with alcohol when he'd been at Rainbow House. He hadn't seen any other attendees flee the room, and enough waiters were strolling around in skimpy getups collecting them to dissuade people from leaving champagne flutes laying around willy-nilly.

Riley's or not, they left a sour feeling in Lennox's stomach.

The bathroom was easy to find, only a dozen feet down the hallway and visibly labeled, but Lennox hesitated outside, hearing low voices behind the door.

Riley's was easy to recognize but the other was unfamiliar. Whoever it was sounded older, his voice deep but words too quiet to make out. Riley, though, sounded upset.

Lennox pushed the door, hinges silent as it opened, and the words grew clearer.

"Have you been writing in your journal?" the stranger asked, and the words were so different from what Lennox expected to hear that he stopped to listen.

"No, I didn't think I'd need it. I'm not a kid anymore, I guess...I guess I thought that moving out and...and being a real adult and stuff would be enough." Riley was quiet but his voice dripped with shame.

"It's deceptive like that." The older man's voice was calm and free of accusation. "Sometimes, the disease is tricky. And," the man continued, speaking louder when Riley drew in a breath to interrupt, "alcoholism is a disease. You have nothing to be ashamed of. The cravings sneak up on all of us, and they can be demanding. You know I've been sober for twenty years and just last week, I had a bottle of Jack in my cart."

"Did you drink?" Riley asked, so quiet Lennox almost couldn't hear him. Guilt at eavesdropping overtook him, but it wasn't strong enough to convince him to shut the door.

"No, but not because of some magical inner strength or anything. I got lucky that my card was declined. The card reader beeping just happened to be enough of a wakeup call for me to walk away. It's not your fault that the card reader didn't beep." Another indrawn breath by Riley had the man interrupting again, "I mean a *metaphorical* card reader, kid."

The sound of Riley huffing made Lennox smile and finally, he stepped back, letting the door swing shut.

Right now, Riley didn't need him to burst in on his white horse with his savior complex. Lennox didn't know who the man was, but Riley clearly did. If Riley wanted Lennox to know he was struggling, Lennox needed to trust that he would tell him. Otherwise, it wasn't his place to demand answers or explanations.

He went back to his seat.

Riley joined him a few minutes later, his knuckles swaddled in clean white gauze. Lennox just carefully brushed a kiss over Riley's fingertips before setting it gently back in his lap, a silent promise that he was there, if and when Riley wanted to talk.

And that he was still there if Riley never did.

Chapter Thirty-Two

"Dude, this room is rad!" Tweety spun around Riley's bedroom fast enough that he stumbled, clearly dizzy. How he saw anything like that, Riley didn't know.

"What are you, Tony Hawk?" Riley teased, flopping down on his mattress to watch his friend inspect everything from the curtains to the makeup scattered on top of Riley's vanity.

"More like Tony Alva," Tweety said as he snagged a bottle of nail polish and chucked it toward Riley.

He barely caught it. "Tony Alva?"

"Yeah." Tweety gave him a funny look. "From His Eyes Have Fangs?"

Riley stared blankly back, not in any way sure how that odd sentence had anything to do with...well anything. Tweety huffed, pouting as he dropped on the bed beside Riley. "Come on, really? The band? You're *such* a millennial."

"Uh, excuse me! I'm Gen Z, fuck you very much!" Riley protested, shoving his friend in fake anger.

"Your boyfriend would get jealous," Tweety immediately denied, then stuck his nose in the air as he ran his hand down the front of his glittery crop top. "Besides, you wouldn't know how to handle all this."

"I'll have you know, I'm an award-winning porn star now," Riley teased, sticking out his tongue.

"For *solo* performances," Tweety clarified, grabbing Riley's foot and yanking it into his lap. Riley laughed as he lost his balance and toppled over, nearly kicking Tweety in the face by accident in his haste to right himself. Semi-pro athlete that he was, Tweety somehow managed to avoid not only Riley's flailing appendages but *also* kept his grip. "Stop moving and let me paint your toenails."

"I think you have a foot fetish," Riley huffed but obediently stopped moving. They needed a fresh coat of paint anyway.

"All this curiosity about my sex life makes me think you forgot our disastrous attempt at playing Seven Minutes in Heaven." Tweety grew quiet and the tip of his tongue slowly slid out of his mouth, sticking out between his lips as he frowned. Carefully, he painted Riley's left big toe. It didn't seem to matter how much he ever concentrated because, like always, a glob of nail polish ended up on the skin near the base of the nail and Tweety huffed.

"We'll get the Q-tips when you're done and clean it up," Riley promised, knowing that Tweety would kick himself for the botched job later, no matter how much Riley didn't care.

Tweety always claimed he chose to try to be a pro-basketball player instead of a cosmetologist because he sucked at pedicures like it was a joke, but Riley knew that deep down, his best friend meant it wholeheartedly. Tweety wanted nothing more than to work in a salon, and no amount of reassurances from Riley had convinced him he was good enough.

"After all," Tweety had said, a smile on his face but his voice sad, *"what person looks at me and sees stylist?"*

Riley wished everyone could just throw away their stereotypes.

Tweety must have been waiting for Riley to relax because he didn't let the bomb drop until he almost done with the nails on Riley's other foot. "I think I'm moving back to Austin."

Riley twitched, accidentally knocking the bottle of nail polish out of Tweety's hand. It spilled over the arch of Riley's foot and onto the white comforter.

"Oh, shit," they said at the same time, staring at the bright blue stain.

"Do you think that'll come out in the washer?" Tweety whispered, cringing as he looked at the door as if someone was going to burst in with a hatchet at any second to decapitate them for the mess.

"I...somehow doubt it?" Riley answered, his own voice creeping higher in pitch. He didn't actually think Lennox would be mad — after all, he'd seen more than enough paint splatters on Lennox's sheets — but he was reminded of the nights he and Tweety had huddled together at the Rainbow Center, their hearts pounding as they waited to see if the Hall Monitors were going to burst in and yell at them for talking past curfew.

"Shit," Tweety repeated, staring mournfully at the stain. "It's worse than lying in the wet spot..."

"Don't change the subject, Tweety bird." Riley flipped the edge of the comforter over the stain. Out of sight, out of mind — or so he hoped. "Now don't get me wrong, I'd *love* for you to move back to Austin. You know I miss you like crazy...but what about the Wranglers?"

Tweety looked away, staring pointedly at the ceiling and humming.

Riley was used to the avoidance technique, though. He reached out and twisted Tweety's nipple through his shirt.

"Ouch! Bitch!" Tweety spat and rubbed the sore spot with his palm. "Jeez, what are you, five?"

"Come on. Spit it out," Riley said, refusing to apologize until he got an answer.

Tweety sighed. "I don't fit in on the team, and that's all I'm going to say on the matter." He sounded unusually solemn, a state of being that didn't fit Tweety at all.

Riley opened his mouth to press again, but before he could say anything, he heard the front door open and Mike's booming voice yelling something about a pizza. Tweety smiled too bright and shoved Riley's foot out of his lap. "You're a mess and so am I. Pip, off you go."

Riley sighed and rolled off the bed, heading toward the door. He paused halfway into the hall, turning to look over his shoulder. "Tweety?" he said, his voice quiet but filled with a plea. "You'd tell me if there was something really wrong, right?"

Tweety waved his hand in a half-hearted thumbs up. "Of course."

Riley didn't believe him. Reluctantly, he closed the bedroom door behind him. As he walked into the room he'd slowly, piece by accidental piece, moved into with Lennox, he couldn't help feeling like he'd made a mistake not pressing the issue. The feeling lingered when he cleaned the nail polish off his skin and touched up his nails, as he left the room to greet Mike in the kitchen, even as Tweety joined them a few minutes later.

And it only grew stronger when he saw the way Tweety, a man normally bold and fearless, flinched away from Mike like he'd been burned before brushing it off with a laugh.

* * * *

"I just don't understand why he won't talk to me," Riley confided to Lennox later, after they'd covered Tweety, passed out on the couch, with an afghan and retreated to their room. They'd offered to let Mike stay as well, but he'd insisted his fiancé would miss him.

"Give him some time. I'm sure he will when he's ready," Lennox murmured, rolling onto his side and curling his arm over Riley's waist.

Riley sighed and snuggled in closer. "We've just never had secrets from each other. I'm worried about him."

"I'm sure he knows. Let him sleep on it, and maybe he'll be ready in the morning," Lennox suggested, and Riley agreed.

But when Riley woke up, Tweety was gone. The only sign he'd been there in the first place was the rumpled bed and a balled up, bloody Wranglers shirt with a tear in the sleeve crammed into the trash can.

And it was only then, staring at the torn shirt, that Riley realized how much his best friend reminded him of his *first* friend, the boy he met on the streets and only knew for a month and yet still, the older boy had saved his life.

Then he cried for the missing boy they'd never found again.

Chapter Thirty-Three

The set was prepared when Riley spilled out of the locker room, five minutes late with an erection hard enough to pound nails, courtesy of Lennox's over-enthusiastic fluff job while they were changing. Graham, the director, opened his mouth to scold him — he could tell from the furrow on the bear of a man's brow — but then he smirked.

"Better late than never," Graham said instead. He nodded at Lennox over Riley's shoulder. "He just here to watch or are we getting another cameo? The views on the last shoot were through the roof."

"Riley's going to fuck me," Lennox chirped, sounding far too enthusiastic.

"I haven't agreed yet," Riley pointed out, trying to hide his grin. Like there was any way he could resist his boyfriend's —

"You can't resist a go at this ass," Lennox said, seemingly finishing Riley's thought out loud.

"Who can blame him," Graham said, quietly enough Riley wasn't sure he was supposed to hear.

Riley frowned at the director. He was twice Riley's size and counting, but that didn't mean Riley wouldn't at least try to put him on his ass if he tried anything more inappropriate than watching.

"Oh, wipe that jealousy off your face. I'm happily married." Graham rolled his eyes, then paused. "Actually, no. Go ahead and keep it. I'm revising the script. Hey, Colton!" He hollered toward the next set over, where one of the other entertainers had just finished a scene.

"Yeah, Boss?" Colton hollered back, rounding the divider in the nude, swiping a terrycloth towel through sweat damp hair.

"You up for another scene while you're here?" Graham asked.

Riley immediately protested, "No way. I *told* you solos only. You're lucky I brought Lennox. I'm *not* doing a threesome!"

"Don't take your panties off yet, Mr. Scott." Graham rolled his eyes and waved away his anger. "You wear jealousy better than Versace."

"These panties won't come off *ever* again if you don't explain yourself real quick," Riley grumbled, crossing his arms over his bare chest.

"I'm thinking we switch to the gym set." Graham waved off to the side where a weight bench and rack, treadmill and pull-up bars set the scene. "Your boyfriend is on the weight bench, then Colton comes over to spot him, maybe puts his groin in his face a bit but no contact. You come in all jealous-like." Graham spoke quickly, his eyes flaring as he mapped out the scene in his head.

He got carried away easily and quickly. It made Graham a great director, but right now, Riley hated that the man was right. It *would* sell. But he didn't want Lennox uncomfortable—let alone the fact that seeing another man's dick that close to his boyfriend would leave him pissed off for real.

Riley looked at his boyfriend for help, certain Lennox would be uncomfortable at the least, downright livid at worst. Instead, Lennox was grinning. "Oh, this seems fun."

"Well, shit," Riley groaned, knowing that if his boyfriend was up for it, he had no real excuse. "Fine, but Cupid"—he used Colton's stage name and punctuated it with a glare— "had better keep his hands and *dick* to himself."

Colton laughed. "Oh honey, you know I only bottom." He winked and slung his towel over his shoulders. "Let me go find some shorts."

It was probably a good idea, since Riley had already watched Lennox struggle to avoid staring at the massive schlong more than once. He wasn't even upset because god*damn*, the man had a giant dick. It was almost a shame that Cupid never topped. Oh, not that *Riley* would want to partner with him, even if he was single—which he wasn't—but it would be a hell of a thing to watch.

"You boys go change costumes as well. Riley, get your boyfriend the blue trunks. I want you in green," Graham suggested. Riley sighed but tugged Lennox back toward the locker room. "Not the long ones," Graham hollered after.

Riley gave the man a nice look at his finger.

* * * *

"You should get jealous more often," Lennox said between pants, sprawled out on the sticky weight bench. He didn't seem to care that he was nude and a dozen men fluttered around the set, cleaning up props and taking still photos for the website.

Riley was sitting on the floor, leaning against the weight rack with his legs splayed, his dick sore but sated. He hadn't taken it easy on Lennox, not after watching the way his eyes locked on Colton's shorts — more specifically, the tight imprint of his dick and balls as they strained the fabric.

He was a jealous fucker when it came to Lennox.

Something he'd never thought he'd know about himself.

He learned new things every day.

"Look at another man's dick like that again and I'll fuck you so hard you won't be able to sit down for a week," Riley promised. Lennox laughed like Riley was joking, but Riley wasn't so sure he was.

"Promises, promises." Lennox winked, rubbing his hand absently over his stomach, smearing the still-wet semen on his abs.

"Mr. Scott?" a man only a few years older than Riley said, his voice nervous and hands fumbling with a clipboard. His cheeks were pink as he glanced at them then looked away quickly, like he wasn't sure he was allowed to stare. He must be new if naked men on a porn set left him embarrassed.

"Yeah?" Riley stretched to hook his finger in the leg of the green boxer briefs he'd started the shoot in, dragging it over to pull them on. One perk of working for OnlyStiXXX was the vast amount of free underwear he was accumulating, since the studio let them keep what they filmed in. Most of them were donated anyway by designers hoping to advertise to the horny men watching.

"There are some people here to talk to you. Mr. Graham said you can use his office?"

Riley frowned. Who the hell would come to see him on a porn set? And *why*?

"I can go with you as soon as my legs work, if you want?" Lennox spoke up, sitting up on the weight bench with a groan. He stretched his back, the vertebrae popping.

"Nah, I'm sure it's just about my contract or something." Riley waved him off. "Go take a nice hot shower. I shouldn't be long."

"Oh, a shower sounds nice..." Lennox didn't bother putting his own briefs on. He just slung them over his shoulder and hopped off the bench. "If you hurry, you can help me wash my back." Lennox winked over his shoulder as he left the set.

Riley stood, readjusting his flaccid dick. "Don't suppose you have a towel anywhere?" he asked, grimacing as the lube and cum made his panties stick to his skin.

"Oh, um...right. One sec." The man patted his pant pocket, then pulled out a crumbled brown napkin. "All I have is this?"

"Well, beggars and choosers, I guess." Riley grinned as the man turned bright red again when he took the napkin and shoved it down his underwear, cleaning up as best he could. It would work for a temporary solution, he supposed.

He headed toward Graham's office, not thinking too much of it until he opened the door and spotted the three men in suits standing in a triangle formation. He froze, his eyes skipping from one familiar man to the next. He didn't have time to run before they moved, herding him out and separating him from the main studio. Behind him, the narrow hallway was mostly dark. It led to an out-of-use bathroom and an emergency exit. That was it.

"You've been a naughty boy, Mr. Scott," the man in the middle said, in a gritty voice that spoke of years of tobacco use. Riley shivered. He'd thought he left these men behind when he'd fled his father's house, the dirty guards who stuck with the senator because of the perks the job brought with it.

Perks like getting to '*visit*' Riley in his room when either he'd been bad or they'd been particularly good.

Heart pounding in his chest, Riley discreetly looked for a way to get around them. Hoping to stall for time, he sucked in a breath, grateful he only stuttered a little as he spoke. "I'm surprised you're still alive, Ricky-dick. Thought those cigarettes would have killed you years ago…"

"Still a mouthy fucker, I see. Don't worry. I'm sure your daddy will have it cleaned up in no time." Rick didn't even bother faking anger. The guard knew he had the upper hand.

"Didn't take long before." The dark-haired man to Rick's left chuckled. He'd been newer when Riley had fled, and he couldn't recall the guy's name. He remembered the guy had a tiny dick and a sadistic streak to compensate.

"Oh, that's right. You had him right trained up, didn't you, Jimmy? Even had him saying 'please' and 'thank you' for your dick." Rick laughed, slapping the sadist on the shoulder.

The three men kept moving forward, forcing Riley to step back if he wanted to avoid them. They stayed too far apart for Riley to get around them, but too close together for him to risk darting between.

His only hope was the emergency exit, but he didn't know where it came out. Onto a street or an alley? He guessed alley, considering how the studio was set up. A long or short one? A dead end?

He turned and sprinted, shoving open the door and cursing when no alarm sounded. He was right that it opened to an alley, but apparently, his dad's bodyguards had expected him to run because a black SUV idled right outside the door, a fourth man, a stranger in a leather jacket, standing in wait.

The musclebound man snagged Riley with ease. In his panic, half his self-defense lessons fled his mind and the ones that remained did nothing to free him.

They had him bundled up in the backseat in seconds, his arms cuffed behind his back with professional-grade handcuffs. Jimmy shoved him to the side, forcing his face into Rick's lap.

Probably to keep him out of sight, despite the tinted windows, but Riley cringed at being so close to the man's dick.

"I'm not some scared little kid anymore," Riley hollered, squirming to sit up with no luck.

"Bet your ass is still nice and tight." Rick laughed crudely, reaching down to squeeze it over the panties. Now Riley wished he'd gone to shower first, so he was wearing…anything else.

He cringed away from the touch. "Fuck you."

"Na. I ain't no faggot," Rick lied. "But be a good boy and I'll fuck you real nice before I take you back to Daddy."

Chapter Thirty-Four

Lennox waited in the shower long enough that the water ran cold, then regretfully spun it off. Shivering, he stepped out to grab a towel, guessing his boyfriend got held up with whatever he was dealing with. He just hoped it wouldn't take long, because he was ready to go home and cuddle.

He got dressed, noticing Riley's clothes still in his cubby, and headed out into the main studio. He glanced around, frowning when he saw Graham by the sound...boom...mic thingy, but still no Riley. He walked over, hands in his pockets. "Have you seen Riley? Is he still in your office?"

"Hm? Oh, Riley? No, I just came from there, and it was empty. I figured he was with you." Graham frowned and swiped a hand through his hair. "Not like him to just disappear. You check the car?"

"He wouldn't have left without getting dressed. He does porn but he's still weirdly shy about public nudity," Lennox shrugged. He'd tried getting Riley to go get the mail in his underwear last week, mostly because he thought it would be fun to traumatize the bitchy mail lady who kept throwing his mail on the porch instead of using the mailbox, and Riley had turned red as a lobster.

"Let's go to my office. I can check the cameras. The studio isn't that big. Unless he's hiding in one of the bathrooms, we should be able to find him," Graham suggested.

"Who was he meeting, anyway?" Lennox asked as they walked toward a narrow hallway in the back of the building. He'd have thought the studio director would have a fancier office, but it was just a small room with a desk and two chairs, along with a single abstract painting that could have been bought at any supermarket on the wall. There wasn't even a window.

"A few men from some senator's office," Graham frowned as he logged onto the computer. "That's odd…"

"What?" Lennox rounded the desk to stare at the two staticky squares that should have had video feed. The main studio and the front sidewalk were playing video fine, but…

"Something's interfering with the cameras. They were working fine this morning…"

"It's just the back hall and the office that are out, right? So probably not an accident," Lennox mused, something close to fear coiling in his belly. "You said a senator? Was it Senator Scott?"

Graham shrugged. "They just said 'the senator,' I didn't think to question them. Figured they were in suits and all, and I know Riley's dad's one of them. Figured they were secret service, so it was probably important."

"Riley doesn't get on with his dad," Lennox heartbeat quickened. "He's supposed to be doing an interview tomorrow, exposing his dad as a pedophile..." Something told him that the timing wasn't a coincidence, nor were the broken cameras. "Could they have tampered with the feed from in here?"

"Anything's possible, I suppose, especially if they could get into the system. I have a password, but a dedicated hacker wouldn't find it difficult..." Graham dropped down in his seat and swiped a hand over his face. "Do I need to call the police? Don't you have to wait twenty-four hours to report a missing person?"

"Not if you have cause to suspect foul play," Lennox replied, already digging out his cell. He felt numb. Fear would come later, he was sure. He couldn't think of what Riley might be going through now, not with what he knew about his asshole father.

The 9-1-1 dispatcher who took his statement seemed too calm, and Lennox struggled not to snap at her as he relayed that his boyfriend had gone missing from his job and that they had reason to suspect foul play — that the cameras had been cut, his things were still there and there was a motive to harm him.

He didn't know if the woman believed him or not, but she promised to send an officer over, regardless.

It took almost an hour.

Lennox paced the office, doom scrolling through social media in hopes of seeing... What? A statement from Riley saying exactly where he was and how to rescue him? Honestly, he was more afraid he'd see something from the senator's office lamenting Riley's 'sudden tragic death in an accident.'

He saw neither, just a dozen ads for various jock straps and video games and a slew of inane posts about peoples' cats, which he normally loved but weren't really on his radar right now.

The officer who showed up was young. He was clearly not new to the force, since he was a detective, but likely new to his shield. He took Lennox's statement easily enough, and seemed concerned, but when he left, Lennox felt like he'd accomplished nothing.

There was no step-by-step plan to find Riley and bring him back home. No reassuring promise that they'd be rolling up to the senator's door with a warrant. All he got was a, "Thank you for your report, Mr. Nakayama. I promise our department is taking your concerns seriously."

Basically, a whole ass full of fuck all.

"So…" Graham cleared his throat awkwardly beside him as the officer left. "I want to be kept in the loop. Riley's a good kid, and I hate to think of anything happening to him."

"God, there better be a loop to keep you in." Lennox swiped a hand over his face. "They were like…way less than helpful." Now, panic swirled in his chest, rising like the tide. What was he supposed to do now?

If he jumped in his car and drove to the senator's mansion, what would happen? Would they let him in? Would he get arrested? Would it be enough to draw attention to the senator to keep Riley safe?

Attention…

Lennox frowned. "I have an idea, but I don't know if it's a good one…"

"Wanna run it by me?"

"So there's this reporter…"

Chapter Thirty-Five

Riley thought he'd left this life behind.

Some small part of him must not have realized that, because his years'-old coping mechanisms came roaring back to the surface as soon as Rick's hands groped his ass. Immediately, Riley sagged, his body limp.

Years of self-defense lessons rendered useless in a moment.

"Daddy said you'd still be a good boy. Said he trained you too well for a few years absence to ruin you." Mr. Rick—fuck, even his mind was regressing, addressing the fucker with an honorific he didn't deserve—dug his fingers into Riley's panties to grip his flaccid penis.

Riley endured the unwanted touch in silence, though salt burned his eyes and a lump hardened in his throat, making it hard to breathe. At least he was spared the indignity of an erection, since Rick had no true desire to give him pleasure. He pinched and prodded with glee, going so far as to twist Riley's balls in his fist.

"Damn," Jimmy cursed. "We're going to be there any minute. You hogged him."

"Can't help it." Rick yanked his hand free of Riley's panties and fisted it in his hair instead. "See how sticky he is? Little slut didn't even wash up. You know I like him dirty. Oh, stop whining. You'll get your turn soon enough. You know the boss isn't stingy with his toys."

Riley hated when they called him that, but his anger faded quickly when he realized Rick had said *toys,* plural. He wasn't surprised. He'd heard about the trafficking ring the bastard had been involved in. Even if he hadn't, some part of him had always known that his dad wouldn't stop just because Riley wasn't there anymore... It was a thought he'd always struggled to push down.

He'd never wanted to acknowledge that he'd gotten his freedom — short-lived though it may have been — at someone else's cost.

Riley struggled to look up when the car slowed, hoping for a chance to flee. Instead, all he got was a good view of the familiar circle drive and, beyond that, a set of normal wooden doors that starred in his nightmares.

He sucked in a breath, preparing to run when they opened the door. It was his only chance — get out now before they could drag him in — but his body wouldn't listen. Just being back here had him frozen. By the time he started to struggle, he was halfway up the stairs and all he'd succeeded in was banging his shin on the stone step.

He sucked in a breath as the third guard, the one who'd driven them here in silence, shoved the door open. "Mom!" he screamed, struggling against Rick's hold. He didn't know what else to do. "Mom, please don't let him do this again!"

Rick laughed. "She's not here. Daddy sent her on a little vacation. Don't you feel special that he wants you all to himself."

Jimmy made a crude grab for Riley's dick while Rick held him still. "Come on. Cry for Mommy again. You know it gets me hard."

"What's going on here?" A booming voice had them all stilling. Riley couldn't move, not even to look toward the stairs. It sounded the same, despite the years since he'd last heard it in person.

His dad never got angry. Instead, he had this way of filling his voice with dry disappointment that scared him more than if he yelled.

"Just telling your boy how much we missed him," Rick answered, grinding his erection against Riley's ass.

"Well, I hope you didn't get too carried away. Wouldn't want him to regret coming home to visit." Dad didn't smile. His face was blank as he started down the stairs. He was in a plain black suit that could have been bought anywhere, his clerical collar stark white around his neck.

Damn, how Riley hated that thing.

Riley strained harder against the guards' hands as his father got closer but couldn't get free. "Sorry... I'm sorry." Riley rambled apologies he didn't mean. "Sir, please, I'm too old for you now. You said I was getting too old, and you know I'm not your type anymore. Please just let me go. I won't say nothing. I won't..."

Pain flared through his cheek, stunning him into shutting up. Dad was speaking, his voice chilly, before

Riley even realized the man had slapped him. "Anything, Ryland. You won't say *anything*. I didn't waste my money on tutors for you to speak like some street hooligan."

"Sorry," Riley whispered, cowering back against Rick. Inside his belly, though, anger kindled — just a spark, a tiny little flame, but it reminded him that *this* wasn't him anymore.

He wasn't a scared little boy afraid of his daddy.

He'd dug and clawed his way out of this shit once. He wasn't going to let himself be dragged back now.

"Oh, son, don't worry." Dad shook his head, and on anyone else Riley would have thought his eyes kind. "You can repent now. On your knees."

Riley gathered the shreds of his courage and straightened his spine, but the move was useless. Rick kicked the back of his leg and it crumpled, landing him down on his knees anyway.

Dad loomed over him, grabbing a tight fist of his hair and yanking, forcing his head back. "You don't seem that sorry, son."

Riley cried out as he felt strands of hair yank out. "You're an asshole," Riley ground out through clenched teeth, grabbing for the thick wrist keeping him in place, practically hanging off it to try to relieve the pressure on his scalp.

His father just gripped him tighter and shook his head. "All those years I spent washing out your mouth wasted. Can't have that..." From the way his eyes darkened, Riley knew what was happening next, unless he could think of something, *anything* to change the man's mind.

"I'm not a kid anymore," Riley scrambled to point out, clutching the man's hand even tighter as he started pulling Riley closer. It didn't matter, Dad had always been bigger than him...and stronger. "You...you said I was too old. And...I've slept with lots of people now. God doesn't like whores, you wouldn't...you wouldn't want to fuck one, right?"

"Isaiah 1:2. *'I reared children and brought them up, but they have rebelled against me.'*" Dad's hand was unyielding. *"A father who loves his son is diligent to discipline him."*

Proverbs 13.24.

Riley hated that verse.

"But don't worry," Dad added. "Isaiah 1:18. *'Says the Lord, though your sins are like scarlet, they shall be like snow; though they are red like crimson, they shall become like wool.'* The Lord forgives, and so shall I."

"I'm too old," Riley repeated, holding on to the only argument he had left.

For the first time, Dad smiled but it gave him no comfort. It was a cold, wretched thing, a worm crawling upward. "I won't hold it against you, son. I'll lead you to repentance."

There were so many Bible verses Riley wanted to spit—from Genesis to Leviticus—but he clenched his jaw shut tight as his father undid his belt and lowered his zipper. He'd screamed the verses before, and his dad had pretended not to hear or talked himself around them. Once, his father had just laughed—because *"God had made him this way."*

"Open up, son." Dad let go of Riley's hair to pull out his dick.

Riley shook his head, his lips sealed shut as tightly as he could. He leaned back, struggling to get away, but Dad grabbed him by the jaw, squeezing until the pain grew too much. He had to open his mouth or shatter his teeth.

He gagged at the cock that invaded his throat, bile rising. Maybe it was the bitter taste. Maybe it was the lack of oxygen— Without thinking, Riley bit down, digging his teeth into the tender flesh.

A garbled, angry scream echoed through the room as his dad flung him off. He landed at one of the stunned guard's feet, copper on his lips. "You little *bastard*," Dad snarled, hand cupped over his dick defensively. His face was red—darker than Riley'd ever seen it.

"Shit," he cursed, regretting the impulsive decision he hadn't even meant to make.

"Grab the brat," Dad ordered, and the silent guard did, holding Riley in place.

"I didn't mean it. I'm sorry!" Riley cried, scrabbling to get free, terror filling him at the look on his dad's face. The man's nostrils flared as he struggled to catch his breath. When he pulled his hand free of his dick, Riley could see the pale flesh spotted with blood.

"Not yet, but you *will* be," Dad snarled, straightening to his full height. "Rick, go to my office and bring me down the cane." He glared at Riley as he spoke. "I can't mess with that pretty little face of yours, but I can make sitting something you only do in your memories, little boy."

The room swayed around Riley, and it got difficult to breathe.

Of all the various implements his father had liked to use on him, the cane was the one he remembered hating the worst—the sound of it cracking against his skin nearly as bad as the way it whistled through the air, and neither sound loud enough to mask his screams when it landed.

"Just kill me already and get it over with. It's what you always threatened me with." Anger sharpened the words into blades that just bounced, useless, off his father.

"Waste not, want not, son. You have something I need. Find yourself grateful that the Lord blessed you with two kidneys. Perhaps, if you curb your tongue, I'll only have my surgeon take one."

Chapter Thirty-Six

"Ryland, your hair's a mess. Sit, and let me straighten it." Mom urged Riley onto a stool in the dressing room backstage, pointedly ignoring the way Riley winced when he sat—the way she'd ignored it for years. "Honestly, dear. It's like you *want* your father to look bad. First running off like a spoiled brat, now this. I hope you realize how hard it was to cover for you."

"You know, Mom? I really hadn't thought about how hard it was for *you*," Riley snapped, fisting his hands against his suit pants. "And I go by Riley now."

"Hmph. Sure, except when you're smearing our name through the mud on that *disgusting* website." Mom yanked on his hair in her anger.

"Ouch," he yelped, tugging his head away. "I can do it myself, Mom."

She chucked the comb at his chest. "Make it quick. We go onstage in five."

He made faces at her back as she turned to her own mirror, touching up her lipstick. "Where's Annie?"

Riley asked. Surely, if this was meant as some sort of forced family bonding moment for the cameras, his sister should be here, too.

"Anna-Grace," Mom corrected sharply, "will be unable to make it today."

There was something in the way Mom said it, a twist of her lips as she averted her eyes, that made Riley narrow his. "You're hiding something."

"Let it go, Ryland. It's none of your concern." But Mom's knuckles were white on her tube of lipstick.

Ryland rolled his eyes. "Whatever. I have to take a piss."

He *did* have to pee, but he really just wanted a few moments alone. Mom, after another lecture about his mouth, waved him off. As he stood, he noticed her phone peeking out from under her purse and his heart leapt into his throat. A covert glance at the guard in the corner—he was chewing gum and thumbing through his cell—had Riley reacting quickly.

He never was a very good pickpocket, but Mom seemed to be almost pointedly ignoring him. He slid the phone free and shoved it in the pocket of his suit jacket, his heart thudding.

He opened the door to the dressing room, coming face to face with a scowling Rick. "Where you think you're going?" the guard demanded an answer with crossed arms and a scowl.

"I...I have to go to the bathroom," Riley answered, hating how small his voice was. He didn't *want* to be afraid.

He especially didn't want the man to get suspicious and pat him down or anything.

"Make it quick. The senator is waiting for you"—Rick grinned lewdly—"on stage," he added after a long gap. Riley bit back his snide comment. He wanted to question how many pounds of makeup his super-straight dad was wearing in order to keep his secret — that his every-other-day prayer session was really a façade to cover up his dialysis sessions.

Apparently, people might be a bit reluctant to vote for a governor who could drop dead at any moment. *Weird.*

But he knew better than to say anything. Instead, Riley skirted by the large man, goosebumps erupting on his flesh as the man followed too close.

Thankfully, they really *were* expected on stage any second, so Rick wouldn't have time to do anything, even if he *would* risk it in a public bathroom.

"Yo," Rick snapped, waving toward the urinals when Riley went to move past them to the single stall.

"I... My stomach feels funny." Riley widened his eyes, trying to look as weak and innocent as possible. He pressed his hand to his belly for proof.

The guard rolled his eyes but finally acquiesced. "I'll be right outside the door, so don't try any of your shit. Got it?"

What shit the guard meant was anyone's question, since it wasn't like the bathroom had a window he could crawl out of. Still, Riley gave a small nod.

As soon as he heard the door shut, he pulled the cell phone out and crouched down, quickly thumbing Lennox's phone number into a new text message.

He didn't even know what to say, or how to explain. To Lennox, it probably looked like he'd just vanished — walked out and never came back. He'd been stuck at his dad's for three days now, with no clue how to get himself free.

Dad had made it crystal clear what would happen if he opened his mouth about anything. It wouldn't be Riley who would suffer — or at least, not *just* Riley.

He didn't have time for regrets or second-guessing. He thumbed out the message and sent it.

I love u and I'm sorry I can't explain but u need to leave town don't tell anyone where u r. u r going 2 b watched

Riley was going to do something stupid, and he didn't want Lennox caught up in it. He deleted the evidence of the conversation, then hesitated when his eyes landed on the last message between his mom and sister.

Curiosity bit him and he clicked. The earliest message was from this morning — likely because his mother had cleaned out the earlier ones, since it sounded like it picked up halfway through a conversation with his sister.

It's been two weeks.

Don't worry so much. The nanny said she's having the time of her life at Disney.

You said I could see her if I did the interview. I said everything you wanted.

Your father wasn't happy with the blouse you picked. You looked like a trollop.

I'm sorry, I'll do better next time. Please let me talk to her. Two minutes, that's it. Just have them put her on the phone. I won't even say anything. Mom, please.

Your father says you can have a photo if you spend time with Landers today. 2pm at the Commodore.

I thought we had an interview?

It's no longer your concern. 2pm or no picture.

I'll be there.

[image]

The last message was a picture of a little girl. She was five, maybe six, and Riley knew immediately that she had to be his sister's daughter. They had the same wispy blond hair, the same button nose. She had a small pink scar from just below it to her upper lip — faded, like it was years old.

Riley touched the tip of his finger to the picture. She was lovely, but Riley had so many questions. He racked his brain, almost certain that he'd never heard about his sister getting pregnant or having a kid. He'd followed the news religiously those first few years, waiting to see if there were any hints that his dad had tracked him down.

Or, that anyone was looking for him in general.

For the girl to be this age, she would have been born while Riley was on the streets still — or just after he'd found the Rainbow House. He would have heard about it. The only thing about his sister he could remember being talked about was her mission's trip to Afri —

Riley cursed.

There was no mission's trip, was there?

It didn't make any sense.

Why would they have sent Anna away to have a baby? His dad was all about family values, and it wasn't like she would have been some teenage pregnancy statistic. She'd been happily married — still was, to the same creepy old friend of his dad's.

Riley squinted at the picture, knowing he was running out of time but knowing *also* that he was missing something. It niggled at the back of his brain, telling him that it was important.

Immediately, it clicked. Those blue eyes... Like Riley, Anna had brown eyes, lighter than chocolate but darker than gold. The bastard she married had eyes like coal. How had Anna ended up with a blue-eyed kid, unless her husband wasn't the father?

If Riley's dad knew — and Anna's husband — then he could guess what had happened. Oh, no abortion for Anna, not with the risk of it coming out and ruining their dad's political chances. No, better to send her away to have the baby in private. And what better way to keep his sister in line than hold her baby against her?

Riley pinched his nose.

God, he hated his family.

The bathroom door opened and Riley panicked, realizing how long he'd spent in here. He grunted loud, then dropped the phone into the toilet. It plopped audibly, and he hoped it sounded enough like shit to give credence to his alibi.

He flushed the toilet, crossing his fingers that it wouldn't flood. He held his breath as he watched the narrow phone spin, then get sucked through the hole at the bottom. He let out the breath with relief as the toilet filled normally, then stepped out of the stall.

Rick was glaring, his arms crossed, by the door. "Took you long enough. Your father is waiting to speak with you."

Riley washed his clammy hands quickly, his blood pressure rising. He could tell from the way his ears pounded and the uncomfortable band tightening around his chest.

Was he really going to do this?

He hoped Lennox got his message in time.

He hoped Lennox didn't try to play the hero.

Rick led him backstage, where his dad was standing alone. In his black button-down and suit pants, the white clerical collar was impossible to miss where it wrapped around his throat. Riley hated it — the way his dad wore the thing like armor, a mask to hide his evil deeds behind. And he hated how many people bought the lie.

Dad frowned at him. "You look like shit."

Riley bit back the desire to talk back. His back was already bruised and welted and only the years of practice from *before* let him sit down without screaming, as it was. Being on set wouldn't stop his dad from finding a way to punish him. It would just encourage him to get creative.

Instead, Riley ran a hand through his hair in an effort to straighten it.

Dad sighed. "Leave it. There's nothing to do about it now. We go on in less than two minutes, but Rick here has something to show you. Rick." Dad waved to the guard, who pulled out his phone.

He held it out to Riley, not letting him take it but making sure the pictures were obvious. They were all of Lennox.

Lennox leaving the studio four days ago, his face determined as he stared at the screen of his phone.

Lennox getting out of his car in the driveway that same day, based on his outfit.

Lennox talking animatedly into a phone in the living room, the photograph shot through the front window.

Lennox sleeping.

Riley hated this. Dad didn't need to say anything for him to see it as the threat it was. Keep his mouth shut, stick to the party line, be a good boy and do what you're told.

Dad said it anyway.

"He's quite pretty, for his age," Dad said, staring at the photos with a bored expression. "Would be a tragedy if anything happened to him."

Riley closed his eyes as pain flared in his chest like someone struck him with a hammer. He was stuck between a rock and a hard place and, no matter what decision he made, someone was going to wind up hurt.

Keep his mouth shut and Lennox walked away. Maybe Riley would never see him again, but Lennox would be alive and unharmed. *But,* his dad would win the election and who knew what kind of damage he could do in that position. And Riley wasn't stupid. He knew his father hadn't given up his predilections. How many more kids would suffer because Riley kept his mouth shut?

Speak up, say what he should have said years ago and know he was putting the man he loved in the line of fire.

It was an impossible choice.

Unfortunately, he had to make one.

Chapter Thirty-Seven

Lennox fidgeted with his cufflink. He hated suits, hated everything from the way the button-down shirt felt like it was choking him to the stupid crease down the front of his pants. And he hated that the pockets were too flimsy to hold his phone without a bulge, since it meant security had confiscated it upon entry to the studio.

For Riley, he would wear it. Lindsey, the reporter Riley was supposed to meet with before everything went to shit, said it was important that he look as credible as possible. That while he likely wouldn't have to speak, since she would be fielding the questions to the senator, there was always a possibility one of the cameramen from the other studios attending the press briefing would catch him in frame.

Riley didn't need a hair-brained artist right now. He needed the lawyer.

"Remember," Lindsey said, abruptly enough he startled in his seat. "Let me do the talking. It's important that our questions hit the right note immediately. We need to keep as many of the cameras on and recording as possible."

Lennox nodded, pressing his lips together tight. It was ridiculous how biased the media had become. He hated knowing that when they accused the senator of not only kidnapping but rape, the conservative news stations might just stop filming rather than risk letting the senator drop in the polls.

It shouldn't be this way.

He expected the lights over the press to dim, or for there to be some sign that things were starting. Instead, he had no warning. No time to prepare himself. Senator Scott walked directly to the wood podium at the center of the stage, his steps measured and confident, a wide smile on his handsome face.

Lennox clenched his fists. He'd never *wanted* to witness an assassination before, but now… Well, there was a first time for everything, he realized as Riley followed the man out.

He looked…fine. Pale, but alive. There was a stiffness to his gait that Lennox didn't recognize, though he didn't know whether to attribute it to anger or pain. He hated to think of what his boyfriend might have gone through.

Silently, he promised Riley that it was almost over.

He was so fixated on Riley that he barely realized a middle-aged woman in a dark green suit and skirt followed him out, ushering Riley to a pair of white chairs to the left of the podium.

"Gentleman of the press," Senator Scott greeted with a smile that highlighted his straight, white teeth.

"Asshole," Lindsey muttered, quiet enough that the camera filming over her shoulder likely wouldn't catch it.

"It is my great joy to be here with you today, and I would like to start by reading a verse from Mathew 18:10. '*For where two or three gather in my name, there am I with them.*' And I am glad to say we have more than that here, praise be." The bastard laughed.

Lennox tuned him out, not needing to hear the man's lies about his dedication to 'keeping Texas on the Lord's path.' Instead, he watched Riley. The younger man sat ramrod straight, his face blank. His eyes stayed on the podium, and if Lennox *didn't* know him, he might have thought Riley was focused on the speech.

But Lennox did, so he could tell that Riley was stuck somewhere in his own head. At least, until Senator Scott pounded his fist on the podium and Riley flinched. "As your governor, I will lead this country *back* onto the path of righteousness. There *will* be a return of family values, and —"

Lennox jerked forward as Riley stood quickly and shouted, "Family values? Where were your *family values* when you did *this* to me?" Riley twisted, yanking up the hem of his suit jacket and shirt in one go, revealing... *Oh God*. Lennox gagged at the bruised, tattered skin. He didn't even know what would leave marks like that or how much pain Riley had to have been in — and still *be* in.

"And," Riley shouted over the noise of the shocked crowd, the muttering and jostling as people tried to get closer, cameras aimed right at him, "if you had *family values* — "

"Ryland, sit *down* — " The woman in green, Riley's mother Lennox realized, was hissing, grabbing at his shirt.

"My son has some mental health issues," the senator was trying to say, talking into the microphone even though the press weren't listening, "His wounds are self-inflicted, an unfortunate issue he's been receiving treatment for."

The senator kept attempting to speak but everyone in the room knew he was lying, if not why. Layered in hatches over his spine, the marks could never have come from Riley—not unless he was a contortionist.

Riley twisted, staring directly at the senator with a challenge in his eyes. "Why don't you explain how your '*holy seed*' ended up in my ass?" Riley dropped his shirt to make air quotes around the words. "I want a rape kit. Whose DNA is going to show up, *Dad*?"

Chapter Thirty-Eight

The words spilled from Riley's mouth like spoiled milk. He hated himself for speaking out when he knew what it meant. What it meant for *Lennox*, the danger it put him in. But he knew he would hate himself more if his dad got elected.

If he could have stopped his dad from hurting others and didn't.

Riley refused to look away from his father to see why the press was clamoring, or answer any of the dozens of questions they were screaming at him — not because he was brave, but because he wasn't. He was terrified that he would look away and the man would stab him in the back, cameras be damned.

"My son is not well," Dad repeated himself, and his expression was supposed to be kind. To people who didn't know him, it probably was. To Riley, it was a threat. He could read it in the glint of his eyes, the lines that tugged at his mouth. It was written in the tread of his steps as he abandoned the podium, his approach forcing Riley backward.

"Don't worry, son. Though no one who practices deceit shall dwell in my house. I'll make sure you go somewhere nice to get the help you need." Dad was too close. Riley couldn't keep backing away, not when his bodyguards were waiting to grab him in the doorway.

He dodged out of his father's grasp, panic tightening like a belt around his throat. "Don't touch me!" Riley yelled, then his Mom was there, and that was so much worse. Her lips were pursed and white, and she was quicker than Dad. Her sharp nails dug into his forearm, blood pooling around her fingertips.

"I *said*" — Riley shoved her away, tearing himself free — "don't *touch* me!"

Mom stumbled back but he couldn't enjoy the sight, not with the fear clawing at his ribs, and not when he backed into a strange man who quickly wrestled his arms behind his back.

Riley fought until he realized it wasn't one of the bodyguards on his dad's payroll. It was a police officer in full uniform. While his dad had his own protection, the station had requested backup from the police. He'd heard his dad complaining about it in the car but now, Riley sagged in relief.

"Am I going to jail? Please, take me to jail. *Get me out of here.*" Anything to not end up back at his dad's. There were enough cameras here, so he wasn't worried that they would keep him.

He was more worried they *wouldn't*.

He'd kill himself — hang himself with a bedsheet if he had to — before he would let them release him back into the 'safety' of his dad's custody.

* * * *

The metal handcuffs keeping Riley hooked to the frame of the hospital bed made it difficult to find a way to lie without pain, but he didn't protest as Officer Preston snapped it around his wrist. He accepted it quietly — until the cop headed for the door.

"Wait! Where are you going?" He yanked on the silver bracelet until it bit painfully into his wrist. "Don't leave me here alone."

Officer Preston hesitated, clearly torn. As Riley's movements grew more frantic, he spun on his heels and came back, dropping into the chair by the bed. "Wasn't going anywhere, kid. Just planned to stand in the hallway, give you some privacy with the doctor is all."

Riley bit back his protest that he was an adult. He also stayed silent about the fear that the doctor could be one of his father's lackeys. As a senator, he had connections everywhere. This wasn't Riley's first trip to the hospital for injuries caused by his father. Plenty of doctor's had looked away from the abuse, paid off in bribes or favors. This very hospital had a chapel they'd paid for with his father's dirty money.

"Was it true?" Officer Preston finally asked, after the nurse came in to take Riley's vitals and left again. "What you said at the press briefing?"

Riley gave a jerky nod.

The cop stared at him for several seconds, not asking any of the questions Riley expected. Eventually, he leaned forward and unlocked the handcuff, giving Riley a *look*. "Don't run or anything, though."

"Are you kidding? Why would I run? You can't charge me with anything since it was *clearly* self-defense, and my dad can't beat the shit out of me here."

Riley pulled the pillow down so he could curl around it, hoping to relieve not only the pressure on his back but the pain in his chest.

He needed to talk to Lennox, make sure he got his message and left town. "I... So, I'm not under arrest, right? Can I still make a phone call?"

Officer Preston leaned forward and grabbed the hospital phone off the hook. "Tell me the number. I'll dial it for you." He met Riley's eyes, his gaze kind. "You're right, you're not under arrest, but I would still suggest calling a lawyer, too."

"I plan on it," Riley promised. He struggled to relay Lennox's phone number, something he didn't usually have to actually dial. He'd been spoiled.

Lennox answered on the second ring, voice strained. "Hello?"

"Lennox?" Riley said, voice breaking as tears burned his eyes.

"Riley? Where are you? Are you calling from the hospital? I saw the police grab you, and I swear to God, I've been freaking out!" Lennox's voice was high-pitched and panicked. Riley could hear noises in the background, a cacophony he couldn't unravel.

"What do you mean, you saw? On TV?" Riley cringed at the thought of Lennox seeing his back, the marks that would scar and wreck him.

"No, in the audience! I had it all planned out. I reached out to that reporter, Lindsey? And she was going to ask the senator all kinds of questions until he had to admit that he knew where you were, then we were going to go to the police. I honestly didn't think he'd be stupid enough to have you right on—"

"Lennox!" Riley finally interrupted. "You were supposed to leave town. You're in danger. My dad has people watching you!"

"Oh, you mean that big guy in the car with the camera? He got picked up by the officer on your case a few minutes ago. I only let him hang around long enough that I could have proof of stalking," Lennox said.

"Officer on my case?" Riley frowned, glancing over at Officer Preston, who was glaring down at his phone screen, tapping quickly on the keyboard. He looked up briefly, meeting Riley's gaze with a curious expression.

"Yeah, the one investigating your kidnapping. I mean, not that he believed me that you'd been kidnapped since the footage got erased, but—"

"He might not have been the only one, Lennox! My dad said if I didn't keep my mouth shut, he was going to *kill* you, and he has the money to pay people to do it!" Riley panicked, pushing himself up even when the move sent agony rippling over his back.

Officer Preston jerked forward but didn't grab him, most likely startled by his sudden movement.

"Don't worry about me," Lennox brushed him off. "What room are you in? I've got you a lawyer, like…a good lawyer, not a me kind of lawyer, and we can be there in fifteen minutes. Unless there's traffic…"

"Lennox, sweetheart…" Riley closed his eyes, burying his face against his knees. He wanted to see him, touch him…*hold* him more than anything, but… "It's not safe. You don't understand. Please don't come."

"I'm coming, Riley. I don't care if it's dangerous. I'd rather die with you than live alone. So stay in that fucking hospital bed and goddamn it, *wait* for me."

Lennox's voice was deep. It sent shivers down Riley's spine.

"I'm...I'm in room..." Shit, he didn't even remember, couldn't get his brain to work. Lennox was coming, going to be here just when Riley felt like he would shatter without him, but *shit*, Lennox was coming. It was dangerous, short-sighted on Riley's part to let him.

Carefully, Officer Preston worked the phone from Riley's hand and lifted it to his ear. "He's in room 304."

Chapter Thirty-Nine

The hospital parking lot was a madhouse, and Lennox was beyond grateful he hadn't driven. The rideshare dropped him off at the entrance, and he walked straight into a circus.

The waiting room was packed with reporters, cameramen and agitated security guards trying to escort them out. Everyone was yelling, trying to be heard over each other, and people with *real* emergencies hovered in corners, trying to stay out of the way while holding dishrags to bleeding cuts and cradling broken arms, as if afraid to be jostled.

Lennox didn't even bother trying to go to reception. He didn't have time to waste. Riley needed him *now*. And, if he was honest with himself, *he* needed Riley. If the check-in lady noticed him sneaking through to the elevators, she ignored him. In the chaos, he couldn't blame her.

The elevator doors closed, muting the cacophony of the lobby, but even as it started ascending, he could still hear it. Compared to that, the third floor was quiet.

He didn't even need to look for the number to find Riley. The police officer sitting in a folding chair served as a beacon. It was all Lennox could do not to sprint. His suit pants—tighter than he remembered them being—strained over his thighs as he hurried.

The officer stood abruptly, a frown creasing his already stern face.

"I'm here for Riley." Lennox tried not to sound panicked but the longer he went without seeing Riley, the more anxious he grew.

"Can I see some identification, sir?" the officer asked.

"Oh, of course!" Lennox fumbled with his wallet, dropping his license and having to pick it up with shaking fingers. He shoved it toward the cop, who barely glanced at it before his face softened.

"Ah, Lennox. Riley's been expecting you. The doctor will be up shortly for his exam, and I think he'd like you to be with him for it." The officer handed his ID back and Lennox shoved it in his pocket without looking.

"Can I go in then?"

The cop stepped aside. His heart thudding, Lennox hurried in.

Riley looked tiny in the hospital bed, lying on his side with his knees pulled to his chest. He had a bruise-mottled arm curled over his eyes, giving Lennox a second to school his face—replace the fear and horror with something closer to the love that inspired those feelings.

Lennox was allowed to stay in the room with Riley while they did his rape kit, though he wasn't allowed to hold his hand, not until the tech left and they started working on Riley's back, instead.

It meant trying not to cringe when they took a needle to the welt that needed stitching, ignoring the strong scent of antiseptic that made him want to sneeze, and trying not to cry when Riley *finally* started crying.

But it meant Lennox got to hold him, and it meant that he was there for support while Riley finally told Officer Preston about his abuse — what he suffered as a child as well as during the three days he was missing.

When he was finished, Lennox's stomach churned with acid and the cop was stone faced. He stood and tucked his notebook in one of the utility pockets of his black cargo pants, excusing himself to call his boss.

It didn't take long for the officer's raised voice to filter in. Thankfully, Riley was sleeping deeply. Lennox tucked the blanket tighter around Riley as he listened, careful to avoid his bandaged back.

"I'll sign whatever write-up you want if you get your ass to the court for a warrant. Senator or not, I want that bastard in cuffs."

Yeah, Officer Preston could join the fucking club.

Personally, an arrest seemed too easy for the bastard.

* * * *

Riley loved Lennox.

Riley loved Lennox so much…but if Lennox didn't stop babying him, Riley was going to smother him with his body pillow.

The body pillow Lennox bought for him and insisted he use for 'lumbar support', which only made Riley think that Lennox didn't know what lumbar support was.

Oh, it was nice for a day or two, having Lennox wait on him hand and foot. And if he were honest with himself, for the first day or two he really had needed it. He'd poured a fifth of vodka down his throat, until Lennox had called Riley's sponsor from his days fighting alcohol abuse — a man Riley hadn't even realized Lennox knew about.

Dean had shown up less than an hour later with a pint of Superman ice cream and a DVD copy of *The Wiz* — with Michael Jackson and Diana Ross, of course. Lennox sat between Riley's knees and munched on popcorn, silent support until the movie ended. Then, he'd left Riley with a kiss on his cheek to talk with his sponsor.

And Riley couldn't deny that he'd spent more time in bed then he'd care to admit, huddled under the blankets in hopes that his dreams would help him forget.

But now, it was like that was all Lennox saw when he looked at him — a broken boy who needed to be coddled.

He didn't seem to realize that Riley had gone back to therapy and, while he wasn't fully recovered — might never be able to truly move beyond his painful past — he was, by and large, a functioning adult again.

So, when Riley woke up with an erection throbbing between his thighs, the last thing he wanted was Lennox stuttering his way through an apology and sprinting off to the bathroom.

Riley cursed and collapsed back against his pillow with a groan, glaring at the closed door. A kernel of resolve started growing in his chest. If Lennox thought

Riley was too traumatized for sex, well...Riley would just have to prove him wrong.

Abstinence was the *last* thing he needed right now. He needed Lennox to touch him, kiss him...needed Lennox's hands on his skin to brush away the memories of the *last* hands that touched him.

Far from traumatizing, even his therapist had agreed that sex could be healing if it was with someone he trusted.

And there was no one he trusted more than Lennox.

Mind made up, Riley pinched himself for luck then slid out of bed. He didn't bother dressing. He strolled, nude, to the bathroom, reclaiming his confidence in his body.

He had new scars on his back, ugly yellowed bruises on his skin, but they were signs only of what he survived. Signs that he was strong.

He wasn't ashamed of them, and he wasn't going to skirt around under the cover of darkness and oversized clothing as if he was.

Even though he hated that they were the first thing Lennox looked at when Riley pushed his way, uninvited, into the bathroom... Riley snapped his fingers in front of Lennox's eyes, breaking the wide-eyed gaze fixed on a particularly ugly bruise over Riley's ribcage.

"I'm not a china doll," Riley promised, his voice strong as he broke the silence. "I'm not made out of porcelain, and I won't break if you touch me."

"I don't think that," Lennox protested, but Riley saw the way his eyelids fluttered, recognized how he tucked his lower lip between his teeth and bit.

"You do, and that was okay at first. But I need you to see *me* now, not the past. Stop looking at me like a victim." Riley backed Lennox up to the counter then curled his hands around Lennox's bare hips, lifting him with only moderate difficulty onto the marble top. Lennox had to fumble to grip the edge to keep out of the sink.

"I just don't want to do anything to hurt you," Lennox whispered, leaning down to press his forehead against Riley's. Riley allowed the contact for a moment before he gently nudged Lennox back.

"Trust me to tell you if I need you to stop. Trust me to not do anything I'm not ready for. Just…trust me," Riley pleaded.

Because to him, that was what it boiled down to. He'd been telling Lennox for days that he was ready, telling him with his body and eyes and everything but his words. Each time Lennox pulled away, it felt a bit more like a rejection.

"I *do* trust you," Lennox promised, reaching his hand up to cup Riley's cheek. His palm was warm and the skin was soft.

Riley covered Lennox's hand with his, holding it in place. "Then prove it. Let me take care of this." Riley lowered his other hand to Lennox's dick. He wasn't fully hard but not fully soft, either.

Lennox hesitated long enough that Riley's shoulders drooped, and he almost gave up. Then, almost imperceptibly, Lennox nodded.

By the time Lennox spilled down Riley's throat, Riley was confident that the only thing that was thinking now was *Oh God*, and *Don't stop*.

Chapter Forty

Riley stared, unseeing, through the window into the backyard, absently stroking the cat's belly as it sprawled on the counter. Simba knew he wasn't allowed up there, but Riley was too distracted to nudge him down.

Something was wrong with Tweety. Not physically, or at least he didn't think so, but he definitely wasn't his usual self. He was too quiet, too reserved — a shadow of the bright kid Riley knew.

"Everything okay?" Lennox's voice startled Riley and he flinched, spooking Simba, who hissed and leapt off the counter like he was offended.

"Sorry," Riley smiled at his worried boyfriend and walked over, curling his arms around Lennox's waist. "I was just thinking."

"About anything interesting? Cause if it's that we need a bird feeder, I tried that last year, but the squirrels kept getting into it," Lennox rambled, making Riley's smile turn genuine.

"Sounds like you had a squirrel feeder then, love. But no," Riley sighed, resting his head on Lennox's shoulder. "I'm just worried about Tweety. Doesn't he seem like he's acting weird?"

"Yeah, a little bit. But you know, if he's giving up on a dream he's had forever, that's a hard thing. Maybe he's just struggling with the decision to leave the team?" Lennox suggested, rubbing Riley's back.

"Yeah, maybe." But Riley couldn't stop thinking about that jersey—the blood and tears. Basketball was a physical sport, but it wasn't like they were boxing or anything.

He just had a feeling...

"Do you think we should invite him and Mike over for a game night or something? After Mike's honeymoon, maybe?" Riley asked, stepping back a bit to look Lennox in the eyes. The wedding was next weekend then the happy couple was going on a cruise to somewhere in the Caribbean. *Jamaica, maybe? Puerto Rico?* Honestly, it had been hard to follow the conversation because Mike kept interspersing the explanation with random screaming at the football game on TV.

"We can have pizza," Lennox mused, and Riley laughed.

God, he loved Lennox.

* * * *

The wedding was lovely. The ceremony itself was short and small, consisting mostly of the bride and groom, their parents and a handful of friends. Riley and Lennox sat together in the first pew and Riley tried to ignore the fact that he was in a church. He only ended up in the bathroom once with Lennox talking him through his breathing techniques, but then the ceremony was over, and they were able to leave.

The reception was a-whole-other story. All of Lennox and Mike's college buddies had shown up, and all of Wendy's coworkers. The hotel ballroom had been decorated with sparkling white lights and several gauzy white drapes waterfalled down from the ceiling. Fake snow decorated the center of the round tables lining the edge of the dancefloor, which turned a hazy-yellow under the flickering candlelight.

Riley thought it was too reminiscent of winter in a dog park, but other than that, the rest of the decorations were gorgeous.

He couldn't help but laugh as he saw the buffet. "Only Mike," Riley muttered to Lennox as he filled his plate, "would serve pizza, pigs-in-a-blanket and barbecue ribs at his wedding. There's not even a vegetable."

Lennox pointed at the halved tomatoes on top of the pizza. "That's a vegetable."

"Technically, that's a fruit," Riley said. It didn't stop him from adding two pieces to his plate, beside half-a-dozen of the crescent weenies.

"I've never seen tomatoes in a fruit salad." Lennox's plate was filled with a half-rack of ribs so smothered in barbecue sauce that Riley wished they had wet wipes.

"I've never fucked you in a hotel bathroom, but that doesn't mean it's not going to happen," Riley said with a wink. Lennox flushed scarlet red and stammered what sounded like an agreement before fleeing to the bar.

"I like you," a familiar female voice said from directly behind him, "But that's more than I needed to know about your sex life, Riley."

Riley cringed, then plastered on a smile as he turned to face her. "Hi, Ms. Ally."

"Oh, Christ." She laughed, wrapping an arm around the beautiful Black woman at her side and pulling her close. Riley had only seen Ms. Ally's wife in passing, and up close the tall, bald woman was even more intimidating. "You hear him, Pookie? Makes me sound old with all his 'Ms.' crap. You're not a resident anymore, dear. Please call me Ally. And this is my wife, Zada."

"Call me Pookie one more time, *lollipop,* and you'll find out how comfortable the couch is," Zada said, but she was chuckling as she spoke.

Riley bit his lip to stop from smiling. "Somehow, it feels a bit weird to be on a first-name basis…"

Ally smirked. "How do you think I feel, dear? When I sent you to live with my brother, I never expected you'd be playing 'show me yours' in the bedroom. I certainly didn't need to know the many ways you'd be defiling public bathrooms. But it seems we both need to be a smidge uncomfortable in this relationship."

"Ally it is."

She clapped him on the shoulder. "And look, the world kept spinning. Best run along now. It looks like my dear brother is about to fall into the fondue fountain."

Riley spun on heels to find out that yes, Lennox was indeed about to topple in. Who in their right mind thought putting a bathtub sized tub of melted chocolate in the middle of a ballroom was a good idea, he didn't know, but of *course* it was Lennox leaning into it, up on his tiptoes.

Maybe they'd be visiting the bathroom even earlier than he'd planned.

* * * *

"Better stay quiet, Kitten," Riley whispered as he lifted Lennox's right hand to his mouth, slowly running his tongue along the slender length of his finger. The chocolate was sweet, but not as much so as Lennox's skin. Riley reached the tip and sucked it into his mouth.

Lennox moaned loud, the sound echoing off the stall. No matter how nice a bathroom was, it didn't change the fact that the cubicles were tiny. It was a tight fit, but as far as Riley was concerned, it just meant that he and Lennox had to press even closer together.

Win, win.

He especially liked the hint of danger, the knowledge that anyone could walk in at any point, that too loud of a sound would give them away. Of course, he'd put an 'out of order' sign on the door, but Lennox didn't need to know that.

Like Riley, Lennox enjoyed the thrill of possibly getting caught.

Also like Riley, neither of them actually wanted to *be* caught.

It was a fine line.

Riley reluctantly let Lennox's finger slip free of his lips. He could suck on it all night, but they didn't have time. Mike had promised them ten minutes. Fifteen, maybe, but he couldn't stall the best man speech any longer than that without drawing suspicion.

Riley's goal was to leave Lennox too tongue tied and weak-kneed to be nervous. So, it was a purely selfless move when he took Lennox's hand and shoved it into his suit pants, allowing him to jerk Riley.

And his motives were definitely pure when he bent Lennox over the toilet and fucked him hard, filling him up with cum and leaving him sticky. The thought that in just a few minutes, his boyfriend was going to be standing on a stage in front of hundreds of people and none of them would know that Riley's cum was still inside him...? It was enough to make Riley wish they had time for a second round.

As soon as Lennox finished his speech, Riley would hang the 'out of order' sign back up on the bathroom door.

Chapter Forty-One

Lennox stood, hesitant, in the archway of the living room, staring at his young boyfriend. It had been a bit over three months—three months, one week and two days, exactly—since Riley had been taken by his father's goons. Riley was meeting regularly with his sponsor and had started seeing a therapist, and between the two and the fact that he'd finally signed up for his first vet tech course, he seemed to be doing pretty well.

Lennox was terrified that he was about to send Riley spiraling right back down. He didn't ever want to have to do anything that would cause Riley pain, but...their relationship was built on things like trust and communication. If he stayed quiet, kept their heads buried in the sand, what would that do to them?

So he cleared his throat. "Riley?"

"Hm?" Riley looked up from his textbook with a smile.

"Have...um, have you been watching the news yet this morning?" Lennox fidgeted with his off-the-shoulder top, scraping at the long-dried paint just to have something to do with his hands besides wringing them.

"You know I hate the news. Why, something fun on there?" Riley was still smiling.

Lennox bit the bullet and walked over, sitting down close to Riley's side. He reached for the remote but didn't turn the television on yet. "You need to see something, but I'm scared that if I show you, you'll be upset."

Riley's smile dimmed and died. He closed the textbook and sat back, crossing his arms. "It's about my dad, isn't it?"

Lennox nodded. There'd been a lot of coverage in the first few weeks, and they'd spent so much time holed up in the house or, if they absolutely had to leave, dodging reporters. It had been pure chaos. With the evidence Riley had, there'd been no way to deny that *something* happened.

Oh, the senator certainly *tried*. While Senator Emerson Scott hadn't been seen much, staying safely behind the gates of the hell house they called an estate, the remaining members of his media team — he'd lost a good percentage of them those first few weeks, unwilling to mar their reputation and future prospects — had gone in front of cameras to claim that Riley must have snuck into his dad's room after a bout of masturbation and stolen the seed that the hospital had found during his rape kit — semen that had been definitively DNA tested as belonging to the senator's.

Of course, that had backfired, since the senator had several dozen filmed sermons in which he decried masturbation as a sin. When the allegations didn't pan out—after all, how did they explain the cane marks littering Riley's back, visible on national television for all to see—the senator's team had switched tactics, claiming that the sex between the senator and his son had been 'coerced'—that Riley had, for whatever reason, snuck into his father's bed and corrupted him, teasing a formerly celibate man.

They'd even flung out Bible verses about Lot, as if that would somehow preserve the senator's image. Unfortunately, a core segment of his followers were willing to justify the man's heinous actions, unwilling to believe they'd been wrong about him.

The worst part had been the realization that, unless the senator voluntarily gave up his seat or two-thirds of the body of the senate voted to expel him, there was nothing preventing him from keeping his seat until the next election, which was two years away.

He didn't even have to withdraw his candidacy for governor.

And *that* knowledge had sent both of them into a tailspin when they'd heard.

That wasn't even getting into the fact that the FBI had been hesitant to arrest the senator, and even once they did, the federal judge had just remanded the senator to house arrest pending his trial—hardly a punishment when your house was a mega mansion.

If the senator was suffering, there'd been no sign of it.

Now, though…Lennox didn't know how to feel, and he didn't know how Riley would react. Would he be happy at the news, or would he feel like Lennox did, that the bastard skipped out on justice?

He took a deep breath, then turned on the news.

The scrolling red banner along the bottom of the broadcast read, *"Senator accused of sex crimes found dead of natural causes in his home early this morning."*

Riley barely heard the news anchor relaying the facts of the case for anyone who'd been living under a rock these past months. He just stared at the screen, reading and rereading the words. *Dead.*

His father was dead.

He pressed a hand to his belly as it churned, emotions battling in his chest. *Dead.*

Riley would never have to worry about his dad or his goons following him to campus or snagging him at a coffee shop. He didn't have to sit through a trial and hear his father blame him for everything or try to defend his actions as a child. He'd heard the questions in the media enough already — the speculations.

Why hadn't he gone to the police? Well, he had. But when the officer you ask for help just bends you over his desk in the police precinct before returning you to your abuser for a beating, it takes the shine off the badges.

Why would he do porn if he was really *a victim?* Because not all victims shunned sex, and not all victims stayed victims forever. Porn was nothing like his trauma. It was the validation he needed that he wasn't broken, and that he could still have sex and enjoy it — as long as it was with Lennox. He was pretty sure he was done with porn now, though. When he thought of going back to the studio, he found himself paralyzed by fear, unable to see anything but his dad's bodyguards dragging him out. Maybe someday he could try again…but he didn't need to. He'd broken down finally and agreed to let Lennox pay for his college.

He hated the thought of being a sponge, taking and taking from Lennox with nothing to give back. He'd said as much to Lennox, and his partner had just laughed, pointing out all the things Riley gave him every day—love, support and friendship.

Riley hadn't been able to argue.

The broadcast continued, and Riley finally noticed the video in the corner. Police officers in full SWAT gear raiding his family home, his mom escorted out in handcuffs. Apparently, his parents had been involved in more crimes than just his. He smirked as he realized she'd cut a deal—pleading guilty to a litany of charges, including failure to report and neglect of a child—in exchange for serving her sentence in a high-security prison with the possibility of parole.

"How do you feel?" Lennox said, his voice hesitant, as the broadcast started talking about forest fires in California. "Should I call Dean? Or Emily?" Emily was his therapist.

Riley took a moment, swallowing his automatic denial, to decide how he felt. It was the most useful tool his therapist had given him, the knowledge of how important it was to take the time to examine his thoughts and feelings rather than burying them or drowning them in a bottle.

Finally, he smiled. "No. I think I'm…okay, actually. He's dead, and she's going away for a long time." Riley bumped Lennox with his shoulder, teasing, "And now you can stop flinching every time the doorbell—"

The doorbell rang, interrupting him, and Lennox flinched, glaring toward the entryway.

"Or not," Riley chuckled, patting Lennox's shoulder as he stood and went to the door.

He was still smiling when he opened it, but the expression froze and withered. "Annie?"

Chapter Forty-Two

Riley stared at his sister in shock. She looked older than he remembered, her faux-blonde hair wispy and tangled around her face, falling out of what had probably once been a neat bun. Her expression was pinched, and he flinched back, waiting for the tongue lashing he knew she'd be giving him.

She'd always had something mean to say, some reason he wasn't living up to her standards or was embarrassing the family. Immediately, he wanted to shut the door and go bury himself under the covers, but something stopped him.

The conversation he'd forgotten, the one he'd read between her and their mother while he was locked in a bathroom backstage... It was the only thing that had him gripping the door, holding the door open instead of slamming it.

"Ryland?" Her voice wavered.

"Riley," he corrected. "Better come in." He reluctantly stepped aside, knowing that even if he didn't see them, the media liked to lurk outside their house, hoping for pictures they could sell to the tabloids of the 'disgraced senator's son'.

Like him, she seemed reluctant, but she stepped inside. "Where's your shadow?" Riley asked, surprised that his sister was alone, considering the memories he had of her. She never went anywhere without her guard, a pinched-face man who looked like a weasel and hated Riley without a passion.

"Fired him as soon as" — she took a breath, shoulders slumping — "Dad died."

Riley rolled his eyes, immediately irritated. She'd always been 'Daddy's little angel.' Always had her head so far up his ass she couldn't see what was right in front of her.

"Good riddance to bad garbage. I hope you're not here to get me to do some stupid statement or anything. I don't give two shits what the world thinks of him...or Mom." Riley turned his back on her and headed for the kitchen, yanking open the fridge and grabbing a jug of orange juice, drinking right from the container rather than offering her a glass.

Lennox, he noticed, stood just on the other side of the door that led to the hallway, not coming in but making him feel strong, nonetheless. Annie had followed him, standing awkwardly by the table.

"That's not why I'm here," Annie said, her voice strangely quiet. When Riley looked at her — really looked — he could see that she was out of sorts. Her dress was wrinkled, a coffee stain near the collar, and her makeup was smudged — like she'd slept in it or been crying.

"I'm not defending Mom, either." Riley dropped the orange juice on the counter and slammed the fridge closed, crossing his arms as he glared at her.

Annie flinched, dropping her eyes, and if Riley didn't know better, he would have assumed she was...ashamed?

"I know I deserve everything you think of me. I said...horrible things," Annie whispered, swiping at the dampness glittering on her eyelids. Clumpy black mascara smeared along her cheekbone. "My only defense is that I was young and stupid. James was the first thing I had that was just *mine*, you know? Dad always liked you better — "

Riley flinched, turning his head away to glare at the window over the sink. Dad liked him better because Riley had a dick and Dad was a closet homosexual with a thing for children.

"I promise I didn't know," Annie said, her voice frantic. When Riley finally turned back, he could see the sincerity on her face. "When James said you came on to him, that...that it was all your idea, I *wanted* to believe him. I didn't want to think that he would do something like that, because if he would...what kind of person did that make him? And...I think I knew, deep down, that if I let myself believe you, what that would mean for me."

She dropped her eyes and her voice got quieter. "I just wanted to feel like someone loved *me* — not my money, or...or our name. But I should have believed you. After you ran away, I realized I'd made a mistake."

"Then why did you never say anything? You stayed right there at Daddy's side. You married that asshole. If you knew you made a mistake, why didn't you fix it?" Riley bit out, demanding answers to the questions he'd had for years.

"By the time I realized I was wrong, I was already married and my husband...? Well, James wasn't as nice as I thought he was. He put me in the hospital more than once over such *stupid* things. I forgot to lay out his suit one morning and he broke my arm." She turned her face away, refusing to meet his eyes. "I met someone at the hospital. He was a nurse, and he was so *kind*. We...we made plans. We were going to run away together."

"What happened?" Riley asked, heart dropping. He could guess... The little blue-eyed girl. The texts.

"Dad happened. He couldn't have two children missing, and...and he couldn't have a '*whore for a daughter*'."

Riley flinched, hearing his father's voice beneath the words.

"They sent me away until the baby was born. Mama let me hold her, just for a minute, then they sent her away with one of the servants. If I'm good and do what they want, I get to see pictures of her. They let me see her once, during a field trip. I had to stay in the back, and I couldn't talk to her—even if I did, she wouldn't know it was me, because she thinks that bitch of a woman is her mother—but I got to see her smile."

"What happened to her dad?" Riley asked, though he wasn't sure he wanted the answer.

"The hospital said he joined some nonprofit that provides medical care to kids in developing countries. He..." Annie closed her eyes tight but it didn't stop the tears spilling down her cheeks. "Dad showed me a newspaper from Colombia. He was caught in the crossfire of some drug cartel and the police. He died in the street. Dad...he pretended to be all sympathetic, but...there was something in his eyes. He had something to do with it, and he wanted me to know."

She swiped her hand over her eyes. "And he said...he said that it was the Lord's will, and that if I didn't want to see what the Lord's will was for children born out of adultery, I would re-find my faith and become the obedient wife my husband deserved."

"I'm... Annie, I'm sorry. I don't know what to say." Riley wanted to keep his anger toward her but it drained away, slipping through his fingers, no matter how tightly he clung to it. Their parents were terrible people, and she'd done her best to survive, just like he had. And unlike him, she had a child to worry about.

"No. I don't want you to be sorry. You never did anything wrong. You were a child, and...and if I hadn't been so stubborn, you wouldn't have had to...and I wouldn't...And..." Annie slumped, collapsing back onto the dining room chair to bury her face in her hands.

Slowly, Riley crept forward, awkwardly putting his hand on her shoulder. "It's not your fault, either, you know. You were only eighteen. Now that I'm older, it's easier to see that you were practically a child yourself. You know, I might know someone who could help, if...if you want to try and get your daughter back," Riley offered, the only peace offering he could think to extend.

"Really? Do you think it's possible?" Annie asked, her eyes hopeful as she looked up.

Riley looked over his shoulder at Lennox, who stood in the shadows with a soft smile on his face. Lennox stepped forward. "When your daughter was born, did you sign anything?"

Annie flinched at the unexpected voice but shook her head, staring at Riley's boyfriend with wide eyes. "No, they just...they just took her."

"So even if she was adopted, it wouldn't be legal. You never officially gave up your rights to her." Lennox turned to Riley. "You still have Officer Preston's number, right?" Riley nodded, and Lennox moved to sit beside Annie. He reached out and took her hand, squeezing it reassuringly. "Officer Preston is a good cop. If there are texts between your parents and this woman, he can get them. They should prove that you never wanted to cut contact with your daughter. We'll get her back, I promise."

Chapter Forty-Three

Three years later

Lennox was running late, not that anyone would be surprised. Lennox was *always* running late, but Riley was particularly antsy about it now. It was Lyla's ninth birthday, and Lennox was supposed to be bringing the gift. Riley had a late shift at the clinic and hadn't had the time to run home first.

"He'll be here," Riley promised his sister.

She just laughed, waving him off toward the small table covered in appetizers. "Go get something to eat, little brother. I'm not worried. Lyla's having fun with her friends, so she won't mind playing hide-and-seek a bit longer than we planned."

The apartment was tiny, with few places to hide, but it didn't seem to be slowing down Lyla or her six friends from having fun. His sister had divorced her husband as soon as Officer Preston tracked down her daughter, and thanks to their prenup, she'd walked away with basically nothing.

He'd never seen her happier. She'd sold her dating company and put most of the proceeds into a college fund for Delilah, who everyone started calling Lyla almost immediately. Neither of them had gotten anything from their parents' estate, which had been frozen by the feds immediately after their mother's arrest—and neither of them cared.

They didn't need dirty money, not now that they had each other. Lennox had let Annie and Lyla stay in the guest room—Riley had officially moved into the main bedroom by that point—until they were on their feet.

All of them had expected Lyla to be scared and confused. After all, she was leaving behind the woman she thought was her mother to go live with strangers. Apparently, though, the woman she'd been given to really was a bitch.

Lyla had adapted beautifully. They'd still taken her to a therapist, though, concerned by...well, Lyla's *lack* of concern. It was where they'd learned that the woman who was caring for Lyla had made it clear to the child that she was *not* her mother and that Lyla was an unwanted addition to her household, allowed to live there only because of the paycheck she brought.

Riley could only be grateful that as emotionally neglectful as the woman was, it appeared she'd never laid a hand on Lyla, and at least his precious niece had been kept fed and clothed.

She'd thrived under their loving care, clinging to Annie within hours of meeting her and smiling like she'd won the lottery.

Riley supposed that in a way, she had.

Three years on, Lyla was flourishing and so was Annie.

Riley filled his plate with snacks, taking an extra helping of pickles for Lennox whenever he decided to arrive, and carried it into the living room. He spotted Tweety easily, dressed as he was in a neon yellow dress and lime green leggings, and squeezed himself into the narrow space between him and the arm of the couch.

"Dude," Tweety grinned, shifting to make a bit more space. "Can I have a chip?"

"Get your own!" Riley protested but held out his plate regardless. "Where's your boyfriend?"

Tweety's expression grew dreamy. "Teaching a class. You're lucky I love our niece" — Tweety had claimed Lyla as 'their' niece almost immediately, and no one minded at all— "because you know how hard it is for me to give up the chance to watch him work up a sweat."

"You just like it when he manhandles you," Riley teased.

Tweety winked. "I'm a big man. You know I gotta appreciate the way he can put me on my back."

"Nah, you just like what he does to you once he has you there," Riley snickered.

Tweety didn't bother looking embarrassed. He just nodded. "As hard as it was to woo him, I have to take advantage of him every chance I get."

"Woo?" Lennox's voice sounded close behind them and Riley jumped, twisting to see his fiancé. God, he loved being able to call him that. "I'm not sure I'd call it *wooing*. More like... Hm. What do you call it when you follow someone around a lot, even when they tell you to stop? Stalking?" Lennox teased.

Tweety stuck out his tongue. "He never told me to stop."

"To be fair, he was a little oblivious," Riley mused. "I mean, what did you have to do to get him to realize you were interested? Show up in lingerie?"

"It was a *corset,* and I'll have you know, I was fully dressed," Tweety sniffed, but his eyes twinkled.

Before Riley could keep teasing his best friend, though, Annie stood up and lifted her pop can like a toast. Dressed in stained sweatpants or not, some things never changed. "Lyla and I want to thank all of you for coming…"

Riley snickered and his sister shot him an exasperated look. Riley shrugged and gave her a 'what can you do?' look, since, after all, she'd been the one to say it, not him.

Annie rolled her eyes and continued the speech. Lennox leaned over the back of the couch, resting his chin on the top of Riley's head, until Riley reached back and dragged him down for a quick kiss. It ended when he yanked Lennox forward, until his fiancé fell into his lap, exactly where Riley wanted him.

* * * *

Riley loved being a vet tech. He loved pretty much everything about his job, from the fact that he was helping sick animals to the hours, which let him get back home to Lennox at a reasonable time…most days.

Today, unfortunately, he was late. They'd had a last-minute patient, a pregnant beagle whose frantic owner had rushed in just as they were about to lock the doors. Thankfully, the labor had gone smoothly, and they'd sent the mama home with six healthy puppies, but it meant that Riley was in a hurry as he rushed out of the front door, hoping he could catch the bus before it left.

The glass door was still swinging closed behind him when Riley ran smackdab into a man passing by, stumbling back and nearly falling. The stranger grabbed his arm to steady him, and Riley realized he wasn't a stranger at all.

He blinked at the pink-haired man, his mouth opening in surprise. Of all the people on all the sidewalks in the city… Maybe, it was fate.

Riley grinned at Shiloh Beckett, ignoring the large bodyguard standing a few feet away, and said, "I've been hoping I would run into you again, but I didn't think I'd *actually* run into you."

For a moment, the man looked confused, then a light went on in his eyes. "Riley?"

He was surprised the man recognized him after all these years. How many had it been, almost ten? He nodded and said what he should have done the last time they'd met. "I didn't get the chance to say thank you before. Can I buy you lunch? Or um…a coffee?"

"Sure." Shiloh grinned. "I know a place."

Want to see more from this author?
Here's a taster for you to enjoy!

Demon Daddy:
The Blood Demon's Pet
KD Ellis

Coming October 2023

Excerpt

Eryn

My room is cold.

Not just the bitter cold of winter — though it *is* that, too — but a lonely sort, a chill that starts in my chest and spreads outward. My breath flickers like a specter on the windowpane before turning to frost. I scuff it away with my forearm so I can peer through the yellowed glass.

Two shadowy figures are standing on the wilting lawn, but I know Alpha Carrick must be the one by the porch. I can only see the top of his head, with its shiny bald patch glinting up at me, but I don't think Alpha would let a stranger between him and his pack.

Alpha's shoulders are stiff — tense and strong.

I wonder what he's saying. If he would turn toward the window, I could read his lips. Instead, I'm stuck interpreting his body language.

The other man steps away, shaking his head. His dark hair flops over his face, but I notice the way his lips turn down. Alpha moves forward, but the stranger lifts his hand. He slashes it sharply across his chest in an obvious refusal. I don't need to see any more. My shoulders slump as I twist away from the window.

I've been passed over.

Again.

I wilt against the glass and let my bare feet thump against the wall just *one* time. A single show of disappointment before I swallow it down. It's sour on my tongue, like the sugar-free lemonade Alpha's mate serves at summer's end.

I'm not surprised. Most packs are overpopulated now, with the laws dictating where we can settle. Well, where we can settle *if* we want to be able to shift freely, anyway. I'm not an Omega—one of the rare male wolves able to bear pups—and I'm not particularly smart or strong. I'd be having a hard time even if I *wasn't* a freak.

Maybe I should give up, accept that I'm destined to be on my own. It won't be the first time. I don't need a pack, because lone wolves survived in the wild. I just need...

I close my eyes, trying to find my inner wolf. He's there, somewhere, pacing under my skin, antsy and rabid—a growling mutt. But even though I can feel him, I can't *touch* him. My ribs could be silver bars, as well as they keep the beast caged.

Caged, but not docile.

I slide off the windowsill and dart to the bed, the wooden floor icy under my soles. I dive under the comforter before grabbing my pillow, dragging it over my face so I can scream into the sheets as the beast growls at me, snapping his jaws in threat.

The phantom press of his claws digs into my fingertips. I curl my fingers toward my palms without thinking. They slice into my skin like shattered glass. At least the pain distracts me from the ache in my teeth. I can smell *everything* — the forest through the window, out of reach, the bleeding meat in the fridge, the salt of Alpha's sweat.

Trying to tame my inner wolf is as useless as asking my shadow to dance. Neither listen.

I manage to choke down my scream just as Alpha's heavy boots hit the stairs and start climbing. My door whines as it swings open.

"You up, kid?" Alpha Carrick's voice is deep as thunder. As much as I'd like to ignore him, I know he can hear my ragged breathing. I shove my hand out from under the pillow and give a half-hearted thumbs up. It won't be the first time Alpha has seen my hands covered in blood, and I doubt it will be the last. At least this time, it's my own.

My feral wolf never bothered learning to submit, not even to me.

Alpha is quiet, but then the mattress dips under his weight. I slap my hand against the sheets to keep from sliding into him. Alpha awkwardly pats my back. "I don't think that pack is going to be a good fit for you. Alpha Reed is…old-fashioned."

"I saw through the window." My voice is muffled by the pillow. "He didn't want me. You don't have to lie."

"It's not that he didn't want *you*. He just doesn't have the resources to…" Alpha hesitates so I fill in the blanks for him.

"To babysit a freak." I barely have the words out of my mouth before Alpha slips his hand under the pillow. He pinches my ear and drags me out like an unruly pup, ignoring my yelp.

"You are *not* a freak." Alpha does that thing that all adults do—say something that isn't true, then expect me to believe them. Because for some reason, adults are allowed to lie if it's for your own good.

I'm an adult now. I sit up and cross my arms over my scrawny chest—too small, too wimpy…a runt not even worthy of belonging to a litter.

"I *am* a freak. Everybody says it." Even *she'd* said it, the woman in my dreams. I can't remember her face, but I know she smelled of nicotine and mint, and when she sang, her voice was gritty. And I remember she had kind hands.

Until she didn't.

"If everybody said aconite tastes like cotton candy, would you eat it?" Alpha's question is pointed, his voice cross.

"Maybe. At least then no one would have to put up with me." My jaw juts out stubbornly as I lie.

Alpha cuffs the back of my head. "Eryn Laurier, don't disrespect me with words like that." He grips my nape tightly, forcing my face up to meet his pale eyes. They are stern but kind, lined from years of laughter. "I don't 'put up' with anything I don't want to, and I certainly don't 'put up' with you, kid."

"I'm *not* a kid." I shove my hair out of my face. If I were a kid, I wouldn't have to leave. If I were a kid, the last pack run wouldn't have ruined everything. Instead, at nineteen, I was too old for my wolf's antics to be excused. A wolf who couldn't submit was a wolf who couldn't stay.

The mattress creaks as Alpha stands. He gives a heavy sigh as he walks. I barely hear him mutter, "I guess you're not."

I want to retreat to the safety of my pillows. Hide away from reality and let it pass me by like an autumn storm, but there are chores to be done before dusk falls tomorrow.

* * * *

Goddess Moon hangs pregnant in the sky. Around me, the woods echo with the sound of breaking bones and shifting skin. I watch Old Jeb fall to his knees, his skin rippling over unnaturally bent joints. He makes it look easy, the transition from man to beast happening in an instant. His wolf, with its shaggy, silver-streaked hair, trots off into the woods, snapping at a teenager caught mid-transition, fur sprouting in clumps over his lumpy spine.

Alpha said it takes bravery for a wolf to submit to the pull of the Goddess so fully. That only the strongest wolves, like the pack Beta, who is already shaking out his dark fur, can change so quickly. But only the oldest can resist the pull entirely, like Alpha Carrick.

And me, but not because I'm strong.

Because I'm weak.

Like the rest of the pack, I stand naked in the clearing. The grass, stiff with frost and its color faded, pricks the soles of my feet. I can no longer fight off the shivers. They come, one right after another, until it feels like I'm having a seizure. My blond hair is long enough to tickle my hipbones but does little to shield me from the cold, not even when I curl forward, clasping my arms tight around my waist for warmth. A breeze whispers along the shell of my ear. And the light—

Goddess Moon's light does nothing but paint my pale skin in tones of blue. I feel nothing…just the beast, pacing in my belly. I try to reach it like Alpha says, to put a leash on its neck and drag it into the light. Again, he cowers from me, snapping his jaws in threat.

A frustrated growl slides between my flat, clenched teeth.

Alpha grips the nape of my neck, the only point of warmth in the winter night. "Take a deep breath."

I know it will be pointless, but I gasp one in. The cold air hits my lungs like a lit match.

"Good boy. Now another," Alpha guides me through taking the breaths as slow and deep as I can, despite my body's shaking. Each breath helps a bit more. The cold leeches away until all I feel is numb. The only thing keeping me from melting into a puddle of mercury is the weight of his palm.

Goddess Moon glints through the bare branches above me. Alpha tightens his hand on my neck, his claws scraping my skin where they push through his fleshy fingertips. His voice is deeper now, guttural under her sway. I can tell he's fighting to stay out of her riptide long enough to talk me through this, like he always does.

He is a good Alpha. Even though my wolf doesn't accept him, Alpha still takes care of me. He doesn't lock me in the kennel like *she* used to or drag me down to the lake to…to… I clench my eyes shut and concentrate on anything but the memory.

It feels like hours—like days—but finally, I feel the itch of fur stirring under my flesh. My knees collapse, and I strike the dirt with a cry. The shift is agonizing. I can hear myself screaming as my bones break and mend and rearrange. Skin tears then knits itself back together, sensitive as a sunburn. Twice, the shift tries to revert as I cringe away from the pain, but Alpha growls an order to push through, dragging my wolf from under my skin by his scruff.

Finally, it's over.

The pain becomes a hollow parody. I slowly push myself up onto four paws, my spine popping. Handfuls of fur finish sprouting, and I whine at the overwhelming need to scratch the itchy pelt.

My gait is awkward, a halting stumble toward the woods where the rest of the wolves are already running. Alpha overtakes me quickly. He is twice my size, his fur brindled. The other wolves are quick to move out of his way.

For a moment—just a brief stretch of lucid seconds—I think that this pack run will be different.

I feel my mind blurring at the edges and panic sets in. I whine when my beast shoulders me out of the way, stumbling when he briefly takes control of my forelegs. I struggle to leash him, to keep him chained to my will. In this body, he is stronger than me. The beast growls, the sound rumbling from my chest, and instinctively, my mind cowers back, giving ground before it.

It is a mistake. I don't know why my wolf is so much wilder than the rest of the pack, why he won't bend to my will as he should. Instead, he tamps me down, burying me under the instinct to run, to hunt and claim. It feels like falling asleep, but each month, I slip under easier.

One day, I'm afraid I won't wake up.

About the Author

KD Ellis is a professional cat wrangler by day, and an author by night. She moved from a small town to an even smaller village to live with her husband and wife and their two children. She loves reading—anything with men loving men. She writes queer romance in between working her two jobs and cuddling her pets— all six of them, which confuses the turtle.

KD loves to hear from readers. You can find her contact information, website details and author profile page at https://www.pride-publishing.com

PUBLISHING

Sign up for our newsletter and find out about all our
romance book releases, eBook sales and promotions,
sneak peeks and FREE romance books!

www.ingramcontent.com/pod-product-compliance
Lightning Source LLC
Chambersburg PA
CBHW030401030726
47497CB00002B/429